"Serve the light and seek the truth resting in darkness. Aid those in need, to the utmost of your power. Learn the avenues of magic and protect the secrets of the Association whenever possible. Risk your own life before putting the life of another in danger."

– The Oath of the Association of
Magical Arts and Sorcery

Also by T. Thorn Coyle

Novels

Like Water

The Panther Chronicles

To Raise a Clenched Fist to the Sky
To Wrest Our Bodies From the Fire
To Drown This Fury in the Sea
To Stand With Power on This Ground

Collections

Alighting on His Shoulders
Break Apart the Stone

TO STAND WITH POWER ON THIS GROUND

BOOK 4 OF
THE PANTHER CHRONICLES

T. THORN COYLE

TO STAND WITH POWER ON THIS GROUND
Panther Chronicles, Book Four

Copyright © 2017

T. Thorn Coyle

Cover Art and Design © 2017

Extended Imagery

Editing:

Dayle Dermatis

ISBN-13: 978-1-946476-04-3 (trade paperback)

ISBN-10: 1-946476-04-8 (trade paperback)

TO STAND WITH POWER ON THIS GROUND

"Our struggle is not in Vietnam but in the movement for social justice at home."

– The Chicano Moratorium

"You have to understand that people have to pay the price for peace. You dare to struggle, you dare to win"

– Fred Hampton

CHAPTER ZERO
BROWN BERETS

The Brown Berets came first, two abreast, dark brown trousers with sharply ironed creases. Tan military jackets. Combat boots.

Brown felt berets slanted crosswise on their brows, cream-colored patches stitched with brown thread and bristling with magic power from the sorcerers who had dedicated time and energy to protect these protectors.

Shoulders back. Heads tall. Proud, as warriors should be, they walked down the rolling hill, showing Los Angeles what was possible if they rose up together. One community. One purpose. One fist.

A united people, faces brown and beautiful. Hair long and dark, shining in the December sun.

Behind them were la gente. The people themselves. Following a wide banner they stretched, sidewalk to sidewalk, a mass of movement, color, and fierce anger.

Bold black letters declared the gathering to be "The Chicano Moratorium Against the War in Vietnam." The canvas banner was gripped in the hands of students, and mechanics, grocers, and cleaning women.

The people were as determined as they were tired.

Tired of waiting. Tired of being beaten by police, tired of students being held back in school, tired of never getting ahead at work, tired of stooping over ripe red berries in endless fields.

Tired of being drafted into war.

In September, Rosalio Muñoz had refused the invitation of Richard Nixon and the US government to kill poor brown people halfway across the globe. *No thank you*, he had said, *I defy your induction.* He began organizing the people instead.

And so, just as the Black Panthers had marched on the state capitol in Sacramento, demanding the right to protect themselves from the police, the people of East Los Angeles marched in defiance of sending their bodies to be cut down in war.

Stop Chicano Genocide, read their placards. *La Raza Demanda Justicia. Brown and Proud!*

And the Feathered Serpent, Quetzalcoatl, was with them, its massive, sinuous body flying overhead, feathers wafting in its wake. It offered direction, whether the people could see it or not.

They knew that it was there. It had helped them before in times of need, and so they called upon it now.

Quetzalcoatl moved through their bodies, touching their minds, opening their throats, filling their voices with a power that could shake the sky.

Weaving its way between the astral plane and the cracking tarmac streets of Los Angeles, Quetzalcoatl led the way, trailing rainbows of colored feathers as its serpent body undulated, and impossibly—in the way that all magical creatures are impossible—the serpent flew.

And Tonantzin was with the people too, marching with them in the images of La Virgin, Guadalupe, sewn upon denim jackets and carried on silver medals that rested above their hearts.

The sorcerers were with the people, too. Las Manos. The Hands of protection, and the hands that made the magic the people were slowly coming to realize was not a thing of fables, but a thing that walked always by their sides, just as God did, and the Virgin, and the Feathered Serpent their ancestors worshipped of old.

Sorcery was a weapon to be used in the struggle for liberation. And the sacred beings of their peoples had never left them. Though Toledo steel had mowed their ancestors down, watering the soil with blood, the sacred beings simply shifted shape, changed names sometimes, or hid, and bided their time.

What was human time to Gods and Goddesses? To the Powers, the forces of Nature that could rend a world in two? While human fought with human, these forces did what was necessary to keep the worlds alive.

Boots sounded on the tarmac as the Brown Berets led the people, over two thousand strong, down the streets of East Los Angeles, heading for Obregón Park.

Eugene Obregón, you see, was a Chicano. A Marine sent to Korea to fight and kill, he had died protecting an enlisted brother from a rain of bullets. Using his body as a shield, Obregón, who should have been marching at their sides this day, had taken his last breath in the war-riddled streets of Seoul.

A man's voice called out over a bullhorn, crackling across the sounds of the marching crowd. "We march to Obregón Park because too many of us have already died in these wars! These pinche wars only help the rich gringos get richer off our backs! We march because nuestro carnal, Eugene Obregón, died in a war far away, fighting for this country that spits on men who look like him. He was nineteen fucking years old, just like many of you brothers and sisters here today."

The crowd yelled and stomped their feet.

A woman took the bullhorn. "Why do we march?" she shouted.

"La Raza march against the war!" the crowd roared back.

"Why do we march?" she called again.

"La gente para paz!"

The Feathered Serpent wove and sang, spreading brightness over the mass of people, feeding from their outrage and the fierce joy of being together, marching, on this bright December day. It was ready to do anything to help the people find their way.

To be worshipped was good. To be powerful was better.

And in these streets? Power marched.

Grandparents and babies emerged from modest bungalows to watch and cheer the young people marching by. Shaded by jacaranda trees, and lit by the bright reds and fuchsias of the bougainvillea plants clambering up wooden fences, the old men waved handkerchiefs, and the toddlers raised their chubby brown fists.

Quetzalcoatl brought the wind that raised the people's voices to the sky, the wind that filled lungs and ruffled dark hair, that caused the banners to stir.

The Feathered Serpent brought the winds of change.

These were the children of the Feathered Serpent, and it would draw the boundary around their bodies to protect from those who wished the people harm, be it the serpents of evil sent out from the shadow Temple, or the policía who smashed the eyeglasses of young students in the streets.

It would protect against those who would send their young brown bodies off to war, far from this land, once the fertile home of the Chumash and Gabrielino, now riddled with concrete and stinking of lead and gasoline.

"Viva La Raza! Afuera Vietnam!"

CHAPTER ONE
JASMINE

We were in Obregón Park, following the Chicano Moratorium march against the war.

The energy of the march still lingered, wild and strong. The park smelled of fire and freedom as much as it did sun and patchy, dried grass. It seemed fitting to gather here, in this powerful place that the people had claimed as their own.

The park was named for an ancestor. That always strengthened everything. Ties to the past carried the spirit forward into the future. I'd been learning a lot about that from Rosalia lately. Aunt Doreen, too.

People milled about the park, sun shining on their dark hair. It was mostly teenagers who brought their friends. Some parents had come, too, and a lot of the people who marched had stayed, some of the Brown Berets said.

There were no children yet, but that would come later. We had to get the teens and adults on board first. To keep reminding them that of all the things in the world to be afraid of, this magic was the least of their worries.

They were all smart. They knew the score. And the communal effort at Laguna Park, where we had blasted open the Temple and at least temporarily banished the snakes, had helped the sense of goodwill we were building.

And the readiness to keep trusting that the magic they felt was real.

I grinned. Having the big ancient powers your mami and papi had talked about show up all of a sudden helped, too.

We had been training for an hour already. People were sparring. Laughing and sweating together on the beautiful December day. They were out on the grass, and gathered near the swing sets and teeter-totters, throwing balls of energy at one another. Some of them sat on the grass, or in folding beach chairs, practicing transferring energy hand to hand in a circle. And then weaving it across, building a web.

Wow. That part, they'd figured out on their own. We hadn't trained them in any of the advanced steps yet. Figuring it out on their own? It meant the web of magic, of light and life, was working.

Every time that happened? Felt like another sign that we were on the right track. And just maybe all this shit was gonna work out okay.

"Rosalia?" I said.

She nodded at me, citrine eyes hooded today, as though she were half here and halfway on some other plane. The veils were always thin around her, I was discovering.

The hechicera stood leaning on a staff. Feathers and ribbons flowed down around the dark wood festooned with bells at the top. I hadn't seen her use that staff before. Jerking my head toward it, I asked her about it.

"This staff, Rosalia," I said, "does it mean something? I've never seen it in your shop and I haven't seen you bring it to other meetings before."

She looked thoughtful, staring out over the people, making sure they were okay.

"I don't need the staff in my botánica," she said. "The shop is my own sacred space. Sacred ground. Blessed. Full of my protections."

She looked at me again. "And at the meetings with the union? They would not yet understand. I was meeting them on *their* ground, claro? I needed to face them as a woman, first, and a sorcerer, second. But here among these people? They need to know my sorcery. They need to see my power. And these people. They understand the power of symbols. So I bring my staff. Of my authority."

She shook it then, ringing the bells, and setting the ribbons and feathers moving in the air that was beginning to warm slightly around us. I could feel it then, the power in the wood, and every spell and incantation she must have woven into the adornments.

"My staff," Rosalia continued, "it shows everyone I am a sorcerer. And that they need to pay attention."

She smiled then, and trained those citrine eyes directly at me. "There is one thing you should learn, Jasmine. The more people trust that you are in authority, the more they feel safe around you. And the more they feel safe, the more they will do to help you. Use that knowledge and don't abuse it. Use it only in the service of the people."

I felt like she had just given me a great gift that I would need to ponder. Just like I had pondered the words of Fred Hampton and Huey Newton, and all the rest.

"Thank you, hechicera," I said. "I think I dig that, but I need to think on it some more. And I've got a meeting to get moving here."

"Yes, go," she said.

I had my lover, Jimmy, gather up the Black Panthers present: Jimmy. Geronimo Pratt—I knew he was a shifter, and a head of Party defense down here, but hadn't had a chance to work with him much. Elaine and Ericka, who were also part of leadership.

Gloria, Verónica, Teresa, and Rafael from Las Manos and the Brown Berets were present, so I asked them to join us, too.

"Let's go meet in the center of the park," I said.

"Should we be meeting out open like this?" Rafael asked. Geronimo Pratt laughed. The sound boomed from his chest. He wore a leather cap with a small brim, which matched the long leather coat encasing his broad shoulders. His posture was always perfect—something carried over from his military days, I guessed.

"We're safer out here in the middle of a park than we are in any Panther or Brown Beret buildings, I can tell you that right now. This park is less likely to be bugged, unless it's one of us. And if it's one of us, we're already screwed, right, man?"

"Right," Rafael replied.

I looked around the perimeter of the park where Brown Berets and Black Panthers, all in their wool felt hats, stood at attention. They alternately faced out and faced in, making sure every square inch was protected for the people. My breast swelled with pride. It was amazing what we were doing here. I wanted the whole world to see them with my eyes. To know what we were about. But I supposed that would come later.

So we picked our way to the center of the park and stood under a big live oak tree that spread its branches outward. It was beautiful. I breathed in the scent of grass and oak and moss.

And then noticed everyone was looking at me. Right. Step into my authority. Make them trust me. Let them know that they were safe. As safe as any black or brown person could be in America.

I cleared my throat.

"So. You know about the battles we've been fighting and you know about the magic. Well, we're going to need a series of meetings this week. And I'm going to ask that you all trust me now, and that you trust Jimmy and Rosalia and my friend Carol who is not here today and Ernesto who is also not here today. You've met them both. We're all sorcerers. We're all committed to the cause. To the movement. And we're all down with power to the people."

No one said a word. Just waiting, as a slight breeze creaked the branches of the oak above their heads.

"I need you to know that first. We all need to be clear on that, because what I'm about to tell you is no secret—at least it won't be for long—but it's a powerful piece of information."

"Just tell us, sister," Ericka said.

I looked at her, glancing at the freckles that danced across her pale brown cheeks before focusing on her beautiful brown eyes. "I've been tracked by a federal agent. I've been *attacked* by a federal agent."

"We haven't heard about this," she said.

"You haven't heard about it because I haven't been attacked with bullets. I've been attacked with some weird-ass, twisted Temple magic."

A few people sucked in air between their teeth.

"That's right," I said. "The FBI is using magic against the people and we're beginning to consider that the FBI has been using magic all along. They used magic against Fred, and Huey, and Deborah. They're using magic to spy on us. There are infiltrators connected to this magic, we suspect. And we have proof they're using magic to influence people's minds."

"Lizard," Geronimo said, referencing the man who had been with us as we busted Huey out of the California Men's Colony. He'd ended up choosing death in the end, rather than betraying the Party anymore.

I nodded, feeling as grim as Geronimo looked.

"So what are we doing about it?" Jimmy asked. "That's what they want to know."

"Well, as Fred said, we're gonna have to stop talking and start practicing. So here that's why we're teaching these people magic, to protect themselves, their families, and their communities. Because Panther and Brown Beret security forces can't do it on your own. There aren't enough of you yet. We've been doing it up in Oakland. People are on board. They're happy to have something to do. I think the same will happen now here. You've seen some of that already. In Oakland, we've even been training children, which is pretty powerful juju."

"What do you mean?"

"The children are the best at magic," I replied. "Because the children don't have that much to learn. The children still think everything is possible. And so it is. And we need to get back to that. It's what I've been learning."

"We need to get back to the mind of a child," Geronimo said, then nodded. "The sister is right. We get trapped in our own thoughts. And we think we know how things should be and how things are. But sometimes that's not true at all, and it limits us."

He looked at his people, then back at me. "So, sister," he said. "How are you going to expand our consciousness? How are you going to open our minds today?"

"Well, I'm hoping that seeing people working magic in this park is already opening your mind," I said. "And some of you have been there when we've been fighting and may have felt or seen that we've been fighting both on the astral plane and here on earth. Well, that fight is going to continue. And it's only going to get worse. And we think it's going to get worse *this week*. So we want everyone on board."

"When?" Verónica asked. She had been part of organizing the stand at Laguna Park, and I was hoping she'd remain a strong ally.

Then a chorus of voices chimed in.

"Don't you guys do work on the full moon?" someone said.

"Christmas!"

I held up my hands to forestall more speculation. "All of those are correct. And to be honest, we don't exactly know what the plan is yet. We don't know the timing because we still are seeking out a few more pieces of information, but we're getting there. But what I need is for you all to do what you do best, which is to be ready to move in an instant and to be ready to organize as many people as you can as soon as you can."

"So, we say go, we have thousands of people ready, and we go under whose authority?" Ericka asked.

"Under mine," I replied, planting my boots more firmly on the grass. "But most importantly, under *your own*. Under the authority of every single person here. I'm not talking about a coup. I don't want your power. I want *shared* power. I want *increased* power. It's the only way we're going to change this world. You dig?"

I held up my fist in salute. "Are you down with the revolution or are you not down with the revolution? Because if you're down with the revolution, you know you've got to take risks. And I'm asking you to take a really big risk right now. I'm asking you to trust me. And trust my friends."

"And what if we can't?" Verónica said.

I stared at her and held her gaze until I could feel the tension increasing. I felt her want to look away.

"If you find out I'm not trustworthy," I said, "I give you permission to take me down."

Verónica nodded. Geronimo Pratt nodded, too.

"That's all we can ask," he said. "You have my support."

Chapter Two
Jasmine

Jimmy pulled up in front of the mansion and I sighed.

I could see Doreen and my mother—the Fire sorcerer and the Earth sorcerer—standing on the porch in front of that big, broad, heavy wooden door, neat and well-coiffed as could be. If a person didn't know the power they both packed, they could look like ordinary, middle-class black ladies visiting their wealthy white friends.

I just so wasn't used to this rich person shit anymore. It didn't feel like home.

It didn't feel like that Panther sitting in the car next to me. He felt like home. I leaned in and placed a soft kiss on his lips.

"Wish me luck," I said.

"You'll do fine, Jaz. You always do. Just remember who you are. Remember you're here for the revolution." He gave a little half-raised fist and a grin.

I laughed.

"Cool. That's what it's about, isn't it? The revolution is going down." I looked back out the window toward the Spanish revival building and the two dark women on the half-round, red-tiled doorstep.

"Just wish I wasn't stuck here. These upper-middle-class honkies don't give a shit about the people."

I sighed and leaned my head against the back of the seat.

"Go on, girl. Be strong."

I planted one more kiss on that beautiful mouth, inhaling Jimmy's amber and musk, then pulled back to look into his gold-rimmed dark eyes.

"I love you," I said.

"I know. I love you too. Now get." He gave me a little push. I shoved open the heavy door slammed it behind me.

Damn it.

My mother and my aunt Doreen were still waiting. Must have been waiting for me all along. I'd been hoping I could just sneak in. Avoid the whole thing, really.

I stood for a moment, just staring at them. They stared right back, as the borrowed El Camino rumbled away, taking Jimmy back to the Black Panthers and the Brown Berets. And every place I'd rather be but here.

"Jasmine," my mother said. "I'm glad you're here."

I gave her a kiss on the cheek, and slid my aunt Doreen into a hug.

"So," I said. "I'm surprised you're not already in there."

"When we saw you pull up, we figured we'd best confer."

I grimaced. "Plan of attack?" I asked.

"You might say that," Aunt Doreen said. "Mostly we're just worried about you."

"What, worried that I'm going to start some shit?"

"That mouth of yours, Jasmine," my mother said. "You never used to curse."

"Well, maybe I've turned into a witch," I said. "I know sorcerers don't usually throw curses, but maybe sometimes a woman needs to."

Neither of them said anything. Okay. Not amused. I can dig that. I wasn't too amused myself.

"Seriously though, I'm not even sure why we're here. What exactly are you hoping to accomplish? I already put Terrance in a coma, so he's out of commission. I don't see the Association doing anything about it. I don't see the Association doing much of anything about anything. Meanwhile, we are in the middle of a war, in case you've forgotten. And I'd rather be focusing on that, instead of this Association garbage."

Oh, I could feel Ocean starting to roar inside me. I was pissed off. Pissed off and wasting my time.

"Jasmine," my aunt Doreen said, "I know you don't think this is important, but it is." Her feet in their sensible shoes were planted firmly beneath her. She looked ready for battle herself.

"As important as people getting shot? As important as people getting beaten? As important as assassination attempts and children going hungry? I don't think so. We've had these tired arguments over and over again. I'm sick of them. I've done my part. The Association has nothing to offer me because it has *nothing* to offer the people."

I looked at both their faces, their eyes hard, their mouths tight. When had I become a stranger to my own family?

"I think you both know what I'm talking about. I can't believe you don't agree."

"Jasmine, you should know we're on your side by now, but whether we agree or not," my mother said. "I have to remind you that we've all taken oaths. We need to abide by those rules."

"I've taken oaths to the Party too."

"Yes. But you made oaths to the Association first."

"Yeah, well. Can't see that the Association has held up their end of the bargain much."

"That doesn't mean a sorcerer breaks her word," Doreen admonished. "Just because someone else has. You know that."

"I'm wondering if I shouldn't just let you middle-aged people take care of this, and leave me be."

Doreen sighed. "Jasmine, I respect you. I've stood at your side. We're all tired, and we're all in this together. Please don't act like a child. You're here now. Do your part. Carol's already waiting inside."

Yeah, I thought, and maybe Carol was still a little too much of a doormat for her own good. I know she'd changed a lot over the past couple months, but living inside this organization the way she did? In the belly of the big whale? It was hard to break away.

That was one thing. Living in Oakland had showed me there was power everywhere. Much as the Association wanted to make us think they had that cornered and no one else had power, that was a big lie. And if *that* was a big lie, I wasn't sure anymore what exactly I'd sworn an oath to.

"You know..." I looked at my mother. "I swore an oath to serve the light and seek truth in the darkness. I swore an oath to serve those in need. And to not put others in danger. I didn't really swear an oath to the Association itself. As far as I'm concerned, I'm upholding my oaths. I uphold them every damn day better probably than half the people who just flew in across the country for this Powers-damned meeting."

They just stared at me, and my mother gave a little nod.

"Well, you may think that's true," she said. "And it may even *be* true, but that doesn't mean there's not still work to be done here today."

Doreen put her hand on the heavy brass door knob. "You're here, Jasmine. Let's go inside and see what we can do."

I sighed again. They were both right, in their own ways. But I could feel the pressure building. It was going to be a mighty storm, and I didn't want to be distracted.

Angela Davis said, *"We are never assured of justice without a fight."* I just wasn't sure this fight with the Association would bring any kind of justice I recognized.

Shutting the heavy wooden door behind me, I straightened my back and strode forward behind the two women who had mentored me my whole life.

CHAPTER THREE
CAROL

Carol reached for Earth, finding it in the grain of golden oak planks of the Mansion meeting hall floor.

Taking a deep breath, she reached through her feet, further down, to the soil beneath the building foundation, and outward, to the gardens outside the tall, multi-paned arched windows that opened to the backside of the stately Spanish-style building that had been her home since she arrived in California, a confused thirteen-year-old, afraid of her own power.

She'd rarely had cause to enter this room. School meetings were usually held in the library, with the handful to one dozen students studying Elemental Sorcery in the Mansion at any given time.

The meeting hall was clearly designed for conclaves just like this. Whitewashed walls rose to a vaulted, timbered ceiling. Ranks of wooden chairs with blue-cushioned seats were arrayed in concentric rows around the compass rose inlaid in the center of the golden oak floor.

Terrance Sterling, current head of the Association of Magical Arts and Sorcery, sat in the inner circle along with Jasmine's aunt and mother—Doreen and Cecelia—Ernesto, and some sorcerers Carol had never met before. The two resident teachers were also there, Mrs. Chisolm and Mr. Wong.

Carol and Jasmine sat in the second circle, shoulder to knee with the other sorcerers. The room swirled with the scent and push of magic. Cinnamon. Loam. Ocean. Pine. High desert. Chocolate. And the strange swirl of those who held multiple elements, blending themselves, both subtle and complex. Like Ernesto, both Air and Fire, whose pomade scent made her wish they were back in his bed.

Terrance Sterling, a Master of all Four Elements, known as a Quintessence, ruled them all.

For now.

That he was here at all was a surprise. Up until a few days ago, he'd been in a coma, put there by Jasmine herself, whose sorcery had opted for that instead of outright killing him.

"We *have* to take that bastard down. For real this time," Jasmine muttered in her ear.

"Ssh!" Carol said, when she saw a sorcerer jerk his head toward them. He was from the East Coast, Carol knew. A black man in a Nehru jacket, bald head gleaming in the sun streaming through the arched windows.

Jasmine was right. Terrance Sterling was a menace to the whole Association. He'd opened them to foreign magics, putting everything at risk.

Carol and Ernesto had discovered the what, but they didn't yet exactly know the why.

Other than, the man had always been greedy for more power, and being head of the most potent sorcerous association on the continent wasn't enough anymore. He was working for the government somehow, but not in any way that made sense.

Terrance and Jasmine had already fought some old-school magical battle, right outside on the front lawn. That was freaky. Carol had been sure someone would die.

And he should have, the way Jasmine's bolt had drilled through the gold lapel pin directly above his heart.

As it was, his eyes still looked too black, too blank. Carol knew his soul still wandered the æthers somewhere. If whomever he was working for didn't have it locked away in a box.

It had broken Helen Price, Terrance's right hand, to know her boss and friend, and maybe even her lover, had betrayed the Association in that way.

Or so she said.

Oh, Helen must have known for quite some time. The thing that broke her was other people finding out.

And Helen sure wasn't in the room today. She'd been missing ever since Jasmine had challenged Terrance, and they'd ripped up huge chunks of lawn, as big as the space left where his soul should be. Helen had taken Terrance away somewhere "for healing," and disappeared herself.

Carol snapped her eyes back into focus.

Jasmine's Aunt Doreen had stood, and was smoothing down the creases in her navy dress. Every hair of her new Diahann Carroll cut was perfect, which was not her usual state.

"I want to call this meeting to order," she said. "Thank you all for coming. I know many of you traveled a long way at great expense to get here."

"Aren't you forgetting something, Doreen?" Terrance butted in.

Doreen turned to him, her cinnamon fire crackling close to the tips of her fingers. Doreen was scary when she was mad.

"What might that be?"

He stood then, buttoning the pinstriped jacket of his bespoke charcoal-gray suit. A Tree of Life set with one jewel for each sphere tacked down a burgundy paisley tie.

"I am head of this Association and should be welcoming our guests."

A tiny spark cracked from Doreen's right hand before she regained her composure and shut it down.

"I think you know that you're the reason we called this meeting, Terrance."

He feigned shock. "Really? It wasn't the rash actions of those angry *children* there?" He pointed a slim pale finger toward Carol and Jasmine, using his blue faience scarab ring as a focus to gather his own powers, ready to strike.

What in the Powers? Carol felt Jasmine tense up beside her.

This was enough. Carol shoved up from her chair, tucking her long blond hair behind her ears. Her connection to Earth grew inside her. She built a solid platform of the Element beneath her feet.

Carol wanted to be ready, in case Doreen needed backup.

Doreen held up her right hand. Everyone in the room could feel the Fire banked inside it.

"I think you know that you've put this Association at risk, Terrance. You've brought twisted Temple magic into our holy spaces. You are consorting with beings who attack us," Doreen continued. "You work with sigils not our own."

"Is that so?" he said, voice sharp as a witch's knife.

The other sorcerers shifted in their chairs. The man from New York spoke, rich voice echoing through the room. Whoa. He carried Air, but Carol wanted what he had. Badly.

"I want to hear what our sisters and the *respected* Doreen have to say. We frankly didn't come here to listen to you, Terrance. We came because *something* is *wrong* on the inner planes, and has been, for some time. These sisters got it going on, and I offer them my respect, and my ear."

"I don't know what you think you're talking about, Mr. Oluo, but..."

Carol felt Terrance reach for his combined magics and pull, practically tugging matter from the room.

"You will *cease!*" A woman's voice rolled from wall to wall. Ocean, like Jasmine, but colder, wilder. Like a Northern sea. She stood then, so tall, red hair flaming down her back, strong jaw framing pale lips. Her green eyes narrowed at Terrance as he raised his right hand again.

With a simple gesture from her own right hand, the woman sent a wave of power across the room. Terrance braced himself, angling his body as though he walked into a storm.

"You will *sit!* And you will *listen*. And you will not raise your magic in this room again, or believe me, Terrance Sterling, this convocation will take your sorcery away."

They could do that? Carol thought. Jasmine squeezed her leg. Carol grabbed her best friend's hand, squeezing back. Then Carol dropped her hand again, wanting to be ready to use her own sorcery if she needed to.

The red-haired woman stood in place. Waiting. Staring Terrance Sterling down.

He shook out his hands, as if he could dissipate the energy that was now streaming toward him from most of the sorcerers in the room. Tugging the snowy white cuffs down from beneath his jacket sleeves, he pinched his lips tight, unbuttoned the pinstriped jacket, and sat back down.

"Please continue, Doreen," the woman said.

"Thank you, Eileen. Though before I continue, I feel the need to ask this assembly whether or not Terrance should even remain in the room for these proceedings."

"I don't trust him outside this room, that's for sure," the man in the rust-colored Nehru jacket said. The man had spoken before, in an accent that could only be from New York, though Carol didn't know enough to tell what borough he was from. "Maybe someone should make sure he can't leave his chair."

A huge man with wild, red-blond hair and bushy sideburns and a button-up flowered shirt with a long collar stood up then. "I can make sure he doesn't leave," he drawled. "Want me to fix him to the chair?"

Jasmine leapt up then. Carol could hear the breath rasping through her lungs, and practically tasted the Ocean teeming in her friend's veins.

"No!" Jasmine shouted. "A judge in Chicago ordered a Black Panther shackled and gagged during his trial. Are we going to do the same?"

A sea of faces, black and brown, pale pink, and olive, they all turned and stared at the white girl with her straight blond hair, and the black girl whose dark natural curls formed a kinky halo around her head.

"Speak, sister," said Mr. Oluo. "Why shouldn't we do this thing?"

Carol heard Jasmine reply, but wasn't following, because answers to one thousand questions suddenly thrummed through her entire being. She reached for words and the puzzle pieces that had been floating in the air suddenly snapped together. And Carol knew. She knew why the spiders and the sigils. She knew why the mention of government, and the taste of strange power.

"Terrance Sterling is working for the United States government *against its own people.*"

A wild wind rushed through the room, whipping up magic, rattling the window panes, increasing the heady mix of scents until she almost felt sick with it.

"Do you have proof?" the red haired woman—Eileen?—asked.

Jasmine stood strong beside Carol. Water and Earth formed a solid boundary. A cup. A dam. A force to be reckoned with. And then Carol's best friend threw back her head and laughed.

"Do we have *proof?*" Jasmine asked. "Just look at him! Look at the sphere of Earth in his Tree of Life. Carol can tell you all about it. What's missing there?"

No one spoke. Jasmine looked at Carol then, waiting.

"That's right, the tiger eye that represents the balance of the elements on this plane is gone. What's there instead? Hematite. It's the only thing keeping him in his body." Carol swallowed. Thinking. "And while you're at it, go look at the sigil inscribed above the door to his suite. You'll find it's Solomonic, and pretty damned disturbing, dig? Though he may have tried to erase it by now. I guarantee traces are still there. This whole place still stinks of it, no matter how hard Mrs. Chisolm and Mr. Wong have worked to cleanse this space."

Every head snapped from Carol to Aunt Doreen, seeking confirmation. She just nodded.

Then Jasmine's aunt spoke. "You may as well go check both things, though."

A skinny white man in a denim suit rose and left the room.

Terrance stood up, too.

Ernesto stopped him, hand gripping Terrance's shoulder.

CHAPTER FOUR
DOREEN

Doreen hated the big, echoey room. It always felt too formal, like most things about the Mansion. She put up with the Association because that was what hereditary sorcerers did.

Most of them, anyway.

Doreen knew this meeting would be difficult, and would most likely be the first of many.

She also knew she had to lobby for her sister, Cecelia, to become head of the Association. Other people could do the job, for sure, but Cecelia had the stability of her marriage to William, and was both a strong sorcerer and a mediating force.

Cecelia would never be one to add oil to fire. Her deep Earth power was steady and smooth as it came.

But looking around the room, feeling the agitation bursting and crackling around her, Doreen also knew she was going to need help.

She couldn't put Cecelia forward herself, and had been out of the game for too long. Her alliances were all ten years old.

Doreen wrapped her left hand around the metal disc that rested just above her breasts, suspended from a silver chain. It was a full moon amulet from her mother—known as Momma Beatrice to the community when she was alive—and it had become a gateway for Doreen.

As she held the amulet, her vision shifted, and Doreen felt herself walking on the astral planes, through a thick, gray mist. Walking toward the realm of her ancestors. Not the distant place and time. Not all the way back to Angola, and the woman with the chipped tooth and red mud covering her hair. She was headed someplace more familiar. And a little more real.

Momma's distillery. The room where she dried herbs and flowers, and made tinctures charged by sun and moon. The place where she kept her most prized magical object, a perfect crystal sphere.

The same sphere that now rested on an altar in Doreen's attic, waiting for the next full or dark moon.

Momma was there. Doreen could almost smell her, and smell the bitterness of the herbs and the sweet stink of drying flowers.

"What do you need, child?" her mother asked.

"We're in big trouble, Momma," she replied.

Irritation crossed her mother's round face. *"Well then, do what needs to be done!"*

"...do you think, Doreen?" Ernesto was asking as she snapped back into focus. The room had grown still in her absence. How long had she been gone?

And what was the question?

It didn't matter. Talking didn't matter. Doing mattered. Magic mattered.

Her niece was always quoting Fred Hampton, the Black Panther leader who had just narrowly escaped assassination.

"We're gonna have do more than talk. We're gonna have to start practicing," Jasmine would quote, *"and that's very hard."*

Well, Doreen was just going to stand here in this room filled with sorcerers and practice, then, wasn't she?

She smiled at her niece, sitting in the second round of chairs, and then Doreen closed her eyes for a moment, testing out the edges of the room. Tasting the air. Feeling the pressure of the Elements, and all the potential magic gathered in the space.

Meanwhile, she stoked the Elemental Fire inside her belly, fanned the flames. Let the scent of cinnamon rise up on her skin.

She walked across the compass rose in the center of the floor, sensible heels striking at the wood, straight toward Terrance. Holding out her right hand, she palmed his forehead. He flinched back at her touch, but only for a moment. His skin felt clammy. Disgusting.

Doreen closed her eyes again, one hand on the metal moon disc, the other on Terrance Sterling's head. The power from every sorcerer in the room felt as if it rushed toward her. But she also felt that wasn't true.

She felt the pockets holding back. Earth there. Fire here. Air. Air. Water. Some of the weaker men and women. Maybe. Doreen was too wrapped up in what she needed to do to tell, but she filed the knowledge away.

Her Fire flowed down her right arm into her hand until it began to warm, then grow almost hot. Terrance hissed out through his teeth and tried to move away again.

"You. Will. Be. Still," Eileen said from across the room. Terrance subsided.

Doreen rocked forward and backward on her heels, swaying toward Terrance and away, always moving with his head cupped in her palm.

She began to croon, a low, eerie sound that filled the room. A few other voices joined her, building resonance. Then more voices joined. She felt Jasmine and Carol, weaving their two elements together. She felt it when Ernesto joined them, braiding Air and Fire into Water and Earth.

Doreen pulled on their sorcery. They fed it towards her. The disc vibrated beneath her left palm, rattling against her fingernails.

"I can't, I can't…please." The words whined low from Terrance's throat.

"Shhhh," Doreen crooned, weaving more energy into and around the man who had been her colleague, and once upon a time, her friend.

She pumped more power into him, not to hurt him, but to *show* him.

He didn't need any more power than this. He never had. He had been a fool to betray the trust.

And one day, they would hold a tribunal on the astral plane, and the bell would toll and strip his sorcery away.

But right now? The man still had a chance. He could redeem himself.

The singing and weaving rose and built, forming one body, one powerful force. This. This was what sorcery could be. They could build anything together.

Including a new world.

The door hit the wall with a boom, and the scent and taste of ice entered the room.

"Stop it!" a woman's voice cried. Helen. "What are you doing to him?"

Doreen kept her hand steady on Terrance's head. She could hear scuffling, and chairs screeching on the hardwood floor.

Terrance's hands gripped her wrist, trying to yank her hand away. The braided sorcery still poured through her, cementing her hand to his head.

"Terrance! Doreen!" Helen said.

What in all the Powers was Helen Price doing back at the Mansion?

Momma, help me. If ever there was any healing, any vision, any sorcerous trick you knew that you didn't pass along, I need it now.

There. There it was. Doreen lifted her hand from the disc and reached, just behind Terrance Sterling's head.

Where a small white spider hung by one silken thread.

She plucked it from the air, and crushed it between her pointer finger and thumb. It sizzled and something jabbed her, like the small prick of a needle or the bite of an ember from a dying fire.

Terrance collapsed, sobbing.

"Terrance, it's time now. You have to tell us the truth. The truth is the only thing that will set you free."

He couldn't even look at her, just leaned so far from her that he was half falling out of his wooden chair.

But there was still power in this room. And the Mansion wasn't clean yet. That spider had found its way in somehow.

But they would deal with that later.

Doreen held up her hands and turned in a slow circle, surveying the room.

Chairs were overturned. Two sorcerers held Helen Price, her creamy, elegant Chanel suit ripped and askew on her shoulders, strands from her dark, Jackie O bob stuck to her too-red lipstick.

Doreen's old friend was so pale. Breath heaving, she was practically panting with the effort to resist the man and woman who held fast to her arms.

"Terrance!" Helen said again, then looked Doreen straight in the face, with a look so filled with hatred Doreen couldn't believe they had ever had affection for each other, once upon a time.

Doreen would likely get a lecture from Jasmine about wealthy white folks always choosing one another, but it gave her pangs of sadness all the same.

"Helen," Doreen said. "Did you really come here to help him? Do you really choose this man who betrayed our oaths? Who lied to us? Who sold us out to who knows whom?"

"He didn't!"

Doreen just shook her head at that. Helen knew it all was true. That was why she went away. She couldn't bear the truth. Turns out, she still couldn't; she'd just decided to turn it into a delusion.

Doreen shook out her hands and spoke to the room.

"I decree, here and now, that Terrance Sterling is anathema to the Association. We must decide his level of guilt and culpability. And then we need to decide who to put into his place."

"You can't..." Helen said.

"She can," said Gregory Oluo, the sorcerer from New York City. "Things should never have been allowed to reach this level of discordance. We should have known. We *all* should have known." He looked around the space. "We could feel something was wrong out on the æthers, but how many of us did anything at all?"

He clapped his hands three times.

"Let it be said that Terrance Sterling, regardless of the facts that we must gather, is clearly unfit to lead. I motion that the floor be open to nominations now."

"You can't do that! We need a proper hearing first, and to weigh the outcomes. We also need to build a proper case for candidacy..." It was a woman Doreen hadn't seen in years, another white woman who worked out of Seattle, Doreen thought.

"Oh, stop it," said Simon Tanaka. He hadn't even left his chair, as though the proceedings were beneath him. Doreen knew, however, that he was just conservative in using his power. Air, she thought she remembered. "You all can see the evidence clear as day. The man is a mess. His aura is shattered. The only thing keeping him together right now is some strange magic. Not ours."

"It's Solomonic," Carol said. "But twisted wrong."

"That feels...correct," Simon replied. Then he stood and walked toward the door. "The rest of you can argue this out if you want to, but I know of only one person the majority of us could stomach as Association head."

He paused at the open doorway.

"I nominate Cecelia. And now I'm going to the library for a drink."

CHAPTER FIVE
JASMINE

There's trouble everywhere, hechicera!" Rosalia said.

We were back in my parents' living room—Ernesto, Rosalia, Carol, my parents, and me—sitting on the navy blue couches, staring at the the white brick fireplace and the family photos grouped on the back wall, drinking the coffee my father, William, had been good enough to make. He'd even put cookies on a white plate, peanut butter, with the crosshatched tops.

My dad was the best. Really. I realized all the little ways he took care of me and my mother, year in and year out. I'd never noticed it before.

The meeting at the Mansion had been a mess. I was glad to leave the sorcerers gathered in gossiping clumps, or using the library as some sort of Association war room.

But that didn't mean my troubles were over.

This was going to be another long damn meeting, and the feeling that we were running out of time clawed at my gut. Something big needed to happen, but with the Solstice and full moon running hard on each other's heels, I wasn't sure how we were going to pull it all together.

Or even what *it* exactly was. We'd called in Rosalia for help with the Association business, and to talk about our next plan for defending the people against the FBI. But she was having none of it.

"What do you mean, Rosalia?"

Huh. That was my non-magical dad asking the question. He usually stayed out of the logistical discussions, preferring to act as an anchor to us all, a role he'd held for as many years as my parents had been married, and done as well as any person could.

I loved my dad. No matter what, he was a rock. His handsome face, slightly scarred with a pockmark here and there. His soft woven sweater, a pleasing shade of orange against his pale brown skin. The dark stubble on his chin.

And the scent of pipe tobacco that always clung to his clothes. I loved it all.

But right now? Him speaking up? It added to my sense of unease.

All was not right in the universe.

I sipped at my coffee. It was slightly bitter, which meant my dad was nervous when he made it. Usually it was smooth as silk on my tongue. I grabbed the little milk jug off the coffee table and lightened it up.

"What I mean is, we fight a war on several fronts. You understand this, yes?"

My dad nodded. He'd served time in the Pacific during World War II. He didn't talk about those days much, the time before he met my mother. But he knew how messy wars could be, first hand.

And he'd seen what this war had done to me already. I rubbed the hollow at the base of my shoulder and looked out the window onto the fading day.

Rosalia was still speaking. "Some of the Aztec dancers who've been going on the marches with the people? They report on their fellow dancers being possessed."

"What?" This was news to me.

"The Feathered Serpent. It seems that it, or he, likes people paying so much attention to him again. He decided he wanted more. So he is taking over the dancers as they practice. As they pray and dance to him."

"Is this a problem?" my mother asked.

Rosalia just raised one sharp eyebrow.

"Of course it is. Yes, I can see that," my mother hurried on. "I just thought it might be something that could help us in this…" She waved her hands around, cutting small slices through the air. "This complicated weave of sorcery, perverted Solomonic Temple magic, Federal agents sending magic snakes after my daughter, and panther shifters running through the streets!"

My mother took a breath. "It just seems to me that if old Gods are flying through the air, maybe a little embodiment will help the cause."

A startled laugh burst out of me. I couldn't help it.

"What's so funny, Jasmine?" my father asked.

"This. Everything. My mother's right. If someone had told me three years ago that the US government was going to be attacking us with magic, that I'd be dating a shape-shifter, and it seemed like the fate of the world rested on a bunch of young revolutionaries barely out of high school, I might have thought they were crazy."

I looked at everyone gathered in the living room. "So a massive ancient Power possessing some dancers who wear his colors and dance in feathered headdresses to honor the old ways? Why not? And maybe it is a good thing. Maybe it's time."

"Time for what?" Ernesto asked, before shoving one of my dad's home-baked peanut butter cookies in his mouth.

"Time for the sorcerers to take over the world."

The words were out of my mouth before I could even think about them, let alone call them back.

Ernesto coughed, practically choking on his cookie. "Not very Marxist of you is it, Jasmine Jones?"

I felt embarrassed and a little pissed off.

"Not from *the people*. From the Feds and the cops. From the wealthy people like Terrance who always end up only caring about themselves."

By all the Powers, I was so tired of sitting in meetings with middle-aged, middle-class people, no matter how much I loved them. Not that it was fair to lump Ernesto in that camp in the first place. For one thing, he wasn't quite old enough.

I stood up and stalked over to the arch of a doorway and leaned against it. "Look. The people dig that we've got magic, right? And they're getting used to having actual panthers running around. They *like* the sense of power and safety knowing they've got a bunch of sorcerers around provides. And they even dig what Doreen and Patrice and all of them are doing. Teaching them actual magic."

Leaning over the couch, I grabbed a cookie for myself.

"*That* is what we're after, right? All power to all the people. Not hoarding magic anymore. Not hoarding money, or supplies. Not hoarding knowledge..." Excitement bubbled inside me like a spring.

I hadn't felt this way since I was fourteen and first learned how to dissolve a rock in water using nothing but my mind and my natural sorcery.

"Don't you see? All the shit on the Panther's Ten Point Program can come true! We can give the people education, and health care, and they can take their own freedom. We can get rid of the cops. We can..."

Rosalia shook her head. "That is a beautiful visión, hechicera," she said. "But you do not know that these Powers of yours? And the beings we call Gods? They hold their own agendas. And they help the people, it is true. But what happens when they want something different? And our people are dependent on them? And some of them are half mad with being ridden by things they cannot comprehend?"

The excitement in me hardened. "Sounds better than being shot in the streets, clubbed half to death, or being sent to die halfway around the world. Sounds better than not having food or clean water, or watching your kids die because you can't afford a doctor."

I took a bite of the cookie. It smelled delicious. It tasted like sand.

My mother spoke then. "I have to agree with my daughter. We are living on a precipice. We all feel the pressure of change. And there's one thing every sorcerer knows about change."

"What's that, my love?" my father asked.

"You never can predict what you'll find on the other side."

The phone rang, shrill and loud from the kitchen.

"I'll get it," my dad said. He patted my shoulder as he passed me. I heard the click of the receiver and the rumble of his voice saying hello.

"Rosalia, you're the one who showed me what was possible when you dragged me to the astral plane that day. You showed me how we can use our power. And what my potential was."

For the first time since I'd met her, the hechicera didn't fix me with her citrine gaze. She just looked out the window at the coming night.

"I don't know if we can do this, but I know we have to try," I said.

My dad came back into the room.

"That was Jimmy on the phone, baby girl. Something's going down at a La Piranya café and they need help."

CHAPTER SIX
JASMINE

By the time we got to the coffeehouse in East Los Angeles, my heart was about leaping from my chest, and I could feel the ocean all around me. My sorcery reached for whatever it could, every water droplet in the air, in my spit, in the roots of plants, in the condensation on the engine block in Ernesto's Mustang.

And of course, in California, the ever-present stretch of ocean. Even slightly inland, I could feel it. I could also feel the tugging of the moon. It was almost full.

We parked two blocks away, down a little alley off the main drag.

"This is not good," Rosalia muttered.

It was just she, Carol, Ernesto, and I. We'd decided to split up. There was just too much work to be done.

So my parents and Doreen remained in Crenshaw to discuss the fate of the Association and Terrance. And how to start dealing with the FBI on a more concerted, planned level, instead of just reacting all the time.

People were out on the streets, some of it the usual evening crush: folks getting off the bus, coming home from work, buying tortillas for dinner if they hadn't gotten them fresh that morning.

But there was something else going on, too.

"Do you feel that?" Carol asked.

"What do you sense, mi amor?" Ernesto asked.

I filed that away to ask Carol about later. Seemed like something else had heated up when I was busy fighting snakes up on the astral. Carol and I hadn't had time to talk about anything but the movement in a week.

"It feels like this neighborhood has..." We kept walking rapidly as she searched for words. People parted for us as though we were the advance team of an army.

We turned the corner onto a busy boulevard, with cars rushing and booming by. It was a long stretch of road. We were walking next to a fence covered with bougainvillea, flashing fuchsia every time a streetlamp hit it. Across the street were low buildings, some industrial, with a cluster of shops just past the next corner.

Carol still hadn't finished her answer. It took me a minute to realize she'd stopped dead on the sidewalk right as we turned onto the boulevard. Damn.

"Rosalia!" I called after the hechicera who was stolidly moving forward down the broad sidewalk, past palm trees and people. She stopped and turned. I waved her back.

Carol tilted her head side to side. A slight breeze lifted her straight blond hair. I could practically feel her rooting into the sidewalk, searching concrete and dirt, and the pipes and roots below, for information.

"It's like the whole neighborhood has shifted sideways. Or like...like someone picked it up and rotated it a quarter turn." Carol said.

I wrapped my arms around my leather coat, and we all looked at Rosalia, who held her hands out, palms down to the sidewalk, head up, nose practically sniffing at the air.

"This is very, very bad." Rosalia dropped her voice. We cupped our bodies closer around her to hear. "La policía y the FBI...they are trying to send us all to El Mundo Malo."

A shock of heat, then cold, ran through me, as if I were going to be sick. Then I just felt angry. Then I reached for the Ocean, drawing as much power into my body as I could.

"Pinche cabrón," Ernesto swore. Guess he was pissed off, too.

"Get ready everyone," I said. "This war is officially *on*."

I knew they could feel the sorcery roiling inside me. I felt the buildup of their own as they drew on their Elements, getting ready to cast.

"Where are we going?" I asked Rosalia.

"It's just there. Up ahead."

And then I saw it at the corner where two boulevards met. A single-story Spanish hacienda-style building with arched windows. Some of them boarded up. Some dark.

But one? Light spilled out from a curved arch and onto the sidewalk. An agitated group of people spilled out with it, some even pushing off the sidewalk and onto Olympic Boulevard.

I began to run, boots eating up the concrete, leather coat flying out behind me. I could hear the heels of Carol's boots beside me, and just hoped Ernesto was with Rosalia. Not that the hechicera needed any help.

Brown Berets were everywhere, and a few Black Panthers, too. Couple of skinny Asian teens. And magic. Bad magic. That strange signature of formal Solomonic working. The slight taint of the astral leaking over into earth.

And the papery scent of snake.

"Powers be damned!" I said.

"The sorcerers are here," someone on the sidewalk said, and suddenly Jimmy was pushing through the crush, coming toward me. He folded me in his arms, just for a moment, wrapping his musk and love around me, his body coiled with tension.

"Jaz. Carol. It's pretty bad."

Rosalia and Ernesto arrived, and the hechicera grabbed her velvet skirts and said, "Take me inside."

A few Brown Berets cleared the way toward the door set into the glass-fronted archway.

And we smacked into a wall of magic.

I shoved through with a blast of ocean blue fire, hoping I didn't hit anyone.

"Stop, Jasmine!" Rosalia said, grabbing my right hand.

We paused at the threshold, looking at the coffee mugs tipped over onto tables tucked into the bright windows on either side of the glass door, dark brown liquid soaking into light brown wood.

There was a small sign in the lower corner of one of the huge window nooks: "Join the Brown Berets and be part of being proud."

A stack of the Chicano paper *La Causa* had tipped over, fanning copies out across the floor. "Free the Biltmore 6!" the hand-lettered headline read.

The place was empty except for two Brown Berets in boots, dark, knife-creased trousers, and tan military style jackets, standing guard over a third man who slumped across a wooden table to the right. His beret had fallen from his head onto the floor. A tan rectangle was next to it. Then I understood.

It was the protective patch Ernesto, Carol, and Rosalia had magicked up just a few weeks ago, ripped off and lying facedown on the tiled floor.

"Can we go in now?" I asked Rosalia.

"Sí."

"Let us all do this together, shall we?" Ernesto said, looking at me. And he was right. Rather than blasting through, we should examine the magic first and see if we could take it down.

The echoes of the Temple pillars we had seen in the battle with the Fed and his minions at Laguna Park were present. I knew Rosalia would already be up on the astral plane, checking them out, so I left that to her.

"What are the corners anchored to?" I asked Carol and Ernesto. "And Jimmy, would you keep people off our backs?"

"These people aren't coming near you, Jaz," he replied. "They know what's going down."

I spared a glance over my shoulder and saw that my lover was right. The people on the sidewalk had calmed down since we arrived, and watched us, most with respectful looks in their brown eyes. A few looked at us suspiciously, but frankly, I would too.

"Okay. Carol?"

"It's in the walls themselves," she said. "Past the opening. Further out, where the support beams for the roof meet the walls."

"Are there sigils?"

Rosalia spoke then. "Yes. The sigils are on the four corners, just like Carol said. But they feel different than the ones we saw before."

She reached out a hand and dragged me onto the astral plane, stars winking all around us, the Temple space a toxic edifice, rising up through stars and mist.

The hechicera was right. It felt different.

"Carol!" I called out. "What do you see?"

Carol, though her Element was Earth, had started having visions a month ago. Her head had cracked open, filled with light and noise, and she saw visions of apocalyptic future and visions of the past. She also began drawing sigils in a trance. Sigils we now knew were connected to these Temple magic spaces.

These Temples we now knew were erected by a government at war with its people.

"These sigils are close. But different," she said. "Oh shit."

"What?" Ernesto said.

I snapped back into my body from the astral. Rosalia could stay in both places for as much time as it took. I had to keep popping back and forth still.

Carol looked even paler than usual under the golden glow of the café lights.

"They're building four temples. And together, the four will build a fifth."

I didn't know exactly what that meant, but I knew we were suddenly playing a game, not just with the lives of our people at stake, but a game with implications so huge, I wasn't sure that we could stop it.

Not in time.

CHAPTER SEVEN
SNAKES AND SPIDERS

*S*he came to him as though he had called her on the phone himself. He could feel the place he'd sent one of his magic serpents to lodge inside her sweet brown flesh.

It was gone now, but the trace remained. Just enough to keep the connection open.

He watched her run toward the café, long leather coat trailing out behind her. As if she were Superman or something.

That Panther bitch. She thought she could outwit him. Thought that she could kill him. Thought that he would fail.

The barbed cincture around Samuels' right thigh itched and burned, reminding him of his duty. Reminding him of his discipline, honed and practiced over years.

His magic fed on blood and will. Nothing would take that away. Not even the Master.

He knew exactly what the girl would find when she got inside that bright café. One of those Mexicans, playing at revolution. Dead. With one of Samuels' sigils carefully carved into his chest.

Inhaling car exhaust and night blooming brugmansia, Samuels couldn't wait to get out of this town. Too bright during the day. Too dirty at night. At least the interesting places were. The places where magic actually did its work. Not that Mansion, stuck in the hills, playing at sorcery.

Playing at power.

"Should we attack?" one of his operatives said. Sullivan. A slightly portly man with a bull neck. Sharp mind, though. He needed to learn patience.

The dark glasses on Sullivan's face, which was ruddy from too much Southern California winter sun, reflected the passing cars as he waited for Samuels' answer.

All the people in those cars, they knew nothing of the battles going on. Nothing of the quest for dominance. They thought their petty ladder climbing or their "sticking it to the Man" were struggles for sovereignty.

They knew nothing at all.

Samuels shook his head. "Not yet. I want to see what they do first. Is Hopkins still in the æthers? On the astral?"

"Yes sir."

"Good. We need to keep an eye on that Temple. Make sure they don't get close enough to crack the pillars like last time."

What was she waiting for? The sorcerers were doing something outside of the café. They hadn't gone in yet. Samuels knew they felt the magic they'd left there. He felt it when the Panther slammed up against it, trying to blast through.

So why the silence?

"Boss!"

"What is it?" he snapped out.

"It's Hopkins…what he's showing me right now…" Sullivan's broad white forehead was beading up with sweat. "It looks like they're trying to take down the pillars."

"What?"

"That's what he's showing me. The blond girl…it looks like she's got some key into the sigils. She's taking them apart."

Samuels felt wild inside, and knew a grin had split his face.

"Boss?"

"Perfect. That's just perfect." Samuels turned to him, to the shocked look on his face. "That's just what I needed to know."

J. Edgar Hoover wasn't going to know what hit him.

"Tell Hopkins to keep shoring up the Temple. I'm heading in across the street."

"Alone?"

"Yes, alone. We should have brought more men for this job, but three is what we have. So I'm going in alone."

And he was going to enjoy it. Every minute of it.

CHAPTER EIGHT
CAROL

Ernesto tapped his Elemental sorcery and began the technique they'd practiced, battle after battle, over the last few weeks.

Carol drew on the power of Earth from everywhere around her, and stored it in the place between her navel and her spine, consolidating. Waiting.

The sorcery bumped against the edges of her skin, wanting out. She waited until Ernesto was ready.

He was. She opened herself to him as though opening to a kiss. Ernesto braided his twin energies of Air and Fire, feeding them into the opening in her energy field, braiding Water from Jasmine, until all four Elements met in Carol's body and combined.

Carol opened the energy centers at her feet, the crown of her head. And then she opened up her hands. That was where sorcery flowed most easily, here on earth and on the astral planes.

Rosalia kept watch in two worlds, guiding the careful placement of Carol's hands.

They needed to do this right.

Carol slowed her breathing, and rooted her energy more deeply into the ground that rested far beneath the concrete and cables and sewers. No matter what, Earth was always there.

The sigils glowed in her mind. Deep black, limned in golden white.

She paid no attention to the cars going by, or to Carlos Santana's rapid-fire guitar blasting into the street. She couldn't even feel the people she knew must still be gathered on the sidewalk.

All Carol felt was the flow of combined Elemental sorcery moving through her, enabling her to do magic that shouldn't be possible for a person like her.

Sending out a thread of green-tinged light toward the pillar, she felt. And tried to See.

There. In the black and tangled shape that looked like a strange piece of art absentmindedly drawn while a person's mind was occupied with something else, she began to see the form.

She saw how this shape fit into another. How those two lines formed a Hebrew letter. How that sweep made a clear image. How they all combined to form the whole, locking in the magic words, the secrets, the combination none but the magician who made this thing should know.

She just needed to…erase the top bar of the sigil on the pillar in front of her. Now that she saw how they fit together, it should be easy. But she wasn't used to working on the astral plane like this, and began to sweat a little under her rust-colored leather coat.

Ignoring the sensations riddling her body, Carol focused on the astral plane and the clarity of vision Rosalia was lending her.

Here. Now. She sent a thread of green fire toward the sigil, and saw the top bar flare and wink out.

"We're in!"

The magic shields collapsed. The men inside the café staggered. One reached for a knife, the other pulled a gun.

Ernesto called out to them, "Vamos a entrar!"

The man with the knife looked panicked and a little ill, but the other one holstered his gun and nodded.

Carol realized she'd been holding her breath, and fought to breathe normally again, shaking off her hands and stomping her feet.

Rosalia took her hand. "Good work, maga."

Carol licked her lips, not even able to speak as the Elemental sorcery slowly drained from her body, pooling toward the sidewalk before dissipating as it hit the air.

She was left with Earth. Her Element. And that felt normal. And good.

"Okay," she said. "I'm ready to go in."

Jasmine stomped across the tiles and knelt in front of the table where the man was slumped.

It was clear that he was dead.

"How?" Ernesto asked one of the Brown Berets.

"We have no idea, man. All we know is the men in black showed up two hours ago and started a freaky light show, tu sabes?"

Ernesto nodded, waving a hand for the man to continue.

"And then, it was like a force field shoved us all out toward the walls. Our man Luis slammed into the glass window, almost broke it."

Carol turned and saw a crack in the big window in the nook on the left side of the door. The table was shoved at an angle against the wall.

But that didn't explain the dead man in the tan shirt.

Boom! A bolt from outside cracked the light fixture above Jasmine's head, raining glass shards down on her and the Brown Berets.

Jasmine rose and spun, turning toward the door where a white man with dark hair slicked back in a movie star wave stood. He wore a sharp black suit, white shirt, black tie, and glasses as dark as the sky outside perched on his narrow nose.

People on the sidewalk were screaming, and Carol heard Jimmy calling Jasmine's name.

An astral snake slithered out into the air, heading straight toward her friend. Jasmine was ready, and countered with a bolt of ocean-tinged blue fire.

Ernesto yelled, and shot yellow and red fire bolts toward the man, but they bounced off some sort of shield.

Only Jasmine's bolts hit true. The smell of singed wool hit Carol's nose. She shook her head to clear it, then crouched down and scooted toward the body at the table, rust knee boots crunching on the glass.

All of a sudden she just knew there was another key here. Trying to avoid touching the glass peppering his back, she attempted to lever the man up. She needed help.

The sorcery in the café grew thicker as Jasmine and the Fed began circling the small area in front of the door.

"Jasmine! I've got your back!" Jimmy's voice again. Carol looked, and all of a sudden, black paws replaced hands, a leather coat and green T-shirt slowly shifted into fur.

She froze in shock. Carol had never seen the actual change before. A bony hand shoved her, then slapped her face. Rosalia. She didn't even know the older woman had moved toward her.

"There's no time for that, maga!"

The hechicera yelled at the two Brown Berets, who had wisely crouched near the café counter, avoiding the sorcerous fire.

"Soldados! We need you!"

The men moved toward them in the same low crouch Carol had used. No one wanted to crawl over the shattered glass on the wood floors. No one wanted to stand up, either.

Between the four of them, they managed to drag the man onto the ground, partially hidden behind the tables and chairs, laying him on the floor, face up.

The room was darker now, lit only by the fixtures in the window seats and the sorcerous fire.

But there was enough light for Carol to see the sigil carved into the dead man's chest, in the vee of his tan shirt, just where the silver cross on the chain around his neck would have rested when he was still alive.

"Is it a sigil you know, maga?"

Carol searched her mind impatiently, then deepened her breathing again and sank her attention down. Down to the place in her center where she stored her power. She needed to access the seat of her power. To See what needed to be seen.

She thought of the journals where she'd drawn the sigils over and over, black ink scoring the white paper, pen nib practically ripping its way through.

"This…feels like a perversion of one of the sigils I've seen before. It's a sigil I think is… for building."

She looked up at the sorcerer's citrine eyes.

"But it's been changed. This one is designed to tear things down."

"What do you think it means, maga?"

Carol spared a glance to Jasmine and the man in black. It almost seemed as if he was letting her friend win. Or as if he didn't want the fight to end.

They were caught in a dance of magic and sorcery. A dance so close to love it was hard to miss. Carol squinted and saw the slender thread that held the two together.

From Jasmine's shoulder, to just over the federal agent's heart.

"I think he wants our help somehow."

The hechicera gripped her shoulders. "What do you mean? The pendejo is trying to kill us all!"

Maybe he was. It felt like that to Carol, too. The earth plane was still shifted slightly askew, like the café tables. Something was definitely wrong.

But this thing? It should have felt more like a trap.

Instead, it was beginning to feel a lot like an open invitation.

"I don't know," Carol said. "But I think he's changing the rules of the game. And he wants us all to help."

"Help how?"

Carol gave the sorcerer a tight little smile.

"He thinks we're going to be his pawns."

A massive wave of energy slammed into the room and shattered the front door.

Carol and the men ducked their heads into their arms.

Jimmy roared.

Rosalia stood. Carol heard the clamor of the silver stack of bracelets up the hechicera's wrists, and felt the velvet skirts slide across her arm.

So she looked.

And saw Jasmine standing there, a big black panther standing next to her, shoulder to her hip.

Voices shouted just outside the door. Then the sound of running feet.

The man in black was gone.

CHAPTER NINE
DOREEN

"Cecelia, Simon Tanaka is right. You have to do this," Doreen said, perched on the edge of the navy couch in her sister's living room.

William was clearing the coffee table and had been making noise about starting in on dinner.

Cecelia stood up suddenly, grabbed the coffee tray from William's hands, and headed for the kitchen.

"I don't have to *do* anything. You think I want to be head of the damn Association?"

Doreen sat in the living room, gobsmacked, staring at her sister's retreating back as she rattled the tray back down the hallway toward the kitchen.

Doreen leapt up, slamming her shin into the coffee table.

"Damn it!" she said. That was going to leave a bruise for sure. "Sorry, William, I know you only allowing cursing in the yard."

He just shook his head.

Following her sister's trim figure down the hallway, past the watchful gaze of Dr. King, Doreen wondered how she could have been so wrong.

Or was she?

Cecelia had flipped on the overhead light against the coming darkness. The kitchen, as usual, was neat as a pin. The blond wood cabinets gleamed, and the blue dish towels and curtains matched the blue lino-leum floor as always.

Funny, Doreen had never noticed it before, but Cecelia's kitchen should have been done in shades of green, like Doreen's was done in red.

Doreen had even decorated her Oakland kitchen in fire colors when she'd forsaken sorcery forever, she thought. And she still had a red table and red-patterned curtains.

Why in the world was Cecelia's kitchen—and living room too—Association blue? Not sapphire, it was true, but navy and pale blue.

She shook her head. It didn't matter what color Cecelia painted her damn walls!

"I thought you wanted this, Cecelia. I'm sorry. And you really are the only clear choice. Do you want everyone fighting over scraps or blowing up the peace that Powers-be-damned Terrance and *Helen*—oh she makes me so mad—forged all those years ago?"

Her sister practically flung the coffee cups into the sink, until William pushed his way into the room and gently steered her away, turning Cecelia as he did so that she faced Doreen again.

"You and Jasmine are always talking about how you hate that peace, you think it's a sham! You want to shake up the *damn* Association! Join the *revolution*!" Cecelia practically spat the words out into the air.

"Sit down with me. Please."

Doreen led her sister to the built-in benches and table near the back door. She finally got them both sitting down.

"Cecelia?" Doreen put her hand over her sister's smaller one. Cecelia drew her hand away. "What's got you so afraid?"

William bustled around, putting the kettle on for tea. He set the remaining cookies on the table between the two women, and put a smaller plate in front of each of them, to catch the crumbs.

Doreen nodded her thanks. Cecelia just stared past the blue curtains at the reflection of the ceiling light on the glass. It was winter dark, despite it only being 6 p.m. Solstice was coming tomorrow, and they didn't even have a plan to mark the turning of the solar tides.

"I never wanted this, Doreen. And I'm not afraid. I'm angry."

Cecelia broke off a piece of one of the cookies, then crumbled it to orangey dust on the small white saucer.

William nudged her over and squeezed his tall frame into the booth, big hand picking up a cookie, gentle as you please.

"Never wanted what?" asked Doreen, once he was settled.

"People looking at me so hard. More power than any one person should need." She dropped the cookie back onto the plate and looked around for a napkin.

"In the basket," William said.

"I still don't understand, Cecelia. This isn't about power. It's about service. Or it should be."

Cecelia's delicate hands dabbed the white paper napkin on her mouth. Doreen knew her sister was stalling because she hadn't taken one bite of that cookie before crumbling it to bits. Doreen just didn't know why.

"Please. Tell me."

Cecelia looked at Doreen with such pain and fury in her dark eyes, it almost felt like a slap in Doreen's face.

"This was supposed to be *you*," Cecelia said. The rich scent of loam perfumed the air. She was drawing on her Elemental power. "*You* were supposed to be the challenger. *You* were supposed to bring change when it was time. Not me. *You*."

Doreen's Fire flared up in response. How could she think that? Doreen wasn't fit for anything after Hector died. Nothing.

William covered Cecelia's hand with his own. Doreen and Cecelia both just sat there. Staring. Breathing. Cinnamon and loam. Fire and Earth.

"But I left," Doreen said quietly.

"But you left."

"No one blames you for that, Doreen," William said.

"It sure seems like *she* does."

Doreen got up, cinnamon stinking up the room around her. Too hot. She took a water glass from the dish drain and filled it at the sink. Then she drank deep, trying to cool her Fire.

"Hector died…" Cecelia began.

"My husband was slaughtered in the hills by the Los Angeles County Sheriff's department!" Doreen slammed the tumbler on the countertop. "I went a little crazy, okay! I think I had a right!"

Cecelia started to cry. Silent tears running down her cheeks, black mascara dotting itself on the brown skin around her eyes with every blink.

"*You're* crying? What do you have to cry about, Cecelia? I truly don't understand."

William cleared his throat.

"Those years were hard on us, Doreen. We were so worried about you, and you just cut yourself off. Even Terrance and Helen were concerned. We understood at first, of course, though Cecelia wanted to get in the car and drive north about once a week that first year. Just to make sure you were okay."

Doreen sagged against the countertop.

"We figured that once you healed, in a year or two, you'd come back," her sister finally said. "Or at least open up to me again. But you never did. Not for *ten years*, Doreen."

Doreen slid back into the booth and watched Cecelia blot her face with the white napkin.

"So you sent Jasmine to me."

William nodded. "It was the only thing we knew to do. For both of you."

"We thought if you saw Jasmine needed help, it might bring your sorcery back, Doreen."

Doreen was quiet for a moment.

"Thank you," she finally replied. "But don't you see, Cecelia? That all changed me. Hector's death. The years away. Even working with Jasmine and the Panthers now. I'm different. It isn't *me* anymore, this wanting to lead the Association. This diplomacy. It changed you, too. You're the right one now, Cecelia. You're the only one we've got."

"I still don't want it."

Doreen nodded at that. "I can't blame you for that. But Terrance Sterling wanted it *too* bad, and look where that led."

"Please don't make me do this. It's been bad enough seeing my own daughter in danger, let alone becoming the person who might send her in harm's way someday."

Doreen sighed, all her anger leaving in a rush. When had she become the strong one of the family? What had happened to them all?

"Cecelia. If the Association is going to survive, it needs an even touch. It needs a healer as well as a leader. It needs Earth. Not Fire. You're all that. And you were certainly the only diplomat in that room today. At least, the only one I'd trust."

William stood then. "Anyone want that dinner now?"

Doreen looked at her wristwatch. "I don't have much appetite, to be honest. Not after today. And I need to get back to the Mansion, then to Oakland. I've left things too long up there, with Patrice and Drake in charge."

Cecelia looked forlorn. Not a state Doreen had ever seen her in. Her sister looked up at her, eyes naked, washed free of makeup from her tears.

"Do you think we can fix things, Doreen?"

"Fix them? I'm not sure. But we can fight like hell to try and make things right."

Tugging on Cecelia's arm, she coaxed her sister up out of the booth. "You're strong, Cecelia. You always have been, and you know it. Just ask that handsome husband of yours."

"You leave my handsome husband alone." Cecelia smiled. Finally.

"Promise me you'll think about it."

Cecelia sighed. "I'll do it, Doreen. I know I have to. But I don't have to enjoy it."

"If you did, we'd start to worry."

She hugged her sister, breathing in the loamy scent of her skin. Remembering what it was like to grow into sorcery at her side.

There was a new generation of sorcerers now. And they needed training. But first, they needed a chance to survive.

"I have to get back. I'll tell Simon that you have my vote."

"I'll drive you to the Mansion," William said.

Doreen kissed her sister on the cheek and said goodbye.

CHAPTER TEN
JASMINE

It was late. I should have been tired, but I was hopped-up on sorcery. I knew that I would crash hard later.

We were back in the union hall. The big, blocky building off the freeway. The room was only half full tonight, not packed like it had been when we planned the march on Laguna Park.

Some people had dragged the orange molded-plastic chairs into rough concentric circles. Carol, Ernesto, and Rosalia all sat in the inner row. I stood at the outside edge with Jimmy, too keyed up from the battle with the Fed to sit quietly and wait my turn to speak.

I'd speak or not, no problem either way. But I wasn't going to be docile.

Local 535, staunch supporters of the Black Panther Party and the Brown Berets, agreed to let us have a private meeting here, which was a good thing, since Rosalia's shop was too small, the Mansion was currently a buzzing hive of jive, and Panther HQ had been blasted apart by the cops during the standoff.

The chairs were filled with Brown Berets, Black Panthers, a few members of Las Manos, and some close in folks who'd been at the café.

I would have been fine with the union organizers joining us, but people who'd been at La Piranya were feeling skittish about dealing with anyone not directly involved.

I didn't blame them.

David, part of Brown Beret leadership, stood on the other side of the circle from Jimmy and me. He leaned against the beige wall, next to a corkboard filled with announcements and notices.

He looked grim. Stern. Hands gripped behind his back, he turned to me and then looked to Carol.

"Did you bring this battle to our door?"

I could see why people followed him. His posture was strong. He carried himself like a man who knew what he was doing. And I suspected he had some hereditary magic in his family tree somewhere. There was a shine about him I couldn't place.

But none of that meant I was going to take any hint of disrespect. And his tone was sharper than I wanted, despite the fact that if I were in his position, I'd be asking the same question. And likely using the same tone.

But he needed to know he wasn't boss.

"Are we the cops?" I asked. "Are we the FBI? Are we Richard Fucking Nixon?"

He looked startled and took a step back. Then he threw his hands toward me in impatience. "We are not talking about the systemic oppression of all our peoples right now. We are speaking of one of my men ending up dead, with a symbol carved on his body that only your friend there seems to understand."

I stood a little taller.

"I feel that, brother. But you need to know that this shit has been happening to us for the past three weeks. I've been attacked myself, and have the scar to prove it." I rubbed the spot on my shoulder that was aching once again. That damn Fed was still attached to me somehow.

"But you are still alive."

"She is still alive because she is a trained sorcerer." Rosalia's voice cut across the room. "She is also a member of the Black Panther Party and my friend."

The threat was clear. Back off, or answer to the formidable woman with the citrine eyes.

"Trust me, brother," I said. "We want to know what the hell went down as much as you. And I'm sorry for the loss of your comrade and will do what I can to make sure justice is served."

"How are you going to do that?" A Latina in the inner row asked. She was sitting between two Brown Berets, but not in uniform herself, instead wearing bell-bottom jeans and a purple peasant blouse beneath a denim jacket. Large silver hoops winked from beneath the fall of her dark brown hair.

The rims of the big eyes staring at me were red, as was the tip of her light brown, aquiline nose.

Carol spoke in response. "I am personally going to crack the code of that sigil and trace it back to the magician who made it, and make him burn."

The woman nodded and crossed her arms over her chest.

"And the rest of us are going to keep working together, to make things right," I said. "To make the streets safe for the people."

"To make the Feebs and the pigs afraid!" shouted one of the LA Panthers.

The people liked that. A lot. And no wonder. Brown Beret headquarters bombed two year ago. Panther headquarters assaulted by a SWAT team just last week. And now the attack at La Piranya, the main organizing hub for radical students and Brown Berets.

"Las Manos is with you," Rosalia said. "And Jasmine, Carol, and Ernesto are as trustworthy as the Panthers or the Brown Berets."

A woman in the back row across from me, wearing a brown and gold poncho that matched her light brown, wavy hair, snorted. Then she laughed. "And what if they get infiltrated too? What then?"

My blood froze in my veins. I called up Ocean to soothe me again. Did these people know something in particular? Or were they just aware that every organization was at risk right now?

We'd dealt with plants before, and all too recently. No one was safe, that was all. I relaxed again.

"We will deal with it," Ernesto said. "Claro?"

"Don't you challenge me," she said. "You don't know me. You don't know my family. And I don't know *you!*"

Ernesto held up his hands, palm out. "Peace, sister. I meant no disrespect. It has been a trying day and a difficult evening. We're all a bit on edge. We just ask that you give us some time. We promise to consult with leadership of all organizations present, and to keep la gente well informed."

One of the Brown Berets began passing around mimeod sheets of paper, still damp and curling from the machine.

"There will be a series of town hall meetings here, every Tuesday or as often as we need them. Keep your ears to the ground. Organize your families and your neighbors. Don't go anywhere alone."

"But my Chuy *wasn't* alone," the woman with the red-rimmed eyes said. "He was with his comrades. So how are we supposed to protect ourselves? He even had one of your pinche patches!" she said to Rosalia. "The magic you said would protect him! Instead, it drew El Mundo Malo closer in. It whispered his name to some bad people. A magician, you say."

She gathered up her woven purse and stood. Then she looked at Carol again.

"I hope you do what you say. I hope you burn whoever did this to my Chuy." She raised her chin, and fixed me with those sorrowful, angry eyes, then turned her gaze on Rosalia. "But I don't trust your magic anymore."

Shoving her way through the chairs, she slammed into the cross-bar of the exit and hurried clicked out of the room The door slammed behind her.

The room took in a collective breath. I sent out a soothing wave of Ocean, just to set things a little bit more right.

I felt the room exhale.

"What's next, then?" said Wayne, one of the local Panthers.

I stepped forward again, and motioned for Jimmy to join me. "We've been organizing patrols up in Oakland."

"And we have those here, sister."

I nodded. "What you don't have are patrols where the shape-shifters among you show people they're being protected not only by muscle, community, and guns, but by actual cats. Big, black-furred cats."

There was a buzz of conversation after that.

"You mean you cats walk around Oakland buck naked?"

We all laughed. And that felt good.

"Naked as the day I was born!" Jimmy said. "But seriously, man, Jasmine is right. When I've shifted and gone out on patrol, I felt the difference from the people. It took them a little time to get used to you damn sorcerers flinging magic bolts at the sky, but once you directed them at the pigs, they was cool with it."

He looked around the room, that beautiful, proud lover of mine, until he saw everyone in the room was with him.

"And now Doreen there is training ordinary folks in magic. Parents are bringing their children to be trained in the playground on Saturdays and after school. And hell yeah, we shifters are out on patrol. You know what that does to the people?"

"What does it do, brother?" someone asked.

"It gives them confidence. It lets them know we got their backs, but it also lets them know they've got their own."

I raised my hand then, to butt in. "And more importantly, it lets them know another world is possible."

"Right on."

David stepped up again, arms crossed over his chest, but nodding. "Thank you for speaking. And thank you for showing up for la gente. We have a lot of thinking to do."

"As do we," said Wayne from the Panthers. He stood, hands on skinny hips, and looked around the group before speaking again.

"We all have a lot of thinking to do. Planning, too. But I want you to know, we've got plans I can't talk about even in a semi-private meeting like this. And we're going to need some of you to help. Raise your hand if you're in."

There was a pause. Then, one by one, every hand was in the air.

"All power to the people," I said.

"All power to the people!" they answered back.

CHAPTER TEN
JASMINE

Jimmy and I crowded onto my twin bed, under the quilt from Momma Beatrice that I'd slept under my whole childhood.

My parents weren't too thrilled with my boyfriend spending the night, but I didn't give them much choice. I'd been in more danger in the past month than my entire life, and I wanted my man by my side.

And I wanted all the love I could grasp.

So, in my favorite green Black Power T-shirt and underpants, I climbed into the narrow bed with my lover.

Curling into the warm crook where his arm met his shoulder, I rested my cheek on his bare chest. Jimmy was small but muscular, with smooth dark skin. I could roll in his scent like a cat. But *he* was the cat. I smiled, for what felt like the first time since that damn Fed blasted his way into my life.

Jimmy stroked my shoulder, then ran his hand down my arm before sliding his fingers up again, under the sleeve of my shirt.

"What you smiling at, Jaz?" His voice was as warm as his hand on my skin.

"Nothing much. I'm just happy you're here. It's good to be alive, you know?"

I felt a kiss on the top of my head. So sweet. I sighed. I wanted this to last forever, but I knew it wouldn't.

It couldn't.

I frowned.

"Hey," Jimmy murmured. "I don't know what's going on with you now, but I coulda sworn you were smiling a minute ago."

"Leadership wants me in Chicago, Jimmy. But there's so much to do here. And in Oakland. If I leave now, how are we going to get any traction?"

I tilted my head up to look at his face. His gold-tinged eyes stared down at me.

"I mean, Oakland will be fine. Doreen's up there, and it sounds like Patrice and Drake are doing a great job with the kids. And they're training more people. But I've barely started any of that down here. And Carol and Ernesto can't do it on their own. The people won't trust them enough."

"Come on up here," Jimmy said, scooching over toward the edge of the bed and making room for me on the pillow. I scooted up until our heads were side by side on the white pillow.

"Can't you tell Chicago you can't come?" he said. "You're right about being spread thin. And now you've got Association business on your plate, too."

I huffed at that. "I'm so sick and tired of that damn Association. They can kiss my ass. But if my mother gets elected as head, I guess I'll figure out a way to give it some time again. If she doesn't? I'm out."

"If she doesn't, you'll either torch the Mansion, or end up running the place yourself, babe."

I kissed his cheek, then lay back on the pillow again. "You really think I don't have to go to Chicago? You think I can say no to Chairman Fred Hampton?"

"Should I be jealous?" Jimmy asked, and poked me in the ribs.

"Hey!"

"Jaz, I think you shouldn't worry about that now. Put one foot in front of the other. You got plenty to do this week. Chicago can wait, don't you think?"

"I don't know. I promised to help them out." I gave him another kiss. His lips were firm and soft as a plum. They were hard to resist. "If I go, will you come with me?"

"That seems to be my job these days, Jaz. As long as we can make it work with the Party, I'm with you all the way. You know that."

"Thanks, baby."

"You can thank me by taking this revolutionary T-shirt off, and making revolutionary love to me, girl."

It was my turn to poke him in the ribs. "Revolutionary love?"

"Everything we do is revolutionary, Jaz. Didn't you know that?" He smiled. I smiled back.

I sighed again, rolling over onto him. "I thought revolutionary love required a lot of shouting. We *are* in my parent's home."

He kissed me, pressing those luscious lips against mine, and then rubbed his head against my forehead like the big cat he was. The scent of musk grew stronger.

"We'll have to be very quiet then, won't we, comrade?"

He lifted the T-shirt over my head. I lay, breasts squished against the smooth muscles of his chest, feeling the water build inside me as he grew hard underneath my hips.

"You ever think you want a child?" I asked.

I felt him grow very still.

"Jaz…"

"Have you?" I whispered.

"I've never even thought about it. I've seen too many people die. I feel like we're in danger all the time. Who can plan a life like that?"

"But if we could? If we defeat the capitalists and imperialists. If we build a strong community for the people. If we get even a slice of our utopia…would you want children then?"

He was quiet. Just his breath, soft and warm. And his hands on my skin. Communicating in a language that I thought I understood, but wasn't sure.

Then he kissed me again.

"With you, Jaz? I want everything. I want you. I want kids. Grandkids. A life. But we got to get through this revolution first."

"Doesn't putting our lives on hold mean that they win?"

He sighed then. "Jaz…"

"Doesn't it?"

"Yeah. You're right about that. But I'm trying to tell you I can't think about kids this minute. I'm trying to tell you I love you and yeah, I would love a kid or two one day. But there's too much at stake right now, baby. Don't you see?"

I did see. And I knew he was right, because most days, I felt the same. I was all in for the revolution and frankly wasn't sure where this having kids stuff had even come from.

But tonight? Tonight I wanted to *know* that what we were fighting for was real, and we could have it. And if we couldn't, what were we fighting for?

Ever since my sorcery exploded into more power than I ever thought I'd have, and ever since that Fed had hooked into me, making me vulnerable, I'd been trying to figure out my emotions.

They were telling me something important and I kept just missing the message because there was always another battle to fight.

I was nineteen years old, and already tired of battles.

"I just need to think of something other than revolution tonight, dig?" Jimmy said.

"So think of making love to me, instead."

I covered his mouth with my own and called up the water inside both of us.

The sorcery rose up inside of me, spilling out of my mouth, my hands, my sex. I rolled over my lover like a gentle wave.

He growled in my ear, fighting the urge to shift, I could tell. Wrapping both arms around me, he flipped us until I was underneath.

"I'm going to make you come for the revolution, girl." His gold-rimmed eyes held a challenge. "Think you can keep quiet?"

My whole body trembled with wanting him.

"I'm very disciplined," I replied.

His tongue traced its way down my body and sunk home.

And that was all I wanted for a while. Discipline be damned.

CHAPTER ELEVEN
CAROL

The Mansion was still filled with sorcerers, and it was making Carol a little crazy. The crush and crash of competing energies was too much. Ernesto said the gatherings weren't usually this bad, but everyone was agitated. Carol knew how she was when she was upset, angry, or confused, but she thought that was just her inexperience.

Turned out even experienced sorcerers sprang leaks when pushed. Especially in close proximity with a bunch of other powerful people under pressure.

But all that wasn't going to help choose a new head of the Association of Magical Arts and Sorcery.

She headed down the long sapphire-blue-carpeted hallway to the kitchen, where she knew Mr. Oluo and at least three of the other visiting sorcerers were having breakfast. The two Mansion cooks had been given their traditional week off while the students were off on holiday. Carol guessed that with Terrance and Helen both gone, no one had thought to call the cooks back in.

Carol had woken up in Ernesto's bed this morning and realized they'd never eaten dinner last night, what with everything going on at La Piranya.

Yeah. She'd have to deal with those strange sigils all day now, along with the house full of random sorcery crashing around.

Plus, there was talk about some sort of Solstice working tonight. As if anyone had time for that right now.

But it was probably not such a good idea to ignore the solar tides right now. Not with what was going down everywhere.

Passing Terrance Sterling's old office, she sighed. Then stopped. The door was ajar, and she could swear she heard something.

Pushing open the heavy wooden door into the sapphire-carpeted room, she took in the heavy walnut desk and the shelves still tastefully arranged with Terrance's magical objects and a few books.

Her gaze swept toward the couch and chairs grouped together around a low coffee table.

And there, huddled on one of the overstuffed club chairs, was Helen Price. Her Jackie O bob was back in place, and her green Chanel suit was perfect, but she was clearly crying.

Carol walked toward her, granny boots sinking into the carpet as her purple maxi skirt dragged against her ankles.

"Helen?"

Her face was ravaged. Eyes bloodshot and swollen. Face gaunt and pale. Mouth pinched and tight, trying to hold back the sobs Carol could feel projected outward.

Helen Price's ice had finally cracked, and all Carol could smell was the arctic sea beneath it. Helen was clearly battling the waves trying to drag her down.

But why here? Why not crawl into a hole somewhere to go through whatever breakdown she was having? It was a little freaky, frankly.

"What are you doing here?" Carol sat down in another club chair across from the woman who used to be Terrance's right hand.

And who Carol had thought was going to help them lead the Association in a different direction. A sorcerer that Carol, Doreen, and others had trusted to do the right thing.

Seemed she was too weak after all.

Carol let her Earth sorcery grow and build, forming a subtle platform beneath her feet and inching it out toward Helen. The older sorcerer clearly needed some stability.

And Carol was glad there was something she could do. These older people? Some of them were just falling apart, leaving it to the young ones to pick up the pieces and figure out how to form something new.

Was that how it always was?

"Helen? What are you doing here?" she repeated.

The older woman looked at her, finally, and dabbed at her eyes and nose with a finely woven white handkerchief.

"He wasn't a bad man, you know."

Carol throttled down her impatience, and sank more deeply into the support of Earth, boosting its power in the platform she was building.

Losing it at Helen right now wasn't going to help. They needed as much information as they could get.

"When did he start to change?" she asked.

Helen clamped her lips tightly together and hunched her knees and shoulders close together, as though trying to cram down a deep secret. Or as though she was afraid of getting struck.

That freaked Carol out a bit. Was Helen Price *afraid* of her? If so, why?

She looked at the corner of the room, where the brown spider and the white spider had made their epic stand, after the white spider had wrapped up Terrance Sterling's body in a cocoon of spider silk. They'd thought that he was dead.

It might have been better if he had died.

The brown spider turned out to have a connection with Jasmine's dead grandmother, Beatrice. And the white spider? They'd thought it had been defeated, but that thing would not go away.

And it was tied in to all the sigils. And the twisted Solomonic magic of the Feds. And their Temple.

But just how, Carol wasn't sure. She rubbed the space between her brows, willing the tension away, and turned back to Helen.

"Helen, you either talk to me now, or I drag you down the hallway for a mini-tribunal. You dig?"

Helen's head jerked back, and she attempted to sit a little straighter in the chair. Carol could tell it was an effort. The woman couldn't even take in a proper breath.

"When did you become so cruel?" Helen asked.

"When did you become a fool?"

Carol could feel Helen calling on Water then, shoring up the ice inside. The air began to crackle. Helen dried her tears.

"There's still time to save the Association, Helen. If that's what you want. But you can't save the Association and save Terrance, too. Where did he go, by the way?"

He was no longer in the Mansion, despite the wards placed around his rooms by four Elemental sorcerers after they'd carted him off the night before. And wasn't that worrying?

Helen shook her head, lips in a line. "I don't know."

Carol leaned back, placing her hands on the arms of the chair. *When you need to feel in charge,* Jasmine had said to her once, *act like you're in charge.*

"Helen. Tell me what you *do* know. I've asked you when Terrance changed *and* where he'd gone and you've avoided answering me both times. I want you to answer me now."

Helen's red-rimmed eyes looked calculating for a moment, then that look was gone. She took in a shuddering breath and dropped her hands into her lap, palms curled upward, a sorcerer's sign of surrender. One hand still clutched her handkerchief.

Carol didn't know if Helen was playing her, but she decided to wait it out.

"It was two years ago," Helen said quietly. "After a trip to Washington DC."

"And what happened in DC?" Carol spoke firmly, but soothingly. Like her mother had when she wanted Carol to tell her what was wrong, but to also know she might still be in big trouble.

"I can't."

"Yes, Helen. You can."

The two women sat in silence. Carol debated calling Ernesto in for help. It might shut Helen down some more. But it might be good to have a witness, too.

"Helen?"

The woman who had been an authority figure to Carol for six years looked at her, practically blank. Despite the sense of ice and Water surging just beneath the surface, she was clearly cut adrift. A sorcerer who had abdicated her power.

"I overheard a phone call. I don't know to whom. But Terrance…he was talking about…" She brought the handkerchief back up to her face and dabbed at the corners of her nose.

"He was talking about Hoover. And the FBI."

All the Earth inside Carol snapped into place, making her feel like an impenetrable fortress.

"Helen…are you telling me that Terrance Sterling met with J. Edgar Hoover?"

Helen nodded.

"Wipe your face off. Blow your nose. Go splash some water on your face if you need to. Shore yourself up. We're meeting with Ernesto, Cecelia, Simon Tanaka, Mr. Oluo, and Eileen. And we're doing it now."

This was one of the pieces they'd been waiting for. This was going to unlock the sigils once and for all. Carol didn't yet know how, but it would.

She sent out a call to Ernesto in her head. He would contact the others.

Carol Johansson had been waiting for the moment when she would become a real sorcerer. A woman with power. A woman who was as certain of herself and her destiny as all the people she admired.

The battles of the past month had nudged her that direction.

But this meeting with Helen Price?

It had brought her all the way there. She finally knew how Jasmine must have felt right before the Federal agent had struck her down. Invincible. Strong.

Pay attention, world, she thought.

And you twisted perversions styling yourselves as Solomonic magicians? Watch your back.

But before any of that happened, she needed to get ahold of Jasmine. Her friend needed the information that Terrance Sterling was involved with J. Edgar Hoover, before she did anything else.

CHAPTER THIRTEEN
DOREEN

It was good to be back in Oakland. Good to taste the brine of the bay on her lips and watch the sun come up over the hills.

Doreen had arrived home late the night before. One of the young men from the Black Panthers had been waiting at the airport to take her home.

Once again, she'd made the Association pony up the money to get her a flight. No way was she driving all that way. She practically felt rich, the way she was getting on and off airplanes these days.

Doreen inhaled the scent of white carnations, red roses, and pine. Christmas at the florist's shop. She didn't care one way or another for the holiday itself, but she loved the lights and the smells that came along with the season.

Her boss had taken a much-needed lunch break, and Doreen was rushing to fill several orders at once. The large green table in the center of workspace was strewn with tissue and flowers, greenery, and boughs. Two wreaths awaited flowers and ribbons, and a phalanx of vases stood on a shelf, needing to be filled.

But Patrice was here, slowing her down. And Doreen could not complain about that one bit.

"We can't stand here in the shop and kiss all day," Doreen said, inhaling the Aqua Net and Queen Helene's cocoa butter scent of her lover. "I have a lot of work to do here, and we have a lot of planning to do for tonight."

Patrice ran her hand across Doreen's cheek, planted one more kiss on her lips, which Doreen was sure had left a plum colored-smudge on her face.

Grabbing a tissue from the box behind the counter, Doreen wiped around her mouth. Sure enough. Plum lipstick everywhere. She smiled.

Patrice slid her curvy self onto one of the high stools at the big work table. Snapping open a compact, she reapplied the lipstick that matched her plum-colored suit and adjusted the braided gold plate necklace at her throat.

Doreen never tired of looking at her, this second love of her life. She thanked the Ancestors for bringing this woman to her door.

"I still don't understand why tonight is so important," Patrice said. "You all seem to act as if we're running out of time."

"We are," Doreen replied.

The shop door clanged open and her boss, Alice, bustled back in, her favorite fake leopard coat swinging out as she turned, arms filled with bags and packages.

"You're back early!" Doreen said.

"There's just so much to do! And I wanted to work on the wreaths myself," she said. "They're my favorite thing about the season."

Alice stopped, and looked at Patrice, then to Doreen, and back again.

Doreen hoped by all the Powers she didn't still have Patrice's lipstick smeared across her face.

"Alice, this is my friend Patrice. She stopped by to see if I had time for lunch. I told her I was too busy, so she sat to chat for five minutes while I worked. I hope that's all right with you."

It better be, Doreen thought. Alice had always been good to her, giving her a job seven years ago when Doreen was ready to claw her way back up from the depths of grief. But you never knew with some white people. Doreen had also learned that the hard way over the years.

Alice gave a little smile. "That's fine, of course! I was just surprised. You've never had friends stop by before."

Alice came through the shop and struggled to open the door to her tiny office while juggling the packages.

Doreen rushed to open it for her. Alice dumped the parcels on an already overloaded desk and turned again.

"Doreen, why don't you go have lunch with your friend? Now that I'm back, we can spare you for a little while."

"You're sure?"

Alice made a shooing motion with her hands. "Go."

Doreen and Patrice grabbed their coats and pocketbooks and were out the door in a flash.

One block away, Patrice burst out laughing. "Oh girl, if you could've seen your face!"

"I don't know what you're talking about," Doreen grumbled.

Patrice just laughed again and patted her arm. There was no time to head to their favorite place in Chinatown, so Doreen steered them around the corner toward Nate's, a sandwich shop she ate at when she didn't bring lunch from home.

Men and women hurried around then, snatching lunch breaks themselves.

A mother pushed a stroller as the toddler inside kicked her feet and shook a bright yellow rattle.

"I was asking about running out of time," Patrice reminded her.

They walked in sync, feet striking the sidewalks in unison. Even though they couldn't walk arm in arm, they could still walk together.

They passed the barbershop, and the nice man who owned it waved through the plate glass window. Looked like business was slow today.

"It's just a feeling. Besides, when we coordinate our sorcery with the big solar or lunar events, it gives everything an extra boost. Solstice is today, and with the full moon coming up, it's a pretty potent time. I can't explain it any better than that. There's just pressure. And the ancestors have been rapping at the back of my skull for days now, wanting to get things done."

"So, Huey?"

Huey P. Newton. Head of the Oakland Panthers.

Doreen had seen a clear aura around Fred Hampton when he'd walked in her door, fully alive after the assassination attempt, on the run from the Feds and police. His destiny blazed like a midsummer sun at noon. She couldn't touch it, though she had offered him a blessing from the ancestors all the same.

Huey, though? He was just as powerful, but shone more like the moon. And the ancestors seemed to think he needed a little nudge to clear the way. Doreen was learning to not argue with the ancestors.

"We're going to try to link him even more deeply to the people and the land than he already is. And connect him more directly to his lineage. So he has the full weight of the ancestors behind him."

"I'm not sure I understand."

Doreen sighed. "I'm not sure I understand, either. But when the push is this strong, I've learned to trust."

"Where are we going?" Patrice asked.

"It's just across the street. The green awning. Almost there."

They crossed the street when the light changed, just as two men in black berets and long leather coats turned a corner and came into view. Following them was a big panther, black coat shimmering even in the gray clouds that covered the sun.

The men smiled at Patrice and Doreen, pleased as punch to see them. Doreen felt that change all the way to her bones.

The Animal People, showing their magic out in the open. Amazing.

"Mrs. Doreen, Mz. Patrice." It was Leroy, which was strange. Panther leadership didn't usually go out on patrol. His ruddy sideburns bristled down the side of his face, and his massive shoulders filled the coat to its seams. The other man was someone Doreen recognized, though she couldn't recall his name.

And the panther. Doreen had no idea who it was. It looked female to her. Perhaps it was Barbara?

"It's good to see you patrolling, bold as brass like this," Doreen said.

"It feels good," Leroy said. "You all were right. Jasmine was right. We need to show the people who we are. Claim the power to share the power, right?"

"Each one, teach one," Patrice replied.

"Right on," said the other man on patrol.

"Will you be coming in to report on Los Angeles soon?" Leroy asked.

The ancestors started tapping again. Something was coming.

A sudden wind blew through the air. The panther raised her head and sniffed, giving a low cough that raised the hairs on Doreen's arms beneath her navy coat.

"She senses something."

"A storm is brewing, for sure. The sorcerers have been feeling it for days."

"Something we need to prepare for?" Leroy asked.

"We're still putting the pieces together. As soon as we have a few more, I'll be at headquarters to let you know."

The sound of children's laughter rang against the storefronts.

"Look, Grandad! It's a panther!"

The small group turned to look at two children, one with puffy pig-tails flying and the other racing behind her as fast as his sneakers would take him. They slammed their bodies into the big cat, who braced herself to hold their weight.

The girl threw her arms around the panther's neck and the boy petted the panther's side and cooed at her.

Doreen was shocked down to her core. Then her eyes filled up with tears.

This. This was the world they were working on. This was the world she wanted.

Where young black men walked the streets, ensuring their communities were safe. And where shape-shifters walked openly, and children loved them.

Patrice grabbed Doreen's hand and gave it a gentle squeeze.

Doreen squeezed back and wiped her eyes.

Leroy grinned again. Another sight Doreen never thought she'd see.

War was coming, a war bigger than Vietnam, you could feel it in the air. But the smaller battles? They were being won.

And the people were building a world worth fighting for.

CHAPTER FOURTEEN
JASMINE

It was time for me to step it up again. My strength was back. And yeah, that spot in the hollow of my shoulder was still bugging me, but you know what? If that meant the bastard could track me through it?

Rosalia was right. It meant that I could track him, too. Time to exploit that business.

We needed to get ready to bring the fight to his door. On our terms this time. Enough of being reactionary.

It was time to get down with being revolutionary. Kick the Feds in the teeth.

The church hall was full up. People had left a space in the center of the wide-planked fir wood floor, but stood three deep back to the whitewashed walls and jammed up against the massive iron printing press in the corner, which cranked out the *La Causa* newspaper, pamphlets, and fliers every week.

We were still waiting on Rosalia, so I was biding my time. Let the people talk to each other for a while. The more they got out of their system now, the less time we'd have to spend on an emotional rehash of last night's events. We'd get to actual debriefing sooner that way.

Carol had called this morning while I was in the shower. My mother said it sounded important. I'd tried to call her back, but the phone just rang and rang. The whole Association was falling apart, and no one was around to answer the phones.

We all were called to a meeting at the Mansion, but I frankly did not have time to deal with Association bullshit. The meeting could wait for me, or start without me.

I didn't really care about that. I just hoped that whatever news Carol had for me could wait until I had the chance to get to the Mansion later on.

Looking up at the big round window set high up on the front wall, I realized that what I *cared* about was being in this old stone church hall in Boyle Heights, surrounded by committed people.

Turned out it was the original church, built more than one hundred years ago. The current church was through a side door, added on when the community grew up around the building.

If you'd ever told me when I joined the Black Panther Party that I'd spend so much time in Episcopalian church halls, I would have shaken my head.

But Father Neil and Father John believed in the people as much as they believed in God. Not so different from my connection to the people and the Powers, I guessed. And if the Panthers had gotten used to me, they'd really gotten used to these radical priests.

Brown Beret leadership and LA Panther leadership were all gathered together, along with some key civilians I'd tapped—black, Chicano, white, and Chinese American—whose magic was closer to the surface than some other folks I'd seen. I hoped to get them trained like Doreen had trained Patrice, Drake, and now Tanya up in Oakland.

Spread the magic, spread the power. Spread the power, spread the magic. Fred Hampton and Huey Newton always insisted that the revolution was built on education and providing for people's needs. You couldn't just go in and lay down a new law. The people had to understand. They needed to feel it was worth it to sign up.

So, Association be damned, Doreen and I were giving magic away to as many people as wanted it.

You didn't have to carry a gun to be part of the revolution. You didn't need to be a sorcerer to protect your community with magic.

The door opened, letting in a small whirlwind of velvet skirts, jangling silver bracelets, dangling amulets, and citrine eyes.

Rosalia had arrived, handing off two cloth bags—stuffed with herbs from the smell of it, and who knew what else?—to the Brown Berets standing security at the door. They fumbled the bags off to some people nearby.

I grinned. You never asked security to carry anything. Unless you were the baddest sorcerer in the LA basin. And maybe anywhere.

"Buenas dias," she said, walking toward me. She'd been doing magic. I could smell the copal scent of it on her hair and skin. Good.

"How do you want to start this?" I asked.

"You go ahead."

Okay, then. In a room bristling with leadership, I was in charge. I took a breath into my belly, planted my army boots on the wood floor, and clapped my hands.

That got their attention. The buzz of talking ceased immediately, and every face turned toward Rosalia and me.

"I am a revolutionary!" I said, raising my right fist. "Say it with me."

"I am a revolutionary!" they all bellowed back, raising their own fists to the sky. I breathed a prayer of thanks to Fred Hampton for teaching us how important it was for everyone to claim the title.

If we didn't claim the title, the revolution was doomed to fail.

Everyone was on their feet, except a white man in a wheelchair who had approached me after he'd seen me do some magic at the Federal Building downtown a week ago.

Dude had serious magical potential. I'd made sure to track him down.

I began to walk, back and forth, across the five-foot clearing in the middle of the room. Right hand gripped left wrist behind my back. My leather coat swung around my green corduroy bell-bottoms, and I'd made sure my natural was picked out to perfection.

Part of doing any sort of magic was learning glamour, and glamour started with how a person carried herself, then moved out to her clothes. You could add anything to it, and convince people of anything you wanted.

As a revolutionary sorcerer, I promised to use my glamour only for the good.

"Many of you were at La Piranya last night. Brown Beret security is looking into the breach with our help. My comrades Carol and Ernesto are working on unlocking the magic seals that allowed the meeting space to become infected and led to the death of your comrade, Chuy."

"We'll be talking about that some more, I promise. But until we have more information, let's not speculate. We have too much other work to do."

I beckoned Jimmy forward, to stand with Rosalia and me. "In Oakland, the Panthers have been doing patrols." I raised a hand to stave off the comments I knew were coming. "I know you patrol here, keeping your communities safe. I know you've got a people's clinic, like we do, and you feed people. We're all doing all the right things to serve the people and support the revolution. But I'm talking about doing more. And I'm about to issue a challenge. So please listen carefully."

Some of local leadership bristled at that. I could feel it. Good. Let them feel uneasy for a moment. Let them feel the shifting of power.

"The challenge is to expose yourselves to the people. To let them know who you really are." I gestured to myself. "Our uniforms identify us. I've got my boots and my long coat on today. But my hair looked too nice to jam a beret on top right now."

That got a few chuckles. But also a few scowls.

"But my uniform only tells people I'm a member of the Black Panther Party. That's important. I dig that. But what's more important is what people don't see. They don't *see* that I'm a sorcerer, and have something extra that can help get them out of danger. Or help train them to defend themselves *in ways the cops can't even see*."

I nodded to Jimmy, who stood, straight-backed and strong beside me. He wore his leather, too, black beret on his head, black turtleneck sweater. Slight stubble marred his face. He hadn't had time to shave.

"This brother is a Black Panther. But the thing the people don't see, and the thing they need to know, is that he is also a shifter. He's a powerful beast who can strike terror into the hearts of those who would oppress us."

Letting that sink in for a moment, I nodded at Jimmy again. It was his turn to speak.

"So we've started patrolling in our panther forms in Oakland."

"And aren't you scaring the shit out of people?" asked a voice from the back of one of the circles.

"As a matter of fact, sister, no we aren't. The people have seen what we can do. They've seen us stop the police in the middle of a firefight, Fred Hampton and others all out in full panther form. Jasmine and her crew organized the people to build a dome of magic."

Rosalia clapped her hands three times. "Some of you were part of the action at Laguna Park. You have also seen what we can do. You have also seen what the people can bear."

She glared around the room.

"Call upon your Ancestors!" she demanded. A few people looked uncomfortable. "Oh! I see! You can talk about La Raza and Africa and who knows what else, but you can't stand in this church hall and call upon the strength and blessings of the ones that brought you here?"

She spat, leaving a white gobbet glistening on the fir planks.

"That is what I think of you, then. Your ancestors believed in magic. They danced on the bare earth. They prayed. They took strength. But you? *Fah.*"

My turn again. "If you think you can bring revolution without using every single thing you are, you are mistaken. We've failed in the past, again and again, because we were not fully who we are. We were too afraid. We *let* them *make us* afraid. Well, no more. The reason we've survived is because our ancestors did everything Rosalia talked about. But they did it in the ways that pleased the masters and oppressors. Or they did it in secret."

I held up both my hands, blue ocean fire flaming from my palms. Tightening up my diaphragm, I put more power into my voice.

"The time for secrecy is done. There's a war being waged on us all. Not just by the police, with guns. But by the government, with magic.

You saw it last night. Some of you felt it in the battle at Laguna Park, and those of you who have been training with the sorcerers have tasted it, too."

Still holding my hands above my head, I cupped my palms toward one another, forming the flames into a blue ball of light, energy, and fire. Then I left it there, floating in the air, and formed my right hand into a fist.

"I want us to not hide anymore. I want us to not just survive. I want us to triumph. And we're here to help you all organize this revolution so that we will win."

"All power to the people!" Jimmy shouted.

"All power to the people!"

"All power to the people!" I shouted.

"All power to the people!"

The sound reverberated in the rafters. And then Rosalia stepped forward once again.

Her silver bangles clattering down her arm, she raised her fist.

"La Raza, por la gente!"

And then she brought the magic down, sending sparks on every head.

And every Ancestor inside every person there, woke up.

Including mine.

CHAPTER FIFTEEN
JASMINE

It was the wildest thing I'd ever felt. My head was on fire, and my skull cracked open. The Water inside me rushed up to meet it, but could not engulf the flames. It could not soothe my fractured skull.

I fought with all my might, reaching for Ocean. Reaching for the streams I knew still ran deep under the ground.

In my panicked haze, I could hear Rosalia chanting some incantation in Spanish. Shoving that aside, I tried to form the power of Water into something I could use to combat whatever she'd unleashed on top of my head.

And then, as though a wave had shoved me deep beneath the surface, everything grew calm. There was pressure around me, and who knew what was happening in the rest of the room, but I felt peaceful.

I never felt peaceful. Not even in Jimmy's arms.

So I floated in the peace for a while. Bathing my cracked and pulsing skull. Washing my battered heart. Bathing the wound in the hollow of my left shoulder.

Washing away all of the distress, fury, fear, and yes, depression, of the past weeks.

And then she spoke to me.

"Jasmine." It was my grandmother's voice inside my head. Momma Beatrice. Even though I'd never met her, I knew it was her. I had felt her in Aunt Doreen, and even in my mother sometimes.

"I'm going to take you further back, baby. Don't be scared."

Floating in this peace, I just nodded. Why shouldn't I trust?

An image of Doreen's Chokwe mask from Angola flashed into my mind, all black with red eyes trimmed in white, red mouth, and the large red-and-black halo around its head.

I was sucked in through the eyes, and landed on a plain of red mud, with grasses waving at the foothills of a mountain in the distance. Tiny red-winged birds flew to and from a tree to my right. And to my left, a woman walked toward me.

She was magnificent. Ochre mud coated the elaborate coils of hair upon her proud head and was smeared across her breasts. Rows of bright beads crisscrossed her torso and a blue-, red-, and yellow-patterned cloth swaddled her hips.

And as she grew closer to me, I could see she flashed me a gap-toothed smile. The left incisor was missing.

This was the woman Doreen talked about sometimes. Our ancestor. Whether she was Chokwe or not, I didn't know. But the mask was the portal to her realm.

She carried something in her right hand. A long spear. Her bare feet sent up tiny puffs of earth as she moved toward me with a rolling walk.

Then she stopped. Smiled big. And threw the spear straight to my heart.

I scrambled to put up a wall of magic, but was too late.

The spear pierced my heart and I fell screaming to the ground.

When I came to on the fir planks of the church hall, the spear was clutched in my right hand and my chest was throbbing.

I struggled to sit up, gasping to take breath into my constricted chest. Jimmy, in his panther form, licked the arm of my leather coat and nudged my head.

Bracing myself against his powerful, black furred body, I slowly shoved myself upright again. But I needed more time before I tried to stand, that was for sure. My head pounded, and there was still a swimming feeling around the edges of my eyes.

I spared a look around the room. Some folks seemed like they were in a sort of trance. Others were curled up on the floor, laughing or moaning.

Rosalia stood in the middle of the room, head back, and arms outstretched. Strange sounds flowed from her lips in a stream.

It didn't sound like Spanish. Maybe it was Nahuatl. Or else she was speaking in tongues. Looking at her was like staring into a heat wave in the Mojave. She shimmered, her edges an overlay of several different images, interposed.

I wondered how many worlds she was walking in. And what the hell she'd done to this room full of people.

The spear began to shake in my hand, snapping me into my body. I used it to help me climb to my feet. Jimmy rose with me, giving a huge yawn of cat breath and musk.

Ancestors or no, we still had work to be done.

I slammed the butt of the spear onto the hard fir planks three times. *Boom! Boom! Boom!*

People slowly shook their heads, rubbed their hands over their faces. Some of them struggled to stand.

Rosalia stopped speaking and opened up her citrine eyes. She looked at the spear in my hand. The shaft was taller than my body, and the spear itself was a long, pounded-iron leaf shape with three long metal thorns at the base.

It still hummed in my grip. My eyes kept wanting to roll back in my head, to let the Ancestors take over. I wasn't going to let them. If they wanted to speak, they could speak through me, when I was still fully present.

I was a Powers-be-damned sorcerer, not a puppet, and they were either down with that or they could leave.

"I." *Boom!* "Am." *Boom!* A revolutionary!" *Boom!*

I could feel the energy build around me. The ancestors were with me like never before.

"*That* is why we organize. That is why we reclaim our magic. That is how we honor our ancestors. That is how we serve the people. All in the name of toppling this sick and crumbling tower to the ground, and building something better. Something more real."

Clarity returned to people's eyes as their souls traveled back into their bodies. More and more of them were standing, and shaking off whatever it was Rosalia had done to us all.

But I could see the change in all their faces. There was wisdom shining in their eyes. And a fortitude that had not been there before.

"Rosalia has gifted us all with a direct connection to our ancestral spirits. That is a powerful force, and a force the FBI, the cops, Social Security, or La Migra will not be expecting. So…" I smiled. "She has given us, not only wisdom and power, but the element of surprise."

Jimmy circled the cleared space in the center of the room, sniffing at the air. He walked slowly, with the same, rolling gait the woman in my vision had.

The words kept coming out of my mouth, goaded on by the Powers.

"The US government? They have spies. And infiltrators. They have tanks and bombs. They have bullets to assassinate, and the power to take our children away or let them starve. What they don't have is our ancestors. What they don't have are shape-shifters who are down with the revolution. What they don't have is the magic *you* all have."

"And they don't know about el movimiento," Rosalia rasped out. Whatever that chanting was must have damaged her throat. "They think they do. But they can never see what we do: that power is built from the ground up, so the people lowest down are the ones to do the building."

I looked at the spear in my hand. It was a tool, for certain, and a weapon. But I realized it was also a message.

"We've talked a lot today. And had our minds blown better than any acid could do. I'd intended to get commitments from everyone here to be more open with the people. To let the revolution rise to the surface on truth, instead of shadows and lies. And I still want that. But the Ancestors have showed me I want more."

"I want us to figure out a way to build a movement that reflects the world we want, not just the world we fight against. This spear? The

Ancestors tell me it represents the truth. And from now on? I'm carrying the truth into every battle I fight at your side."

"Gente," Rosalia said, "today, I cracked you open and took away your fear. There is still magic to be done, and planning. But what we cannot bring into the magic and the planning is the fear, and all the pettiness that brings. The Ancestors have given each of you a gift today. I don't know what those gifts are, but I can feel them in the room now, in your hearts, your spines, your blood."

I saw a lot of people nodding at that. Many had tears streaming down their cheeks, including some of the Panthers and Brown Berets.

David stepped forward then, his brown beret tilted back on his glossy dark hair. "Hechicera—that is the word to call you, yes?"

"Sí."

He started again. "Hechicera, you have given us all a gift today. I know that I have forgotten how to honor our ancestors. But I am willing to learn, if you will teach me. And you—" He looked at me. "You have power. I can taste it. And you are right to tell us to carry the spear of truth into our revolution."

He turned to the rest of the people gathered and held out his hands.

"My hands are yours. My heart is yours. We shall work together in our truth and in our strength. And we will rip these federales pendejos to shreds."

CHAPTER SIXTEEN
CAROL

Ernesto and Carol were taking a break from the visiting sorcerers, the arguments, the counterarguments, and the jockeying for position.

The library was taken over by sorcerers. So was the kitchen.

They retreated to the work room, a place Carol loved, with its high arched windows with lab benches underneath them. Wooden floors. Long wood tables. Strange concoctions ready to be brewed.

Today, the bunsen burners didn't hiss. The gardener had been sent on enforced vacation for the duration, so there was no sound of the lawn mower. Just a jay calling outside, and the chirping of sparrows.

Oh. And the rise and fall of arguing voices down the hall.

Should they have been politicking? Shoring up Simon's bid for Cecelia as head? Or checking in with Cecelia herself?

Probably.

But it was hard to take all of this seriously when people were still dying in the streets. Some of whom were likely dead because of the actions of Terrance Sterling himself.

Carol had marched Helen to the kitchen after giving her time to clean up her face. She couldn't seem to get the words out, so Carol told them.

Terrance Sterling had betrayed them all…to the Powers-damned FBI.

Half of the sorcerers gathered in the fancy kitchen, drinking coffee and eating fruit and cheese, were furious. Others were incredulous. The ones that bothered her, though? They had seemed intrigued.

One of them had even argued that perhaps working with the FBI on magical operations was a good idea.

"Seriously, if you can't feel outrage at the news from the former head of your secret magical organization's *right hand* that he'd been working magic out of bounds and feeding access to government spooks, what's *going* to outrage you?" Carol had said. She was fuming, practically cracking the floor tiles with her anger. "And why should I trust you?"

She was still pissed off, even after leaving the room to cool down.

Carol knew Ernesto was angry, too. His pale brown skin flushed red, and his jaw was tight. But he didn't say a word, just kept calmly laying out white paper of various thicknesses and a variety of black pens.

"Aren't you angry?" she pushed.

Placing a pen carefully down, he made certain it aligned perfectly with a pad of paper on the long table she paced in front of.

He finally looked at her, deep brown eyes hard beneath his glasses.

"Of course I am angry. What do you think? One of the Brown Berets was slaughtered last night, in a magical operation, and we don't know how. But oh! We do know that the man who was supposed to be all high and mighty leader of a clean, upstanding organization might just be at the root of it."

He yanked back a wooden chair and sat down. Carol could tell he was willing his beautiful sorcerer's hands to stillness. That he wanted to cast. To blast something into smithereens.

"All of these years, I've supported the man. Oh, we've had our disagreements, but I was always willing to abide by his decisions for the Association, for my teaching, even some of my *research*." Ernesto looked up at her again, holding her in place with those eyes.

"I trusted him, Carol. Can't you see what that would mean to me?"

Deflated, she pulled out a chair across from him and sat too, reaching across the pens and papers to grasp his hands.

He grabbed back, then pulled her across the table until they met in the middle for a deep, half brutal kiss. Air and Fire met Earth.

And made Carol wish they had time to go upstairs and forget about all of this for a while.

But they didn't.

She broke the lock his warm lips had on hers and sat back in the chair, feeling the hardness of it dig into her back. She reached for the Earth still moving in the woodgrain and steadied herself again.

"Thank you," she said.

He looked startled. "For what?"

"For that kiss, for one. But really? For letting me know how you feel."

He blew out a huge breath, and put his head in his hands for a moment, then raked his fingers through the thick wave of his hair.

It was getting longer, Carol noticed. It almost touched his collar now.

"We have to get to work on these sigils, maga."

"I know."

They worked silently for a while. Ernesto had dragged some books in from the library earlier, tomes on sigil magic and other magical symbols. Sorcerers didn't usually need this sort of magic, so, even though he had studied it, he didn't know it well enough to figure out what Carol saw in her visions.

"Look at this," he said, shoving a book toward her, finger pointing to an image. "Does that look like any of the sigils you've seen? Or that Jasmine showed you?"

It looked like a tree with a broken limb. A central pillar of a line, with four lines crossing, narrow to long, forming a rough pine tree shape. But the longer line at the bottom had one half dangling at a sharp angle from the central line.

"I haven't seen it, but it reminds me of something…" Carol mused. "The book doesn't explain it. That's strange."

"A lot of these old symbols have lost their meaning. It's a wonder we've got records of them at all."

He took the book back and kept looking.

There was something about it, though, that bothered Carol. "Would you mark that page?"

Ernesto ripped a scrap of paper off one of the drawings she'd discarded and slipped it between the pages of the book.

And then the world went black.

Carol was falling, falling, falling. Tumbling through sludge. And stars. And earth. And sky. And day. And night.

She felt a searing pain as bullets pierced her flesh.

Saw her body jerk once. Then twice.

She saw a baby being born.

She saw the planting of the first seed that grew the first tree.

And heard Ernesto shouting in her ear, calling for help, and then a babble of other voices rushing in.

And the tree grew tall and broad, its roots sinking deep into good soil, giving home to creatures large and small, until a man came with an axe to chop it down.

"Carol! Carol!"

There was hideous pressure against her right shoulder. Someone kept punching her and she wanted them to stop. She tried to grab the hands, shove them away, but she was shaking then, as if a thousand ice cubes surrounded her body.

And she was tumbling again, this time flying upward through the air.

A circle of men surrounded the tree. They hung limbs from the branches, like the milagros on the walls of Rosalia's shop. Small animals writhed and squealed and shrieked, hanging upside down in snares. Rabbits and weasels, cormorants and doves.

Fingers snapped in front of her face. "Carol! Come back!"

Another finger peeled her eyelid back, and a white light pierced her head. Rolling forward, she vomited across papers and pens and black ink and arms and hands.

There was vomit everywhere. She had to get it out.

Her right shoulder was on fire. Who had set her on fire? And why?

"Carol, you've been shot. We've got a doctor on the way. You're going to be fine." Cecelia's voice. Jasmine's mother.

"We should get her on the table. Lay those blankets down."

William? Jasmine's father? What was he doing here?

She screamed and screamed and screamed.

And blackness.

And someone putting something soft under her head. And then there was pressure on her shoulder again.

But at least she could breathe now.

"Who?" her eyes fluttered open. She looked up into Ernesto's brown eyes.

"We're trying to find that out," he said, mouth set in a grim line on his face.

Carol closed her eyes again. The overhead lamps were too bright. Too much effort.

"Carol?" Cecelia's voice again. "If you open your mouth, I'm going to give you a tincture for the pain."

Carol did, and tasted bitter drops on her tongue.

"I'm also going to start feeding you Earth to stabilize your body, but we can't work on the healing until we get the bullets out."

"Bullets?"

"Yes, in your shoulder," Ernesto said.

"How?"

"Someone shot through the window."

"Me?"

She was having trouble hanging on to thoughts. The pain was starting to recede, but the numbness was invading her brain.

"The sigil."

"Don't worry about that now," Ernesto said.

William said, "I'm not a sorcerer like you all, but it seems to me if she was working on something and got shot, the two things might be connected."

"It's the tree. The tree is in danger."

And she blacked out.

CHAPTER SEVENTEEN
SNAKES AND SPIDERS

*T*he temple room deep underground was lined with slabs of granite over sheets of lead. The air felt hushed. Dead inside. As though nothing could get in or out, except through the reinforced steel door.

Yet when the Master crooned his syllables of power, when blood drops hissed on candle flames, when the sigils were drawn in the proper order and placed in the center of the circle…things arrived.

Strange things. Twisted things. Things summoned up from depths Samuels did not want to know.

They were things no man should have to see or feel.

Things that drove Samuels back to his cincture and his flail in his narrow, austere bedroom. Anything to regain his discipline. Anything to retain his consolidating power.

Anything to drive away the visions planted in his head. Visions designed to keep him in check and under thumb.

He also used the tools of discipline to drive away the knowledge that the Master was unhinged. It was something Samuels needed to keep at bay for now. Until the time was right.

Until the exact hour.

Samuels needed to be in Los Angeles still, but when the Master called, Samuels was always obliged to attend, so he boarded the fast jet and ate through three time zones to answer the summons.

Samuels stood, dark glasses in the breast pocket of his suit, right hand loosely gripping left wrist, shoulders straight, feet aligned at just under 180 degrees on the gray stone floor.

Just like the other twelve operatives that ringed the ritual space twenty floors beneath FBI headquarters in the center of DC.

They were the elite. Trained magicians, every one. Initiates of a magic that went back to the fourteenth century, to magisters who styled themselves as contemporary King Solomons, building their own astral temples, summoning demons, and consorting with angelic forces. They were said to have only scratched the surface, barely plumbing the depths and heights later generations reached.

And of course, later generations separated, some seeking out the left pathway and others the right, like the two great rivers that flowed through the Capitol. But unlike the magical lines, those two rivers joined forces just below the place FBI headquarters stood on the map.

Samuels wondered if the magic could flow together again, the way it was supposed to.

But the Master had twisted the flow of magic to his own ends. His was a dark vision, and his operatives learned to live in darkness, eyes grown too sensitive for the mildest rays of sun.

Samuels was one of these. He was pretty high up the food chain, but he knew it wouldn't matter if the Master ever grew too displeased.

And the Master hadn't been pleased with Samuels for quite a while.

Stinking with amphetamine sweat, the Master wore his long white robe, showing yellow underneath his arms. Standing in the middle of the circle, surrounded by flaming candles, he raised his arms, then brought them swiftly down, hands cutting the air like knives.

Samuels fought the urge to flinch. He'd felt that swipe as though a knife had crossed his torso, scoring him with fire.

"Come, Oh Intelligence! Now in Time!"

The magic was real, but the ritual was for show. The Master was reminding Samuels that it wasn't just the Master he was beholden to. It was the Intelligence. The Grand Operator. The one whom they all served.

The tattooed sigil beneath his left arm began to writhe and burn. But Samuels was prepared for that. The barbed cincture digging into his right thigh became a focal point, one pain canceling out the other. Samuels had practice with that pain. It only increased his will. It made him strong.

The Master could summon Samuels, but he could not control him.

Not anymore.

"Elevate our Lives!"

At least the Master wasn't making the weird noises anymore. Samuels hated it when the man started crooning. It made the hairs stand at attention on the back of his neck, even after all these years.

He just wished the Master would finish this charade, so Samuels could get back to LA.

Samuels kept those thoughts locked tightly behind several steel doors in his mind.

The Master pointed a hand toward Samuels torso. The tattoo burned more fiercely, giving off the stink of charring flesh. Samuels shut down as many pain sensors as possible, focusing on the cincture digging barbs into his thigh. He would prevail.

Allowing his face to grimace, he shoved out a whimper. Anything to get the Master to stop so they could move on.

The Master smiled, a tight little slit beneath the white potato nose on his squashed, square face.

The burning ceased. Samuels allowed himself to relax.

"Report." The Master clapped his hands.

Hoover. His name was fucking Hoover. Samuels locked that thought away as well. It would not do. Hoover was always and only the Master here.

"We successfully took out a Brown Beret, causing more chaos among the sorcerers, the Black Panther Party, and the Brown Berets themselves, sir."

"You used the sigil?"

"Yes sir. That was the bait to get the Panther sorcerer there."

The Master waved his stubby-fingered hand.

"What else?"

Samuels cleared his throat, squashing down the flare of anger at the interference that was threatening to botch his operation.

"Apparently, a shot was fired into the Association Mansion. A girl was hit, but there does not seem to be a fatality."

"Who?"

"As far as I can tell, it was an LAPD plant inside the Brown Berets. They thought it would be a good idea to sow discord between the sorcerers and the Chicano groups."

Samuels wondered why that particular girl was targeted. Who besides him and his trusted men even knew she had the powers she did? As far as he knew, the Master wasn't aware of her at all. He locked that thought down, too.

The Master's eyes were cold.

"And do you approve of this?" he asked.

"I do not, Master."

"I. Don't. Care," the Master said. "The Panther bitch is still alive. Fred Hampton is still alive. Deborah Johnson is still alive. Huey Newton is out of prison. And there is still a fucking live panther scaring the shit out of guards in Cook County Jail."

The Master's face slowly changed from white, to pink, to red, to purple, each color climbing its way up from the collar of his robe until it reached the top of his head. The tendons on his neck bulged. Power roiled out from his body and thrummed across the floor. The amphetamine stink was almost gagging. Samuels felt the operatives ringing the room fight to stay in place.

The Master's wrath affected everyone. That was how it was designed. That was how they were designed.

"And you have lost plants and operatives. And have failed twice—no, multiple times to defeat spics and niggers and half-trained girls, on the astral. Not only on your own, but with highly trained operatives under your supposed leadership. We have wasted too much time on you!"

Samuels had expected the browbeating. Even expected a real beating.

He also realized he didn't care anymore. Taking in a breath, he relished the pain that kept him focused.

"Yes, Master. But if you would allow me to explain," he said.

He would talk the Master down, the way he always did.

And buy himself more time.

CHAPTER EIGHTEEN
DOREEN

Doreen was in the attic, preparing for a ritual she wasn't even certain was going to happen.

That it *needed* to happen was a certainty. The ancestors had told her so.

But the other person involved? Huey Newton? She wasn't so sure he understood.

These Panthers. They were so bold. So brave and determined. Smart as whips. Unafraid of death in a way she'd never seen. They had to be, of course. Death dogged their heels every day.

But they were also so very, very, young. And the man she waited for was older than the rest. At twenty-seven, Huey P. Newton was practically an old man among the Party. Fred Hampton was only twenty-one. A leader among men if she'd ever met one. As powerful as Dr. King.

Doreen dusted altars and shelves. and then unwrapped the bouquet she'd brought from the shop and started picking through the carnations and roses, enjoying the scent of the pine branches she'd bundled in at the last minute.

It was Solstice and Doreen missed Hector all of a sudden. Her husband had loved the Solstices and Equinoxes, which was funny, for a being so tied to the tides of the moon.

Said they kept him connected to the earth somehow, and he liked remembering that his life depended on the sun.

She should have gotten Drake a present for Solstice, but with everything going on, she had just forgotten. Setting the flowers down again, she rummaged through the shoeboxes on the shelves near the rear of the attic. There was something she thought she remembered…something he might like.

Drake had grown into himself in the past month, and even more so since Doreen had gone down to Los Angeles.

There it was, inside a small, dark purple velvet bag. A brass pendulum, perfectly weighted, on a long brass chain. She'd been meaning to teach the boy dousing anyway, sure he'd have a knack.

A sharp knock came on the attic door, which swung open with a groan. There was the boy himself.

Drake, only thirteen years old, carried himself like a different person than the beaten-up child Jasmine had befriended. He stood in the attic, hands on hips, in his corduroy jacket and his usual red sweater with the same plaid shirt peaking out from beneath.

But he couldn't have been more different. For one, he had the air of magic about him, all from one or two month's worth of hard work. And he was fierce now. No one would mess with him.

Patrice reported that the children he was training adored him. Doreen could see why.

"Come in, Drake. It's good to see you." The boy he had been would have offered her a hug. This boy? Doreen wasn't so sure. She opened her arms anyway, and he walked on in. Briefly, though. A quick pat on the back and they were through.

"Patrice is coming. She's bringing up the pitcher of water."

"And Huey?"

"Said he'd be here if he could."

Doreen sighed. That was the best they could hope for, she guessed. Freshly busted out of prison, Huey Newton answered to no one anymore, except the needs of the Party.

She thought she had convinced him that this would help. But people never fully trusted a magic that wasn't their own.

Despite having been married to Hector all those years, Doreen still wasn't sure how to describe shifter magic. She just knew that it was there, and worked somehow. Only the Animal People themselves knew for sure.

Some secrets you didn't share.

"I have a small present for you, Drake. For Solstice."

A small smile crossed his face. "You didn't have to do that, Mrs. Doreen."

"It's more of a tool than a present. It's something I need you to start working on."

She put the soft bag in his palm and waited while he pulled the brass weight free.

"What is it?"

"A pendulum. It's used for dousing. For finding things. Some magic workers can even locate people that way."

"Far out. How does it work?"

Doreen showed him how to shorten the chain until the balance felt right. How to pinch the chain between his ring finger and thumb, and how to hold his other hand, palm up, under the weight, to test for "yes" and "no."

"That is the very basic method, but there's a lot more you can do with the tool. I'll show you more next week, I promise."

Or whenever the next battle was through. That went unsaid. They both knew it though.

Drake nodded. "Thank you so much," he said, and tucked the velvet bag into the pocket of his jeans.

Doreen went back to arranging flowers on the big ancestor altar in the middle of the room.

"Would you get me the matches?" Doreen asked Drake. He shrugged out of his jacket and hung it on a peg by the door. Then crouched at one of the low shelves along the wall and found a box of matches.

"You want the candles lit now?" he asked.

"All but the candles in front of the mask."

The mask. The big red, black, and white Chokwe mask. The key to the ancestors in Angola, no matter which tribe they belonged to, it seemed. Not that Doreen knew much about the differences. She just knew her people came from there.

She thought maybe Huey's people did, too. When she saw the man, with the soft, slight Southern drawl he'd inherited from his parents, and the bright eyes that saw through a lot, she recognized him. After they'd raised a magical storm to help the Panthers bust him out of the California Men's Colony, she'd felt a kinship there.

An acknowledgement that somehow, they were related down the line.

She heard Patrice's heels on the steps outside. And a heavier tread behind her.

It had to be Huey P. Newton, head of the Oakland Panthers. He'd decided to come.

"Hey baby," Patrice said from the door. Her outfit this evening was the orange dress that hugged her ample curves. Her lips were painted to match. She headed right for Doreen and gave her a kiss that simultaneously made Doreen want to drag her downstairs, and feel slightly embarrassed at having shared such a thing in front of a guest.

Jasmine said Huey was "down with gay rights" but Doreen still wasn't used to being open about her love for the woman who'd become her best friend.

She kissed and hugged her lover anyway, then turned to greet the man filling up the attic doorway, smelling of cigarettes and big cat.

"Welcome back, Huey. Please come in."

"Thank you, ma'am."

Drake hurried over with a folding chair and set it out for Huey. Doreen nodded at him, and he got seats for all of them, snapping the wooden chairs open and placing them in a rough circle on the Douglas fir planks.

"If you don't mind my asking, why am I here, ma'am?"

"The ancestors have been speaking to me again," Doreen said. "Remember how they blessed you all, last time you were here? You, Fred, Deborah, Leroy...?"

He nodded.

"Another big battle is coming."

"There always is."

"Drake here figured out it's coming this week. There is no real time to plan. There is barely time to strategize. We could plan for ten years for this battle and still have things go wrong."

"Ma'am?"

"The ancestors want to give you strength for whatever the Party's role will be. They've already given my niece, Jasmine, a tool of power. But…" How in the world was she supposed to say this to the man sitting across from her? Shape-shifter or not. Used to bullets flying past his head or not. She was about to ask him something very strange.

He just sat. Waiting.

Doreen took in a deep breath, and then asked Drake to light the candles near the Chokwe mask. Then she called upon her Fire. She needed to feel her sorcery flowing through her body and out into the energy field around her. She needed to remember who she was, this shortest night of the year.

The ancestors began tapping at the hollows behind her ears, wanting to come through. Wanting her to let them in.

And so, as Drake lit the red candle, and the black, and then the green, Doreen dropped her attention deeper and opened herself to the voices of those from long ago.

"They want something from you, Huey. They want a blessing, and a sacrifice." She held the palms of her hands to his forehead. Heard him breathing in the small attic room.

"They want your blood." His head jerked beneath her hands, his breathing grew more raspy, but then, she felt the change. Felt something in him decide. And he loosened then, and grew firm again.

Then, he pushed up the black sleeves of his leather coat and held out both his wrists, facing upward so the soft skin was exposed.

Doreen nodded. She knew that he would feel it. That he would know.

"We will spill your blood for the good of the people, like the kings of old. Your sacrifice will be their sacrifice, and you will take on their burdens as your own."

Patrice placed a glass bowl on the floor between them, underneath Huey's outstretched hands.

"Drake? There is a small knife on the altar. Pass it through each of the three candle flames, on both sides of the blade."

The boy did as he was told, smoke guttering up around the knife, candle flames reflecting off the blade.

"Now wipe it on the white cloth."

He did so, and handed her the knife, hilt first.

She breathed across Huey Newton's wrists, and placed a kiss on each one.

"Ancestors! Take this willing sacrifice of blood shed as a promise for a life to come. We do not offer you death, but the gift of life eternal. We offer you our hearts, our goodwill, and a pledge to serve the people as long as we shall live."

"Huey?" she asked.

"I pledge to serve the people, as long as I shall live. I shall live and die for the people."

And Doreen cut a thin slice across both wrists, knife parting the lighter brown skin there, a line of blood welling gently up.

He grit his teeth and shifted slightly in the wooden folding chair.

She handed Drake the blade and ran her hands down Huey's arms, pushing blood toward the two cuts until it ran into the bowl.

Patrice came forward with a pitcher of water and poured it over both their hands, washing the blood off his wrists, and mixing water and blood in the clear glass.

Then Drake offered them another clean white cloth.

And it was done.

CHAPTER NINETEEN
JASMINE

How in all the worlds did *I* join the revolution and *you* got shot?" My boots were practically wearing a hole in Ernesto's rug. I barely saw the altar on his dresser, or the art nailed to the walls, though I knew they were there.

Mouth and stomach were sour, and my armpits stank from the fear that jolted through me when I heard what had happened. Damn. It should've been me.

Carol was propped up in Ernesto's bed, tucked under the white comforter with the burgundy trim, almost as pale as the sheets. Her breathing was labored, I could hear the catch every time she tried to inhale.

And she couldn't sit up yet.

Carol should have been sleeping, but the stubborn thing wouldn't let them knock her out. There was too much work to do, she said.

Wasn't that the truth. The full moon was coming, tugging on every drop of water in my body, practically stealing the spit from my mouth.

"I feel it too," Carol said. I barely caught the quiet words.

"Feel what?"

"The moon."

That stopped me. "You can feel the moon?"

"Of course."

Ernesto came back into the room before she could explain, carrying a tray with what smelled like chicken broth, and some sort of nasty herbal tea from my mother. My mother, Cecelia, was usually good about making healing teas taste comforting and sweet. But some wounds needed nasty, I guessed.

"If you drink the tea, you can have the broth," he said, handing me the tray. "Let me help you sit up."

He very gently and carefully tugged her pillow upward. Carol gasped with pain. I set the tray down on the rug.

"Let me help you!"

Together, very carefully, we got my friend propped up enough that she could swallow without choking.

Sweat beaded across Carol's forehead from the effort. She didn't smell so good. Ernest grabbed a soft white cloth and wiped her face with such tenderness, I needed to turn away.

I grabbed the tray from the carpet, flipped the short, sturdy legs down, and set it across her on the bed.

"What if I don't want either?" Carol finally whispered.

"If you drink the tea, you can have the broth," Ernesto repeated, a big fake smile on his face. "Cecelia's orders."

"Don't cross my mother when you're sick, Carol. It'll be worse than getting shot."

Carol tried to lift her right arm and hissed in pain. "Do I have to eat left-handed? And how am I going to cast?"

"I can feed you, and you're not going to cast until you heal," Ernesto said.

"And if I get attacked again?"

"I'll kill them," I replied. "Or Ernesto will. And you can always cast through your feet. You Earth sorcerers have all that ground-shaking mojo going on."

Ernesto held the cup up to Carol's mouth.

"Gah. Terrible." It took a while, but she drank it all. "I think I need that soup."

Ernesto spooned some into her mouth.

I went back to pacing the room.

"Ernesto, what the hell happened down there?"

He sighed and kept on feeding Carol.

"We were working on the sigils. I'd just found something that stood out to me. Carol didn't recognize it."

"But something bugged me," Carol said.

"What did you sense?" I asked.

"Stop a minute, Ernesto." Carol turned her head from the spoon of broth. He put it back in the cup.

She laid her head back on the pillow and closed her eyes. I waited, listening as my friend labored to slow her breathing down.

"Can't you *help* her, Ernesto?" Seriously, the man needed to get it together.

Startled, he put the cup back down on the tray, and three seconds later, I felt him reach for Air. A slight breeze stirred Carol's blond hair. She opened her mouth and filled her lungs. Then started coughing.

"Ow! That all hurts."

"Try it slower, maga," Ernesto said. "Synch with me."

He touched his fingers to her breastbone and breathed. Slowly. Deeply. After a few breaths, I could feel Carol match him. As if they were breathing the same breath. In and out.

Pretty groovy.

My friend was lying in bed, shot up, and struggling to breathe, and I was still asking her about sigils.

I hated this. But we had to figure out why Carol was a target. And if the information might also save one more black boy from getting shot dead by police? Maybe this was even worth it.

Maybe.

"I am a revolutionary," I muttered, trying to remind myself. "I am the revolution."

"Jasmine?" Carol whispered.

"Yeah?"

"I am, too."

Damn. Right. The skinny white girl from Minnesota, my best friend, had just taken two bullets for the revolution.

It wasn't random. It was war. And that pissed me off even more than I already was.

I turned away for a moment so she wouldn't see the tears threatening to spill from my eyes.

"Tell me about the sigil," I said, pretending to examine the objects on Ernesto's dresser top. Taking in a huge draft of air, I thought: *Be cool, Jasmine Jones. Be cool.* Be. Cool.

So they told me. About a tree with a broken limb. Carol entering into trance.

And immediately getting shot.

"What don't they want us to know?" I asked.

I headed toward the door.

"Jasmine!" Ernesto called out. "Where are you going?"

"To find Helen Price."

I was seriously pissed off now, running down the hallway, shoving past the visiting sorcerers. I turned the corner to the stairs and slammed into a thick black dude in a fancy Nehru jacket that strained at his shoulders. His bald head gleamed in the light coming from the window at the end of the hall.

Mr. Oluo. From New York. That's who he was.

"Jasmine Jones. I've been wanting to speak with you." His voice sounded like thunder.

"What Element do you carry?" I asked, though I had a suspicion I knew.

"Air."

"Good. Let's go make a storm."

He followed after me, thunking down the stairs in what had to be hundred-dollar shoes. How'd a black sorcerer get that kind of bread? That was a conversation for later.

"Where are we going?" he asked.

"I need to talk to Helen Price. Know where she is?"

"I believe she's in a meeting. In what was Terrance Sterling's office?"

Oh. Was she? A woman who should not be taking meetings with anyone, in an office she had no right to anymore.

I slammed down the hallway, riding my fury, and flung open the heavy wooden door.

"How dare you!" It was some white man. I vaguely remembered him from the big conclave. Not even worth my time.

"Helen. What in all the Powers do you think you're doing?"

A wave of ice met me just inside the door.

Helen's face was pinched and white. Even her perfect makeup couldn't cover the strain. She knew she was screwed and was trying to find what alliances within the Association that she could, before it was all over.

She wasn't running with her tail between her legs, I'd give her that.

"I'm simply having a meeting with Tom Xavier, to discuss what direction the Association might wish to head."

"You have no say in the matter anymore."

"Come on, now," Tom Xavier—I guessed that was who he was—shouted.

I held up a hand and snapped some electric blue fire into my palm. "You can get out of this office, Tom Xavier. I don't need to hear from you ever again."

"You're threatening me?" he whispered, eyes narrowed like he was gonna do something about it.

"It looks that way," Mr. Oluo said. "Why don't you go to the kitchen? Fix yourself a cup of tea?"

The sorcerer made sure to clip my shoulder as he passed. Let him. I had no time for slights or posturing. I'd leave that to whichever toadies Terrance Sterling had left.

Helen looked like shit. Which was good. She should.

"How long did you know? When you were meeting with us, oh, so concerned? When you were trying to make nice and conciliatory? My aunt *trusted* you! My mother, too!"

She just sat in the club chair, mute.

"How. Long. Helen?"

Crossing the room, I crouched in front of her until my face was inches from hers.

"Tell me."

"I don't know what you're talking about."

Mr. Oluo stepped up behind her, and put one hand on her left shoulder. He spoke then. Softly. Almost gently.

"I think you had better tell us what you know, Helen."

She burst into tears.

I snorted and shoved myself back up, then onto the sofa. Mr. Oluo took the other end. I just waved a hand.

Helen just kept crying.

"Maybe those tears work on some people, Helen. But I know how powerful you are. I know you have the force of a glacier at your fingertips. Tears? They won't melt too much of your power away. So why don't you tell me—you, who've been one of the most powerful people in this Powers-damned Association all these years—exactly how long you knew Terrance was not only colluding with the Feds, but trying to *take us down*?"

I felt Mr. Oluo flinch and turned to him. "Oh yeah, you didn't put that one together yet? Terrance has been undermining Association magic. Tainting it. We're just trying to figure out why."

"Helen?" Mr. Oluo asked again.

"Power," she said. "He wanted more power."

I leapt to my feet again. "Oh please! Of course he wanted more power. Everyone knew that much. But why, Helen?"

She just shook her head.

"Jasmine."

I turned. It was my mother, standing in the doorway.

"You're back." There was a lot I didn't say there, and wouldn't. Not in front of Helen and a sorcerer I'd barely just met. I knew she'd argued with Doreen about not wanting to be Association head before Doreen left.

What was it with this generation? These people were either ready to blow the world apart or go hide in a hole. My mother wanted my damn participation in the farce, but didn't want to take the responsibility being handed to her.

My mother walked into the room and nodded at Mr. Oluo. "It's good to see you again, Gregory. It's been years."

"We're not here for pleasantries," I said.

Her voice cracked through the room. "You will talk to me with respect."

I winced, but didn't reply.

My mother played with a silver Nefertiti amulet that rested on her peach sweater. I could tell she was trying to keep it together.

"I came back to tell Helen to pack her bags and leave the Mansion. She is relieved of all Association duties."

She turned to her old friend, then. "Helen, we will give you enough money to go far, far away from here. If we find that you are in contact with Terrance Sterling, your funds will be cut off."

"That's it?" I asked. "You're just going to let her go?"

"Don't you think it's best?" my mother said. But she was looking at Helen. That question wasn't for me.

I laid a hand on my mother's arm. "Stop trying to protect her. Please. She has information that we need."

My mother place a hand over mine and removed my hand from her arm. My own mother did that.

"This isn't the Black Panther Party, Jasmine. We don't torture people for information, or whatever it was you thought you were going to do here."

"I wasn't…"

"Oh," she said. "I smelled your magic from a mile away. I think you were. And besides, you're late to the party. Carol already told us about Hoover."

That stopped me in my tracks. Hoover? Terrance Sterling had been working with J. Edgar Hoover? Was that what Carol had called me about? The phone call I'd tried to return?

I had figured I'd find out what she wanted when I got to the Mansion. And then my best friend got shot and the news must have left her head.

My mother turned her back on me then. "Gregory? Would you escort Helen to her rooms and oversee her packing? I want her gone before sunset."

This was all so much worse than I thought.

Chapter Twenty
Jasmine

It was early evening on the Solstice and my mother had all but declared herself head of the Association. And there hadn't even been a vote yet.

I wondered if there would be one now. If the damn conclave of sorcerers would meet to decide whether the Association was going to move forward doing nothing, or…

My head hurt. I thought my mother was down with helping the people. Now? I just didn't know. I wished Doreen was here, but I was going to the next best thing.

Ernesto had offered to drive me to see Rosalia. I'd refused and called Jimmy to come back and pick me up. Ernesto looked relieved. The man was a wreck, and I could tell that, much as he wanted Rosalia's counsel, he couldn't bear to leave Carol's side.

I really wanted to talk to my father, but couldn't risk it. Not right now. I was still too filled with anger. And felt a little bit betrayed.

This was getting to be a pattern.

And then we were supposed to be meeting with Panther leadership, and the Brown Berets again. I didn't know if I was up to it all.

Jimmy's borrowed El Camino rumbled down the streets, heading toward East Los Angeles again. It was so funny: I'd grown up in Crenshaw, and spent a lot of time at the Mansion in the hills around

Mulholland, but I'd been in East LA more since I moved to Oakland than I ever had before.

"I don't know what I'm going to do about Helen Price," I muttered to the windshield.

"Shit," Jimmy said, steering around a corner, barely missing a parked Cadillac.

"That damn car is sticking out too far," Jimmy said. "I don't know, Jasmine. If I was you, I'd be so mad I could spit. But I also have to imagine your mother knows what she's doing."

"Why? Why do you imagine that?"

"Because," he said, slowing down in front of a parking spot between a bakery and the tire shop, "from where I stand? Your mom has more magic than any of those other cats up the hill."

"My *mother*? The healer? The one who barely uses her magic except to make healing teas for people? She's practically an herb woman, not a sorcerer."

"Jasmine, chill out," Jimmy said. Then added, more gently, "I think your mom has more going on than you see. Dig?"

Then he concentrated on parallel parking as cars whizzed by.

Once the El Camino was situated, I heaved the door open, almost ramming it into a baby carriage.

"Cuidado!"

"I'm so sorry!" I said to the mother. She threw me a dirty look and kept walking.

I looked around, but didn't see the blue door with the orange triangle and the gold hand. Carol had told me the store moved around sometimes, but I hadn't really believed her.

"Is that it over there?" Jimmy pointed to a place across the street.

"Far out," I said. This was like some place out of a book. Las Manos were truly the baddest sorcerers in town.

In their poor-ass neighborhood, with flaking paint on their front door, they could shift space and time enough to move a whole botánica and have the rest of the neighborhood remain the same, piñata stores, auto body shops, vegetable stands, and all.

"How much of this is Rosalia, and how much is Las Manos?" I wondered as we waited for a break in traffic to cross the street.

By the time we pushed through the door, and I heard the bells clamoring above my head, I was ready for some magic that tasted clean.

But I didn't know just how much I also needed comfort until the tiny hechicera wrapped me in her arms and smashed those bangles against my shoulder blades.

It was weird to be here. Solstice night. Mad at my mother. My best friend, who was supposed to be the safe one, lying in bed with holes in her shoulder from a .22.

Luckily the Mansion had deep pockets for a doctor who didn't mind dealing with spooky injuries, and could also be paid off to not call in bullet wounds.

Rosalia took me to the statue of the Virgin blazing with candles, that beatific smile on her face as her tiny feet crushed the snake below.

"Make an offering."

"With what?"

She held out a small dish filled with golden pebbles. In her other hand was a small piece of wood with a burnt end.

"Frankincense," I said.

"And Palo Santo," she replied.

I rolled the amber resin beads between my fingers, and went to throw them on the coal burning red in an abalone shell at the Virgin's feet.

"But you must also offer all the pain in your heart."

That stopped me dead in my tracks. *All* the pain? There'd been so much these past months.

"I don't know…"

"*She* knows. Just offer what you can. She'll take the rest."

That didn't make any sense to me, but I decided to trust the hechicera, since she seemed to be right about everything else.

I blew across the frankincense, imagining that my breath carried the pain, the fear, the anguish, and the rage. And my sorrow. Yeah. That was in there, too.

Then, one by one, I dropped the resinous beads onto the charcoal, where they hissed and began to melt, releasing their sweet perfume.

We stood there for a while. Staring at the Virgin's face, and breathing in the sweet smoke. Then Rosalia gestured Jimmy closer. She held the end of the stick of Palo Santo in the flame of a red candle.

The sweet burning-wood smell mingled with burning resin. She began to move the glowing stick around our heads. Her mouth moved as she worked, weaving a spell of smoke and prayer around our heads and down the fronts of our bodies, then up the back.

All of a sudden, everything felt as if it dropped away. The battles. The killings. The imprisonment. The fight with my mother.

"I feel clean."

Jimmy shook himself, flexing his hands and rolling his head on his neck.

"Now we will sit down. Jimmy will pour us each a small glass of wine. And we will talk."

"I don't know about the wine..." I started saying. We still had a lot of work to do.

"Your sorcery will still be there," Rosalia said. "And right now, you are too wide open. The wine will soften the edges, just a little."

We went through a burgundy curtain next to the long counter and into the back room where a small table and four chairs sat in what otherwise looked like a store room for the witch at the end of the road.

Bottles and jars and boxes, all filled with seeds, dried flowers, and some things I wasn't sure I wanted to know anything about. But I looked anyway.

Looking at the jars, filled with physical manifestations of magic, I remembered. It seemed like a year ago, but had only been earlier that day.

"So, I want to talk about my ancestor and that spear she gave me." I turned to Rosalia. "I mean, a real spear? From wherever she is to *here*? How'd that happen?"

Rosalia's face was stoic. Still. But her citrine eyes held my gaze, penetrating as always.

"Yes. The spear. What did you feel when you held it?"

I noticed she wasn't answering my question, but I thought about her question anyway.

"It hummed. Vibrated. It caught people's attention when I needed it. It…" I looked to Jimmy, who was already sitting on a spindly chair at the round table.

"It gave her Authority," he said, speaking to Rosalia.

I could hear the capital letter he gave the word. And I wondered what he'd seen.

"That is the nature of such a gift," she said. "To be honest, hechicera, I've heard of such objects, but have not had the honor to see or touch one before the spear came to you."

What did that mean, then? I'd gotten some object of power that someone like Rosalia had never even seen? Despite the cleansing smoke, it all felt like too much again.

Rosalia gestured to the table. I sat. Jimmy poured a red wine into small, clear glass cups. It was dry. Just a little sweet to cut the tang of tannins.

I relaxed some more. Rosalia was right. I needed this. Just a taste or two. The amount that was in this small glass. If I drank any more, I might start to cry. And if I started crying, I wasn't sure when I'd be able to stop.

And we still had a battle to plan. After we figured out exactly where the target was.

After a few sips, I found my tongue again.

"So, I want more information on the spear, but guess I won't get it tonight. Besides, we've got too much else to do, so I'm not gonna trip on it. I'm not sure where to start, so I'm just gonna list some things out, okay? First, we need to figure out who shot Carol, and why. The timing seems suspicious, right?"

Rosalia nodded, face grave, then sipped her wine.

"Then there's the attack on La Piranya. And the sigils. The Temple sigils. The…" I took another sip of wine. "The sigil carved into Chuy's flesh." There was the anger. Back again.

"And the snakes and spiders, which just won't seem to go away. Which means Federal agents. And who knows what other government spooks."

I set the glass down. It was still half full, but I didn't want any more wine. "Oh. And Terrance Sterling sold us out to the FBI. And not just the FBI, to Hoover himself. And all of this is somehow connected to the assassination attempts, the assault on Panther HQ…probably even the bombing of Brown Beret HQ two years ago. Hell, maybe even the assassination of Dr. King and Malcolm. We don't know how far back this stretches, or how wide it spreads."

"So what do we do?" my lover asked.

"We figure it all out, and then we burn their twisted Temple to the ground," Rosalia said.

"Right on," Jimmy replied.

Huh. Yeah. That deserved a toast.

"To burning their Temple down." We all clinked glasses together. "Happy Solstice everyone."

"Happy Solstice."

"May the light always return."

"Okay. We need to get back to the Mansion now."

"Jasmine," Rosalia said. "You tell Ernesto to come back and talk to me. Soon."

"I will."

I hated to leave, but opened the door anyway, bells jangling to announce our departure.

There was still more work to do.

CHAPTER TWENTY-ONE
CAROL

Carol lay on Ernesto's bed, staring at the cream-painted ceiling and the wrought iron lamp fixture. Through the fog in her head, she attempted to puzzle out the sigils in her head. There was something about the sigil carved into that poor man at La Piranya. The twistedness of it reminded her of what she was calling the broken tree.

Cecelia and some other Earth sorcerers had been in and out, feeding her energy and healing. Her shoulder already felt much better, which was amazing.

Not that she had any idea how long it was supposed to take for a gunshot wound to heal, but this had to be quick.

She was just glad to not be on medication that muzzed up her brain. The pain was doing a good enough job of that right now.

With a soft knock on the door, Ernesto came in.

"You don't have to knock on the door to your own bedroom, Ernesto."

"I wasn't sure if you'd be in the middle of another session with the Earth sorcerers."

She smiled. In the middle of all the drama, it was nice to just look at him and feel in love.

He came over and laid a kiss on her forehead.

"What about my lips? They didn't get shot."

"Getting shot has made you sassy, maga."

He kissed her anyway. She gasped.

"Did I lean on something?"

"No," she said. "I'm just remembering. We kissed. In the workroom. When you were showing me the tree. We were starting to twine our Elements together. Remember? We pulled apart. And then I got shot."

He sat down on the edge of the bed, shaking his head. "No. That's not right. We kissed. And then we said we needed to get back to work. I found that sigil. You said it looked like a broken tree."

"And *then* I got shot?"

"Why are you asking about this?"

"I was just wondering if someone found us because we were combining our Elements. They recognized it or something. I don't know! I just can't figure out why, in a Mansion full of sorcerers from all over the country, *I'm* the one who got shot."

He held her left hand in his.

"Maga, you got shot because all along, you're the one who's been getting the visions. And seeing the sigils. You. Not anyone else."

She flopped her head back down onto the pillow, winced, and then exhaled with a sigh.

"I've been lying here, trying to figure those sigils out, but there's still something I'm just missing. It's so close. I know it's there."

"Maybe you need to just rest right now. Besides, I got you a present."

She struggled to sit up, hissing as she forgot for a second, and used her left elbow to push.

"You can receive your present lying on your back," he said.

"Oh?" Carol arched an eyebrow.

Ernesto was rooting in the top drawer of his dresser. "Not that kind of present. Not until you're fully healed."

He turned, a small package in his hand.

"I got you this."

She unwrapped the pale green tissue paper. Nested inside the paper was a malachite cube, two inches across. Its sides were a beautiful swirl of variegated green. Running her fingers across the polished surface, she closed her eyes.

Even in this altered form, the stone was still alive. Nothing could take away the power of Earth.

She opened her eyes to see her lover looking down at her.

"I love it. It's beautiful."

"Happy Solstice," he said.

"May the light always return," she answered.

Ernesto leaned in and kissed her.

"I'm glad you're still alive, Carol."

She laughed. "So am I."

"I'm serious," he said, rich brown eyes looking concerned behind the lenses of his glasses. "I've been your teacher, your mentor…I feel like I should have been able to protect you."

"From what?" Carol asked. Leaning her head into his chest, she breathed in, then spoke into the soft cloth of his shirt. "Ernesto, we were in a warded building with fifty of the most powerful sorcerers in the world. We were in a room we've worked in a hundred times. They could have just as easily hit *you* with those bullets."

And that terrified her.

He ran a hand over her hair. She felt a soft kiss on the top of her head. Carol wanted to stay there forever, feeling safe and comforted for the first time in a long while.

But her shoulder was starting to scream at the position.

"I need to sit back again."

Ernesto braced her uninjured side and the back of her head and helped ease her back onto the pillow.

"I'm too tired for this. My shoulder feels like a hill of fire ants took up residence, and I can't figure these damn sigils out!"

"Carol, if you weren't an Earth sorcerer, you wouldn't even be awake right now. Your body is repairing itself faster than it should. But that doesn't mean it can heal you without you lying down in this bed and resting."

"Ernesto…" She sighed in frustration. "Did you hear what I said to Jasmine?"

"I am a revolutionary?"

"Did you think I was kidding? Did you think I'm not all in now? I hate this Mansion now. I hate that half the people in it don't care what's been happening. They don't even care about *Vietnam*, which is on the news every night. How are we going to make them see that what's happening in Watts and East LA matters to them? To us?"

"You know, my parents were so proud when we realized I was a sorcerer," he said. "I was born with Fire, you know. And Air kicked in when I was twelve. Their little Ernesto had not one, but *two* Elements! They were so happy to send me to the Hacienda on the Hill, as they called it."

"You lived here?"

"Of course I did. I just assumed you knew that. We were poor farmers in the Fresno Valley. My parents had their own land, which mi papá always said made us rich. And compared to some of the people I grew up around, we were."

"Do you ever see them?"

"I usually drive up every other month. I should be there for Christmas, but…" He raised his hands and shrugged, a rueful look on his face.

"Come sit with me." Carol tilted her head toward the other side of the queen bed, wincing as the tendons in her neck and shoulder moved.

"I hate this," she said. "I thought I was doing well by remembering to not pat the bed."

"At the rate you're healing, you'll be better in a few days," Ernesto said, taking off his shoes.

"I hope so. Before you sit down, is there any paper in the room?"

He disappeared for a moment into the small study that was the other room to his suite. He threw an army-green canvas satchel onto the bed and climbed on top of the comforter next to her.

Digging through the satchel, he pulled out two issues of *La Causa* before coming up with a pad of blank paper and a zippered pencil case.

"Can you draw with your left hand?" he asked.

He put a small burgundy pillow on her lap and propped the open pad on it, then rooted through the pencil case.

"I have no idea."

"You know, the old Spiritualists used to write with their left hands sometimes. They said it helped the Spirits speak more clearly."

"Well, I guess we'll find out."

Carol took a black pen from Ernesto and adjusted the grip in her left hand. Then she slowed her breathing down, calling up the Power of Earth and calling up the sensations she got in her body before the visions came on.

She still wasn't sure exactly how to control the visions, but figured now was as good as any a time to learn.

She remembered a strange tapping feeling at the bottom of her spine. And then there was the tingling at the base of her skull. A floating feeling around her temples. And finally, the sense of energy flowing through the middle of her forehead. The place called the third eye.

She tried to imagine what those felt like. As her breathing deepened, she imagined her vision expanding outward. First from the slight depressions on either side of her eyebrows, right where her hairline began. Then out the back of her skull. And then the third eye.

As she entered a deeper and deeper state, the pen in her left hand began to move across the page, scratching out lines and curves that joined to other lines.

The Temple column. The sun-wheel. The spider. The crescent. The jagged, slantwise N.

The broken tree.

Faster and faster, the sigils came. Carol was barely aware of Ernesto flipping the pages of the notebook when she filled a page.

The slight snick of the paper being moved from underneath her hand, and then the field of white again. White that needed to be marked up.

As the symbols came, so did the image of the Temple, rising. Four Temples. There were four temples.

And the temples formed a diamond shape. She drew the diamond. A square set on each corner. Each square had four corners. On each square sat a temple, built of sigils. Magic. Forming a new form.

Cubes within cubes within cubes.

Building a Temple so majestic, so powerful, no one could deny it anymore.

All would worship at this temple.

All would worship under the Master's guidance.

In this servitude, all would become free.

The Master knew what was best.

The Master held the key.

The pen dropped from Carol's hand and she blacked out again.

CHAPTER TWENTY-TWO
DOREEN

They poured the blood and water on the offering stone in the backyard. It seeped into the soil.

"You're bound to Oakland now. And to the people. It's a sacred pact. The land itself will support you." Doreen looked at Huey's face. He looked serious. Solemn. She placed her hands on top of his head. "The ancestors bless you. The people rejoice in you. Be a servant to your power and it will grow like a mighty tree."

"I have the people behind me, and the people are my strength," he replied.

Doreen walked him through the house to the front door, and Patrice and Drake went back up to the attic to put everything away.

A young Panther was standing on the front steps.

"Emergency meeting, man. We just got the call."

Huey nodded then turned. "Thank you."

Doreen placed a hand on his arm. "It's a burden, but also a gift."

The young Panther looked at Doreen. "You should be getting a call sometime tonight yourself," he said. "They asked me to pass that word along."

"Thank you. Good night."

She stood on the porch, watching the two young men walk away. Everything was moving so quickly. She wanted to hang on to the power of the ritual. The potency of what she'd felt. The joy of the children playing with the panther that morning.

The thought of what the phone call would bring disturbed her.

She sighed. It wouldn't do to borrow trouble. She knew better. Best to let the phone call come when it did, and not worry.

Heading back up to the attic, she found Patrice and Drake were already finishing up.

"Mrs. Doreen, can I talk with you a minute?" Drake asked.

"I'll just carry the pitcher and cloths downstairs," Patrice said. Gathering the objects up, she kissed Doreen on the cheek and headed down the stairs.

"Want to sit on the steps outside?" Doreen asked.

Drake nodded and got his jacket.

Doreen turned out the lights and locked the door, then they sat on the landing, feet on the top step.

For a while, they just listened to the sounds of Oakland at night. Cars playing music. Some voices laughing as people walked by on the street out front.

She smelled night blooming jasmine and the brugmansia whose golden downturned trumpets were her favorite night blooming flower of all.

"Care to tell me what's on your mind?" she asked.

Drake took in a breath as if he was steeling himself. She felt his shoulders grow tense beside her, and just waited.

"It's about the magic. While you've been gone, I've been training the older kids. Some of the adults, too. Patrice can tell you, I've been doing real good at it."

"I'm not surprised. You work hard, Drake. You're focused on what's important to you. And you also have some natural talent. That's a powerful combination for anything, but especially for working magic."

Doreen looked at his profile in the dim light that filtered up the stairs from the kitchen window down below. He gave a quick nod, lips tight and small. She wasn't sure if he was scared to speak, or scared to say too much. Either way, it looked like those lips were locked down tight on a tumble of words.

"Drake...can you just tell me?"

"I want you to initiate me," he said in a rush. "Like you did to Mz. Patrice."

So that was what this was about.

A car horn blew four sharp blasts, then a long one. There was shouting. Then it grew quieter again, so they could catch the sounds of rustling under the hedges at the edge of the yard.

"Can you tell me why you want to be initiated, Drake?"

"You don't think I'm good enough?"

"It isn't that at all. I'm going to try to explain, but it's complicated..."

"That's what adults always say when they don't want to do something." He stood up and started moving down the stairs.

"Drake! Please stay. I want to try to explain, I really do."

He came two steps up and sat down again, as if he couldn't bear to sit so close to her anymore. He was hurting, and she wasn't certain why.

Perhaps it was just thirteen year old angst. The discomfort of knowing there was a whole world out there and you couldn't have it yet. And not understanding that even when you could have it, there was always someone standing next to you, trying to take it all away.

"Initiation is a commitment. To the Powers. To magic. To being responsible for more than yourself. Your life." She paused. Thinking. Hoping the ancestors would offer her the words to explain the unexplainable. "Initiation means you walk through a doorway and your life changes. There's no going back anymore. No saying you don't want to. You live with the responsibility for the rest of your life."

"What happens if you don't?"

That was a very astute question. And one that some of the most seasoned sorcerers never thought to ask.

"Something gets twisted up inside you. Some people go a little crazy. Some just fade away. But other people? They do bad things in the world, and cause a lot of pain."

They sat in silence for a moment, breathing in the night.

"I want...I want to do good, Mrs. Doreen. I've been feeling this... kinda pressure everywhere. Like something's about to burst. It's outside me, all around. In the people. In the sky. But it's in me, too. And I want to help. I want to help people. And I feel like I need something that's going to help me."

Doreen had watched this boy grow into a young man, almost overnight. Black boys often had to, she knew that. The world was not kind to black children. But she could see the shine inside him. And the ways that he was waking up.

She also believed him. He knew what he wanted.

She also knew she wasn't ready to place that burden on him, the way she had with Patrice, and in a different—and in some ways more brutally serious—way, with Huey Newton tonight.

"It's the Solstice, a very powerful time. In a perfect world, we'd be lighting candles and celebrating. But instead, we're preparing for this thing we all feel coming. That's the pressure you feel, Drake. Something's about to change."

"I *know* that, Mrs. Doreen! Why do you think I'm asking?"

"Drake?"

"*What?*"

He must be really upset to be so short with her. She let it slide.

"Will you give me a chance to sleep on this? The reason I'm asking isn't that I don't think you are worthy of initiation, or that it isn't right for you…."

"You just don't want to do it."

"No. That isn't it. It's that I'd hate to put a burden so large—a lifetime's burden—on someone who has such a large stretch of life ahead. Who knows what you'll want to do with your life when you're grown?"

He stood up again and turned to her, face fierce. Angry.

"I thought you understood all this stuff. And I thought you always told the truth. But you're jiving me now."

"I'm not…"

"I don't know if I'll *get* to be grown!" he spat out. His face was mostly in darkness, but Doreen could just see the slight shimmering of tears.

It pierced her heart. Of course the boy thought he was going to die. Why wouldn't he?

"Come here, baby," she said, holding out her arms.

He stood there, stock still. Then his face closed up, as if someone slammed the shutters on a window.

"I'm not a baby," he said. Then ran down the stairs.

"Drake!" Doreen chased after him, running through the open kitchen door.

"What's happening?" Patrice asked.

Doreen ignored her and ran down the hall, hearing the front door slam.

She hauled it open and stepped out on the porch.

"Drake!" she shouted to his back as he ran down the street, lit for an instance by each street lamp, then swallowed up by dark. Light. Dark. Light. Dark.

"Drake! Come back, *please!*"

Then Patrice was tugging at her arm, pulling her back toward the house.

"It's Jasmine on the phone, Doreen. You have to take this call."

Doreen looked at her lover. She was aching now. Too much. She wished she knew the boy would get home safely. That he wouldn't do something foolish in his pain.

But she also knew he was right. They were running out of time.

And no one knew what tomorrow would bring.

She felt every bit of the longest night seep into her soul. There was no light to be had this year.

"Doreen, baby. I'm so sorry. Come on inside. I've got coffee on."

Doreen turned and looked back down the street. A motorcycle with a faulty muffler roared by.

Patrice pulled on her arm again.

"Doreen. We're going inside now. You're going to talk to Jasmine. And then we're going to figure out what to do."

Doreen wasn't so sure that was possible anymore.

And she had no idea how to craft an initiation for a thirteen-year-old boy.

CHAPTER TWENTY-THREE
JASMINE

Not only had my mother gotten Helen escorted off to who knows where, but by the time Jimmy dropped me off at the Mansion and headed to meet with local Panther leadership, my mother had also managed to commandeer Terrance Sterling's office.

I found her in the large, sapphire-carpeted room. Terrance's magical objets d'art were gone, as were his books. The slab of desk had slightly shifted position, as had the sofas and chairs.

The corners had been dusted for cobwebs. You'd never know there'd been a battle by two opposing forces for the soul of the Association there.

All of this meant mother had enlisted several people to help her, and they had agreed.

I leaned against the door jamb, watching her as she stood working behind the walnut desk, dressed tonight in a green, drop-waisted shift with wide pleats that hit just above her knees.

The walnut of the desk complemented her dark skin. I remembered how beautiful I thought she was when I was a child. She was still beautiful, but the planes of her face had hardened overnight.

Always formidable, after her brief moment of weakness, she had returned a veritable mountain.

"When did you decide to stage a coup?" I asked.

My mother looked up, startled. Then tsked.

"It's not a coup. I'm not in charge. The sorcerers who are still here will vote tonight, just as we planned."

I just nodded. Looked like a coup to me. But these days? I knew when to hold my tongue.

"What made you decide you wanted it after all? We were always willing to fight for you, you know."

My mother sighed at that, setting down the papers she was fussing with. There was a file box on the floor next to the desk. Slowly filling with things Cecelia Jones thought she wouldn't need.

Or would need to look into later, once the storm blew through. Yeah. From the way she handled the papers, it looked more and more like an evidence box than deep storage.

"I realized I'd taken vows that included serving the Association. And to work for the good of the people. By offering my name as head, I have a chance to accomplish both."

"Right on," I said. "Welcome back, Mom."

"I was never gone. You know as well as anyone by now that sometimes we need to pretend we can back away from all this. But it's not in us to do so for very long." My mother gave me a sad smile. "So welcome back yourself."

I felt my shoulders hunch a bit at that. I didn't want to think I was back inside the Association of Magical Arts and Sorcery. The Party was enough. I had to do this bullshit, too?

But I also noticed I wasn't saying otherwise. Not yet.

I needed to get out of that office with the taint of Terrance Sterling still in the air. And the echo of the giant white spider battling the brown, webs filling up the space.

"What time is the meeting?"

"In an hour," she said.

"Cool. I'll be up with Carol until then."

I had seen the small white spider Doreen had plucked from the air in the assembly hall. This fortress was still breached, and I didn't like it one bit.

Taking the steps up to Ernesto's suite two at a time, I was struck yet again. How in all the Powers had a shooter gotten close enough to the Mansion to hit Carol?

I knocked on the suite door and got no answer, so I turned the knob and went on through.

Ernesto was with Carol in the bedroom.

"How are you healing up?"

She still looked paler than usual, and seemed weak. But it was a miracle attesting to the power of the Earth sorcerers in the building that she was even here at all. And yeah, that included my mother's work.

As a rule, sorcerers don't do the work of witches, but when we bother to bend the Elements that direction? It's powerful stuff.

"I think I'm okay. Wish I could be there to fight for Cecelia tonight."

"It sounds like she has plenty of support," Ernesto said.

"Hey! Aunt Doreen gave her vote by proxy to Simon. Why can't you do the same with me?" I asked.

"Consider yourself deputized," Carol said. Her voice was so soft, I almost had to strain to hear it. She was weaker than before. Or maybe she was just tired.

"I came to ask if you'd figured anything out, but you really look like you need some sleep."

I caught myself turning my black felt beret over and over in my hands. I willed myself to stop. Breathe in some of the water from the vase of flowers next to the bed.

I hated feeling the huge storm that was brewing, getting ready to break when we didn't know *what* or *why*. It was making everything up to this point feel like small skirmishes.

"It is obvious here that the agents of government speak the language of pure force," Frantz Fanon wrote. What was the force behind their magic? And what was their aim?

What was *our* aim, besides responding to attacks?

Water filled me then, stilling my anxiety, washing away my weariness.

"We need to orchestrate and attack. And we need to do it now," I said. "Ernesto, I need to see everything you've worked on regarding the symbols. They're a sort of language, right? Can you figure out the code?"

It was Carol who nodded, hectic red spots of incipient fever on her cheeks. That wasn't good. But we didn't have time for her to fully heal before moving forward, and she kept insisting on taking part.

All acts of real change required sacrifice. That was another thing Fanon said, that it was our job, not to understand the world, but to change it.

Well, motherfuckers, we were going to do just that.

I wanted Carol to heal. Badly. But I wanted to change the world too, to protect the people—all people—and to build a world where a black child could grow up proud and free.

I shook my head. Damn. My own internal war wasn't helping anything.

Ernesto was already laying papers out on the bed. Papers filled with clear black lines and intersecting curves. The images bristled with power. I could feel the magic encoded in them as if they were embedded in my skin.

"I want a table brought up here," I said. "We need to get methodical about this. And I want Rosalia brought in. And Jimmy. And anyone else we think will fit in this room."

Sparing a glance at my friend, I felt a rush of remorse. "But I'm sorry, Carol. You should really rest. Ernesto can…"

Her lips set in grim determination. "I'm not going anywhere Jasmine Jones. I said 'I am a revolutionary' and I meant it. *You* taught me that, Jasmine. You. Don't take it away from me now."

Ernesto was placing the papers into piles. "I'll go get a table and call the others. Carol can explain what happened to her. She had more visions and…" He gestured at the papers. "Well, you'll see."

With a rake of his fingers through his hair, Ernesto was out the door.

Carol looked at me, blue eyes half clouded with pain. But she seemed…solid. Happy even.

"Happy Solstice, Jasmine," she said.

"Happy Solstice, Carol," I replied. Then I walked over and gave her left arm a light squeeze. "I'm so thankful the Powers brought you here. And I'm glad you're my friend."

"May the light always return."

CHAPTER TWENTY-FOUR
JASMINE

I knew my mother wanted me in tonight's conclave, but I'd be damned if the Association took precedence over this. Let them argue it out. I told her to send a runner when it was voting time.

Both rooms in Ernesto's suite were packed. Jimmy and Rosalia had put out the call and more people showed up than I expected.

Guess we were riding on some goodwill and good old-fashioned rage. A potent combination for preparing for war.

Shifted panthers lay on the floor, guarding the doors and windows.

When they arrived, Ericka and Elaine said no way in hell were they "trusting this motherfucking Mansion when one of your own damn sorcerers just got shot" and proceeded to shift on the spot, startling a couple of visiting sorcerers who were passing through the entryway at the time.

I couldn't blame my Panther sisters one bit.

Rosalia and two other Las Manos sorcerers gathered around a folding card table in Ernesto's small sitting room with a pile of Carol's sigil papers spread out. They were looking at one set that seemed to have similarities, while Carol, Ernesto, and I were working on another set spread out across the bed.

Geronimo Pratt and Jimmy dragged more chairs into the sitting room, and were deep in conversation with Gloria and Rafael of the Brown Berets.

"Carol," I said, leaning forward from the folding chair I'd pulled up to the bed. Ernesto sat by her side on the bed itself. I tapped one of the sigils. "This one. It doesn't look like any of the sigils on the astral Temple the Feds built over Laguna Park."

Remembering she couldn't really sit up any straighter to look at the symbol, I held the piece of paper up.

"I don't remember drawing that," she said, then looked at Ernesto. "Was that one of the ones I just did today?"

"Sí," he said. "The spirits were really speaking through you, maga. I think there were…" He ruffled through the papers on the bed, shuffling the pages, searching. He pulled out one page and held it up to me.

"Jasmine, I think there are two more with a similar feel."

We both searched for them. I finally dropped down deeper into my center and let my Elemental power flow through my fingers, and began to search by feel, instead of sight.

Ernesto did the same with Air.

It felt like sifting my fingers through warm sand. The symbols had weight and density, but there was a lightness about them, too. Following a slight tugging sensation from my breastbone, I reached out with my left hand, resting my palm on the symbol there.

I opened up my eyes, keeping my breathing even and slow. I watched Ernesto seeking, listened to the rumble of Geronimo rapping about something in the sitting room—sounded like strategy—and the low murmur of Rosalia's voice.

"Here," Ernesto said, and opened his eyes. We both held up our sheets of paper. They were of the same family, though I couldn't tell you exactly how.

"Carol?" I asked, showing her the symbols.

"Holy Powers," she whispered, growing paler than before, eyes starting to roll back upwards in her head.

"Ernesto!" I said.

He dropped his paper and put a hand behind her head, making sure she didn't strike it on the headboard. He eased her back onto the pillow. Her eyes fluttered and her breathing came in rapid pants.

"Can you slow her breathing down?" I asked him, starting to panic. This was so not good. How was I going to lead people into battle in who knew how many days if my best friend getting shot and passing out from ink on paper threw me off?

That damn snake of a Fed had a lot to answer for. I wanted my damn bravado back. This feeling everything was the pits.

Ernesto was working with her. I could feel him slow his own breathing down further, and did the same. He sent a soft breath up her nostrils. Once. Then twice. On the third breath, I watched as her chest lungs filled and pushed air upward into her chest.

She exhaled on a sigh and blinked rapidly.

"Holy shit," she said. "I can't believe I never saw this before."

"What is it?"

"Can you help me sit up a little?"

Ernesto propped her up with one arm, careful to avoid the wounded shoulder, as I gently shoved another soft pillow behind her shoulders and head. She needed to be fully supported still. No way she should be sitting up even partially on her own.

"I think these are sounds! They're trying to form a word. Or a phrase or something." She pointed to the shapes. "See this? And this? See how they look like letters? Or those…you know. Like Chinese. Or hieroglyphs."

"Pictograms?" Ernesto said.

"Yes!" Carol said. Her breath still sounded uneven.

"Do you need me to get an Earth sorcerer in here again?"

Carol froze. Holding her breath. She looked scared for a moment.

"How many of them do you trust?"

I sat back in my folding chair again as the enormity of what she just said hit. It was so obvious. I needed to up my strategy game. Of course other people were compromised. I knew I didn't like a lot of the Association members, but had discounted them as foolish, blind, or bigoted.

"After you get your freedom, your enemy will respect you," Brother Malcolm said. I was working on getting free, but I'd forgotten that I had to respect my enemy in order to fight my enemy.

My enemies may have been bigots, but thinking they were fools was a mistake.

"I'll get my mother."

"After," Carol said.

She was right. I couldn't burst into the conclave right now, calling for my mother. That would undermine too much.

"Can I ask Rosalia to help?"

Carol made a small, impatient sound. "I want to finish this," she whispered.

Looking into her blue eyes, past the pain, I saw the determination. If I had to respect my enemies, I had to respect my friends, too.

We all made sacrifices for the revolution.

I cleared my throat and rubbed a hand across my face.

"Okay. What do you think the words are?"

"I'm having trouble concentrating..."

I laid a hand across her forehead, really wanting to send for my mother, but knowing she and Simon Tanaka, Mr. Oluo, and the others were likely embroiled in multiple arguments right now.

And yeah, I wasn't sure who else to trust.

Carol didn't feel feverish. She felt more...absent. As if part of her spirit was fading away. Or trapped on another plane. I sent a prayer out to the Virgin. If she could help me, maybe she'd help Carol, too. Help her to come back. Help her to heal.

"You know those things witches sometimes do?"

"Which things, maga?"

"The chanting. Not words."

"Barbarous words of power," Ernesto and I blurted out at once.

Right then, Rosalia entered the bedroom on a swirl of deep green velvet, holding up a paper inscribed with more black ink.

"Carol! Maga!" She walked into the room, then stopped dead when she really looked at Carol.

"How long has she been like this?" she said sharply to Ernesto.

"She wouldn't let us get anyone," I said.

"How long?"

"Around twenty minutes, mas o menos."

Rosalia shoved me aside and immediately put her hands on Carol's temples. Then she closed her citrine eyes, breathing in through her nostrils. I could practically feel the brace of heavy amulets resting on her chest begin to quiver with sorcery.

Her silver bangles clashed against each other.

The energy field she was gathering tried to push me back.

I stood my ground, and reached for Ocean. I felt Ernesto reach for Wind, and then for Flame. He and I formed an Elemental triangle around Rosalia and Carol on the bed. Ocean feeding Wind, Wind feeding Flame.

"That's right, maga, call your spark back home. It found what it was looking for. You're safe now. Come all the way back in. All the way back home," Rosalia said, never taking her hands from the hollows on each side of Carol's skull.

I saw a glimmering, as though something was moving toward us. So faint. Felt a tugging. Ernesto and I kept pouring Elemental power into the triangle. Stabilizing. Safeguarding. Warding.

I had a vague impression of other people crowding into the room, but had no time to spare to look.

And then the glimmering increased, and stationed itself above the crown of Carol's head.

"Breathe, maga," Rosalia said. "Breathe in."

Carol did, taking in a huge, shuddering draft of air. She coughed, grimacing as her shoulders moved. Then she gasped.

Her color returned. How had she grown so pale? Some peach highlights emerged on her forehead and chin, and the hectic red spots faded from her cheeks.

She was Carol again. My friend.

I looked at Ernesto and his eyes mirrored mine, communicating without words. We slowly dialed back the Elemental flow, letting it diminish, layer by layer, until Wind, and Ocean, and Flame became whispers and trickles. On a deep breath, we drew the Powers back into our own bodies, just as Carol had breathed her spirit back into herself.

"She's back," Rosalia said, as though Carol had just stepped out for milk and returned home. "And once she rests, she should have more to tell us. No es así, maga? Isn't that right?"

Carol nodded, still taking in deep, slow breaths.

Then she started patting her left hand around, as if she was seeking out the papers.

"What do you want, maga?"

"Diamond," she said.

"This?"

I held up a white rectangle inscribed with a diamond, a square traced over each juncture point. A large Y—as if someone had drawn a dousing rod, or an elongated seagull shape—was superimposed over the bottom half of the diamond shape.

Carol nodded again.

"That's it," she said.

"That's what?" I asked. "I don't get it. Can you explain? Is it some information you brought back? Something on the astral?"

"Give her some time, hechicera," Rosalia admonished. "She has returned, but her spirit hasn't rooted itself yet."

Then, dressed in his Nehru jacket, Mr. Oluo walked into the room, pushing past Jimmy and the others, who I only then noticed were crowded in the space. Only the shifters had remained in the sitting room, still guarding the window and the door.

The big magician glanced down at the paper and said, "That's a map of Washington DC."

Then he looked at Ernesto and me. "We're ready for the vote now."

CHAPTER TWENTY-FIVE
CAROL

Carol had to admit her shoulder was killing her. She'd never felt pain this bad in her whole life and she hoped she'd never feel it again.

She couldn't even fathom how ordinary people dealt with it. She guessed that was what morphine was for. Or other kinds of drugs. She was making do with the energy the Earth sorcerers pumped into her, and the nasty herbs from Jasmine's mother, Cecilia.

She could barely access her own Earth sorcery. She had asked why, being an Earth sorcerer, she couldn't do her own healing.

Cecilia had replied that it was always harder to heal physical wounds from the inside out than from the outside in. That healing from the inside out was a stronger sort of healing, but it was also the most subtle. Slower, she said.

Carol *was* healing from the inside out, with the help from outside showing the sorcery the right paths. Showing the energy the way to go.

Ouch. Carol knew she should be patient. She could also feel the intense pressure of the battle building outside. Of the sun and the moon aligning. Of the sigils spinning. And that new pattern, the four-cornered diamond shape.

She could also feel the pressure from the conclave room in the Mansion.

She could feel the meeting starting and resented being locked out. Although, admittedly, part of her was grateful to not have to deal. She knew Jasmine would rather not be there at all.

Jasmine would rather be in Ernesto's sitting room, meeting with the Brown Berets and the sorcerers of Los Manos, plotting strategy, instead of trying to keep this limping Association from completely imploding.

Carol was coming to agree with Jasmine. She wondered if the Association had outlived its usefulness. That this wasn't the dawning of a new day and time for something else to take over. Whether that was this "magic for the people" or not, Carol didn't know. All she knew was the way things have been going sure wasn't working anymore.

She tried to adjust herself on her pillows. Her tailbone already sore from being in one place too long.

"Damn, that hurts," she said.

So what could she do? Carol was alone temporarily. Sorcerers were in the other room still looking at the sigils. Jasmine had her vote as proxy. Rosalia was busy.

Carol slowed her breathing down. The map. She could find out more about the map of DC.

She hadn't done a lot of astral travel before but since meeting Rosalia, she'd learned pretty quickly and, frankly, being in her body right now was the pits, so...

She thought, *I know the pattern itself and I know what part of the country I'm aiming for. Can I just send my astral body there out into the æthers?*

She knew Rosalia would have her head for trying again. She shouldn't spend too much time outside her body in her weakened state. But she couldn't bear to just lie here and stare at the ceiling either.

Closing her eyes, she dropped her attention down into that place between her solar plexus and her hips. Carol began the breathing pattern to regulate her Sight. Regulate her blood flow. Regulate her synapses and keep everything moving properly in her body while her spirit flew.

"Powers, keep me safe," she whispered. "I need help. I need this information. I need to not die getting it, okay?"

She felt the response from her element, Earth, surrounding her. She waited just a moment, listening, then took a deep breath and began to ease her spirit out, trying to stand up outside of her body. One bit at a time, she worked, lifting her head, easing out of her shoulders, her spirit slowly sitting upright. And then her thighs, her knees, her feet, until she was floating above herself.

Her body was still and white on Ernesto's big queen bed. A silver cord tethered her soul to the physical plane. She could tell her body breathed still, but shallowly.

It was going to have to be enough. She rose higher on the astral plane, toward the swirling gray mists of the mutable place many sorcerers called "the astral" or "the æthers." Rosalia had taught Carol that this place was only one layer of many worlds available to those who knew. The veils could be parted if you knew how.

Carol wouldn't need to. Today, she only wanted to focus on the earth plane from a distance.

In her mind's eye, she held an image of the map Washington DC. That diamond shape. The square tilted on its end with four smaller squares, one at each corner. She held the image of the big Y intersecting the shape. The two great rivers meeting, forming one.

"Show me the leylines," she said. And overlaid on top of the diamond shape shone a network of brightness.

Bright gold and purple. Deeper greens. And there sure enough, just underneath the straight line connecting the FBI to the obelisk to the Pentagon, with the Washington Monument smack center, as the fulcrum, she saw it. A deep, pulsing red line tracing underneath.

"Why am I not surprised?" she muttered. "But what's this other thing?"

It wasn't a leyline. It felt and looked different than that. But it was definitely a pattern. It was a great, almost perfectly circular shape moving in and around the big diamond. It flowed in two directions, one inside the other, clockwise and counterclockwise. A steady stream of winking lights, red and white.

I need to get closer, she thought, and guided her spirit body further down, down towards the earth plane. Floating closer to Maryland. Virginia. And Washington DC. And then she saw it all, clearly, and almost laughed.

The moving lights were cars. It was the Capitol Beltway.

And something about that stream of cars also lent energy to the pattern.

She saw the whole thing more clearly now. The temples. The temples in each corner. Building one great temple, together.

The Fifth Temple, which, if built, could wreak more havoc than the world had seen so far.

"Okay. Show me how the magic feeds itself. I need to see it. Powers, help me, please."

She took another deep breath, hoping that her body was getting extra air too. She knew she needed it. There was a slight tugging on the silver cord. The body calling her back. But Carol wasn't done yet. It wasn't time.

"Show me. Show me the sigils," she said.

First the northern sigil. All lit up. The one that looked like a fat spider radiating out from the column. And then the sigil to the east part of the map. The column with the circle in the center, topped by the C of a crescent moon. The two sigils began pulsing together, connecting the diamond shape. The energy flowed downward and connected with the south. To the square centered below. The big I of the column, with a capital N canted toward the side in the middle of a circle. And then the energy…reached. She could almost feel it stretching itself up. Towards the west. The Western sigil was broken.

It was the cascade of lines. The tree shape, with the broken limb. The energy was having trouble connecting and completing the circuit from the west back up to north again.

"Gotcha," she said. "That's our in."

The magical energy looked as if it flowed in the barest trickle from west to north and, in the center of her soul, Carol could feel the perversion of these symbols.

She realized, then, that it wasn't that the energy was trickling from west to north…it had turned itself, like a ribbon, so all she could catch was one slender edge.

The clarity of the original diamond pattern, terrible as it was, was still cleaner than this.

Sleeping underneath it all, she sensed an older magic. A purer magic. The magic of nature, and the way things were. The ebb and flow of seasons and time, birth and death, discord and harmony, day and night.

It was close to the sorcery she wielded, as though all she knew had sprung from this original source. But it was coherent, all of one piece. It was a magic not separated out into elements. It was the magic of the whole web of life.

She knew it was part of the continent, the planetary soul. She thanked and blessed whoever had worked the ways of that magic. The original peoples, whose names she did not know, but vowed to learn.

"We're going to see if we can't help you," she said. "Revive you. Breathe some life back underneath these temples that crushed you and dragged you into this other cosmic war."

The tugging on the cord grew stronger. Carol knew she had to go. She thanked the Powers and begun making her way back along the silver thread drawing her back and back.

Back through the ætheric layers. through the veils of existence until once again she was in. That inchoate, misty place.

Carol continued to will herself down, until she hovered over her bed again. Her body looked so pale and weak, and shriveled, almost half the size of what it should be.

"Damn," she said. "Powers. Fill me up."

She lowered herself swiftly towards her physical body, and tried to ease her way in. She tried to slip into the crown of her head. She couldn't. It was shutting down. *She* was shutting down.

Shit. She shouldn't have gone away.

Her body was trying to close its systems off, to conserve energy. It thought she was dead, or gone.

"I have to get in!" she said. She was starting to get frantic. From overhead, she saw Rosalia burst in through the door and run to her body.

"Rosalia," she tried to say, "I'm here!"

The hechicera didn't look up. Carol just hoped she heard her.

Rosalia scanned Carol's body with her hands.

"No! My crown, my crown, my crown!"

The hechicera snapped her head toward Carol's face. Her citrine eyes practically glowed. And then she lifted a hand until it hovered just above the top of Carol's blond hair.

"There, right there," Carol said.

And with one long bony finger, Rosalia reached for Carol's crown, as if she was poking a hole through a piece of cling wrap.

Carol rushed back into her body. She took in a mighty breath and exhaled. "Again," she heard Rosalia say.

Huuuuhhh, Carol took in a mighty breath, and *whoooo*, exhaled.

"Again," Rosalia said.

Huuuuhhh, Carol inhaled. *Whoooo*, and exhaled.

"One more time!" Rosalia said. "*Breathe*, maga!"

Carol took in another breath and felt her soul slide all the way down to her feet. She exhaled, and coughed, wrenching the bullet wounds in her shoulder.

She could feel moisture. Tears running down her face. Tears of gratitude. Her eyes fluttered open. She saw the hechicera's sharp face and citrine eyes staring down at her.

"Thank you," she whispered.

Rosalia shook her head. "I hope whatever you found out was worth it, maga. Because you went away too far."

CHAPTER TWENTY-SIX
DOREEN

Doreen sat at her red Formica table in the kitchen, head in her hands. A cup of chamomile tea sat on the table in front of her, ignored.

Patrice massaged her lover's shoulders, digging her sturdy fingers in between Doreen's shoulder blades. It felt good, but Doreen couldn't relax.

"How could I have bungled that so badly?" she asked, staring down at gold-and-white–crackled pattern running through the Formica.

"Baby. You've got a lot going on," Patrice said. "I don't think you bungled anything. I just think these are tough times and you're dealing with a thirteen-year-old boy. It can't be easy being that young."

Doreen sighed. "No. No you're right. I need to sit up now, baby."

Patrice gave her shoulders one last squeeze, kissed the side of her forehead, and sat down at the table across from her. She looked worried. There were creases in Patrice's forehead that weren't usually there, and all the lipstick had been wiped from her beautiful, full lips.

All that was left was her dark face, those big dark eyes staring at Doreen with so much love, it almost took her breath away.

"Thank you," Doreen said.

"For what, baby? The massage?"

"Just for being here. For being you. This would be so much harder without you," she said. "You know, I think that's part of why I gave up my sorcery all those years. It wasn't just the grief, though that was most of it. It was that I'd come to rely on Hector to help balance me. To be my partner when things were tough."

She looked into her lover's eyes. "I didn't have that for too long. Patrice."

"Well. You have it now, baby. I'm here." She reached a hand across the table. And took Doreen's in her own.

Doreen could feel the energy they shared. It was so different from the energy of a sorcerer or a shifter. It was something new in her life, and beautiful and comforting all the same.

Patrice took her hand back. "Now drink your tea."

Doreen blew on the surface of the cup. Took a swallow. It tasted of honey and spring grasses. The tea started its work, soothing her, but she didn't really want to be soothed.

"You know," she said. "I feel like a child myself. I want to sit here wallow in my misery when I know there's work to be done."

"You can wallow for another half an hour," Patrice said, and laughed. "Seriously, though, we do have a lot of work. I know it as well as you. But you don't have to work anymore tonight, Doreen."

"I don't? I feel like...I feel like I have to. I can't stop or either I'll never start again, or this storm will roll right over me, laying me flat forever."

"Doreen, I'm new to this magic, but I can tell, that ritual you did with Huey Newton tonight? That was big. It was a lot. And tomorrow there's going to be more. And then two days after that. We're not going have any time for rest. So what do you say we take advantage of this longest night, and make some magic in the bedroom, huh?"

Doreen managed to crack a smile.

"The ancestors surely blessed me when they sent you my way." Doreen stood and reached out for her lover's hand. "You sure are beautiful, Patrice."

Patrice tucked her warm palm inside Doreen's and wove their fingers together. "So are you, Doreen. Now let's make love."

CHAPTER TWENTY-SEVEN
SNAKES AND SPIDERS

The men needed more training still. Samuels wished he had a temple space of his own. A warded, consecrated temple. A place that knew him, as the Master's temple was aware of every drop of sweat the Master dropped onto the granite floor.

He also wished he knew he could trust his men.

But he was making do with an abandoned warehouse on the edges of Los Angeles and the best operatives he could find. He just hoped their loyalty could be bought by the promise of more power and autonomy than they'd ever get under the Master.

Samuels needed sleep. Two flights in one day were taking their toll. But the work had to be done. And be done now.

The Master was right. They'd botched the last two battles. There was no way that Panther bitch should have gotten the amount of leverage against him she did.

He wondered if she would be surprised to see him again. If she thought that she had managed to kill him.

"Again!" he shouted. The men were good. But not good enough.

The warehouse windows were encrusted with years of grime that had kept out most of the dim, pre-sunset light of the shortest day.

It was dark now, but even so, they were working toward the middle of the cavernous space, where even the light from the remaining bulbs in their industrial cages barely reached.

The men still had their dark glasses on.

A person grew used to the alterations. It was hard to change back once the damage had been done. Oh, heightened sensitivity and more acute sense were not considered damage in the Order. How could they be? To see clearly at night was a boon, when one was an agent—just another form of spy.

When people called them "spooks," they didn't know how accurate the description was. For the initiates of the Order, at least. Not every agent was inducted into the sanctum sanctorum.

"You must allow your serpents to flow freely, while still retaining control. They are not entities outside of you. They are you. Spirit of your spirit. They move at your will and your command."

Hopkins, the agent he was yelling at, stumbled over an old piece of pipe. He'd been too caught up in what the ætheric snake was doing. The serpent itself ghosted into thin air. Gone.

The other three agents practiced sending their serpents to strike each other in the air. They were doing pretty well. But not one of them had the magical operation correct.

"Halt!" Samuels yelled into the dusty cavern.

"You are all still treating these snakes as servitors that live outside of you, instead of as part of your own being. The three of you"—he pointed— "are doing quite well."

The men wiped the perspiration from their faces and had the audacity to look pleased.

"And that is a problem. Because you are doing so well at this level, you have locked yourselves into a trap you cannot see."

"I don't understand," said Sullivan, his portly face reddened from exertion.

Samuels consolidated his magic in his breastbone, and drew up another thread of power from his sex.

Then he allowed them to flow up and down, matching each other, linking in his solar plexus and lower, in the seat of his will.

"What am I doing?" he asked the men.

Sullivan answered, "Activating your power centers and linking them together."

"That's right. But that isn't all I'm doing. I am also showing the energy how I want it to move. So when I do this…" He flicked his ring finger and a serpent shot out and attached itself to Hopkins' face.

The man screamed and started tugging at the astral wraith, trying to get it to detach.

Samuels snapped his fingers and the snake fell away.

"That was exactly the incorrect response. The serpents are a part of you, as much as your core energy is. They come from the sheath of ectoplasm just around your skin, and are tied to your animal brain. Which is all information you should have learned in the first six months after your induction."

He flicked his finger again, toward the one black man on his team. Joaquim. The snake flew out. Joaquim tilted his shoulder to the left, jerked his head back to avoid the astral serpent, and flung out a snake of his own.

Samuels grabbed it with his left hand.

"Good. You moved around your core and didn't think. Your body responded and your astral body did as well. That is what I want you all to drill."

The men formed themselves in pairs to practice once again.

"Men. The people out here don't have our magic. They have a sorcery you can barely understand. And they were born with it. Not like you. Don't underestimate them. Ever."

They got into sparring position.

"And don't underestimate yourselves again."

CHAPTER TWENTY-EIGHT
JASMINE

The vote was anti-climactic, mostly because I didn't care about the damn shenanigans a few of the out-of-towners tried to pull when it became clear my mother had won, hands down.

"You all agreed to this conclave and this vote," I said. "So you had damn well better agree to the outcome we all just witnessed here."

As I left the meeting hall, I heard voices raised again, starting up some damn fool argument I had no time for.

Mr. Oluo and Ernesto followed me.

Halfway down the hall, I stopped.

"Gregory, right? No offense, brother, but I need you to look me in the eyes right now, your hand on mine, and tell me whether or not I can trust you, because I'm not letting you anywhere near Carol, or anywhere near those sigils, unless I'm sure."

He didn't even flinch. As a matter of fact, a smile ghosted around the edges of his full lips.

"Thank you for according me the respect of asking. And I commend you for being a general in the army of whatever war I can feel swirling all around you."

He held out his right hand, and placed it over my outstretched fist.

Then he looked me dead in my eyes. Unwavering.

"I, Gregory Oluo, sorcerer of Air, swear that I am trustworthy to those who seek to uphold the vows and precepts of the Association."

I started to speak, but he continued.

"I, Gregory Oluo, sorcerer of Air, swear that I am trustworthy to those who fight for the good of the people."

He took a breath and spoke a third time.

"I, Gregory Oluo, sorcerer of Air, swear that I am trustworthy to those who seek the fires of justice, who forge the metal of righteousness, who breathe the air of truth, and who pour out the waters of love."

"So mote it be," Ernesto whispered.

I nodded, and pulled my fist away. Good enough.

"Right on," I said. "You're in, brother. But fuck the army." I grinned. "I'm a member of the Black Panther Party in good standing."

He laughed.

We hurried back up the stairs to check in with Jimmy, Geronimo, Gloria, and the two sorcerers from Las Manos. Teresa and Rafael.

"Together, we can mobilize two thousand people in two hours, and five thousand people by tomorrow. Maybe more," Geronimo said. "In LA, Oakland, Chicago, for sure. Maybe Philly and New York, or a few other places."

"Las Manos needs to check in with our people, to make sure we have enough trained people on the ground to direct the people showing up to help," Teresa said.

"The sooner you can tell us what the plan is, the sooner we can get people organized," Geronimo said.

I exhaled in relief. "That's good. Thank you."

I nodded toward the sorcerers. "I'll get Doreen to coordinate with you all, too."

Then I squared my shoulders. "Start with the meetings and the phone trees as soon as possible. Within the hour if you can. Let people know to get ready. We don't have all the information yet, but we will."

I thought for a moment. "Frankly, with all the infiltration we've had to contend with, the final plan will have to be communicated in pieces, and at the last minute."

"We concur. We discussed security leaks earlier tonight, Jasmine," Gloria said, "and you're right, there's no way to get them plugged in time. It's clear people are too close in, with what happened to Chuy and Carol."

"We can't take any chances," I replied. "Not with an operation this big."

An image of my ancestor came to me again. And an image of the spear. I looked at each of their faces then, making sure they took in what I was about to say.

"We're stopping with the motherfucking skirmishes tonight. We're going to war. And we're taking it to them, this time. Not the other way around."

"Right on," Gloria said.

Jimmy just squeezed my hand. I was grateful for that. Grateful he was going to be at my side.

"Okay. Do what needs to be done. You're leaders of your own people, but you're also my deputies for the duration. Does that work for you?"

They all looked me in the eyes and said hell, yes. Even Geronimo nodded.

I walked back into the bedroom to find Gregory Oluo and Rosalia, heads close to each other, peering at the sigils.

"Do you need to set those on the table in the other room, so the other sorcerers can look at them, too?" I asked.

"No, hechicera," Rosalia said. "The others, we have many sigils to unlock tonight. It is best to keep on as we were, until the pattern becomes clear."

"What do you have?" I asked.

Gregory pointed at what I could now see was a rough map.

"That's the original Masonic square that surrounded the city," he said, pointing to the diamond shape. "See those smaller squares? They set actual stone markers on each corner, to anchor the energy into the earth. That diamond surrounds all of the important government agencies."

"What's the big Y at the bottom?"

"Two rivers joining. The Potomac and Anacostia."

Ernesto whistled through this teeth. "That's some big power."

"I thought DC was smaller than that," I said.

Oluo nodded, crossing his arms over his chest. "It is. The city itself clusters above the notch where the rivers meet."

"See this?" He pointed to a lower field, just to the left curve of the Y. "This area here is now part of Virginia. It's called the retrocession. Maryland and Virginia ceded land to form the capitol. In 1846, Virginia's land was returned."

"It broke the magic," Rosalia said.

"I never thought of it that way before," Oluo said. "But of course. It's obvious now."

"Does that leave the Feds weaker," I asked, "giving us an in?"

Mr. Oluo turned to me, grinning like a wolf. "It does indeed," he said, looking down at the sigil. "Damn. Whatever you cats are cooking up, I want to know aaaall about it."

"Carol, maga?" Rosalia said.

Carol was obviously Seeing something again. Her eyes flickered beneath her closed lids. There were pale purple shadows beneath her eyes, and the skin on her eyelids was almost translucent, with pale pink blood vessels showing through.

Her lips began to move. "Cooooe."

Oluo moved to close the door between the rooms, blocking out the sound of the comrades working there.

We all hushed and moved in closer.

"Iiiinnn." She exhaled, and was silent for a moment.

"Come. Come. Come," she said, moving her head on the pillow, side to side, as if she was shaking her head no.

Her eyes flew open and she took in a gasping breath.

"Intelligence!" her voice rasped. I reached out for her left hand.

"Now in Time!" She gripped my fingers tighter.

"Elevate us." By all the Powers. Her voice no longer sounded like her own. Carol started to grunt and croon, making unholy noises in the back of her throat. Freakiest shit I'd ever heard.

I held on to her hand. Ernesto, on the bed, had a hand over her right wrist. Not gripping, just making contact.

"Ahhhh! Nnnn. Nahn. No!" She was gasping now, starting to writhe on the bed.

"She'd going to re-injure herself!" Rosalia said. "We have to stop her. Form the triangle!"

Once again, she shoved me out of the way and placed her hands on Carol's head, this time trying to stabilize it.

I moved into position, linking up with Ernesto, forming the triangle of Wind, Flame, and Ocean.

"Cooommmeee!" screamed the guttural voice from Carol's throat.

"It isn't her!" I said.

"Focus, hechicera!" Rosalia snapped.

I pulled on Ocean, hard, then felt Oluo's heavy hand on my shoulder.

"Do you trust me?" he said.

"Yes!"

And Mountain slammed up, knocking another corner into the form, turning the triangle into an Elemental square.

A diamond. Whole. Complete. I looked at him in shock.

"I have small amounts of the other Elements at my disposal, along with my primary Air," he said, shrugging.

Another damn Quintessence. Gregory Oluo had been holding out on me. If I'd had time to think about it, I would wonder why he wasn't in the running for Association head.

"Give me paper!" Carol gasped. It was her voice again. Rosalia shoved a clean sheet of foolscap and a black pen in her left hand.

Carol close her eyes again. We kept the Elemental square humming, feeding one into the next, blending, moving, braiding the energies faster and faster.

She drew the diamond shape. The four squares on the corners. The large Y shape. Then she started scribbling and scratched other forms, arrayed within the larger shape. I couldn't tell what they were, she was drawing so fast, only her hand moving as she lay back on the pillow, eyes flickering behind her eyelids again.

I could practically feel the energies gathering around us. That storm that had been brewing on the æthers. The energies *we* were calling, I realized.

Not an outside force. The storm was us.

The pen dropped from Carol's hand. Her breathing slowed.

Ernesto, Mr. Oluo, and I began to ratchet down our construct, allowing the energies to recede again.

Carol was asleep.

And on the white paper, spanning the left line—the Potomac River—was a five-sided shape, a tower, and an X. In the space above the tower was a temple.

"So...that's the Pentagon," I said.

"And the Washington Monument." Ernesto said. "And the temple must be the White House, right?"

"So what's the X?" I asked.

Mr. Oluo shook his head in disbelief.

"That right there would be the FBI."

CHAPTER TWENTY-NINE
JASMINE

We met and planned long into the longest night, crowded in Ernesto's sitting room, with Carol sleeping a doorway away.

Jimmy and I finally dragged ourselves off to my parents' house, where we snuggled together before falling into fitful sleep. The sigils chased me all night long. At one point, I was climbing the sheer walls of the Washington Monument. It seemed very important to get to the pyramid at the top.

Though the midwinter dawn came late, it still came all too soon.

Jimmy kissed me awake. I wanted nothing more than to stay in that too-narrow bed and make love to him all day.

I groaned. "We have a meeting with leadership in an hour."

"Hour and a half," he said, a hand running up my naked thigh. "Plenty of time for me to do some of this…"

"Jimmy, I can hear my father in the kitchen."

"So, we'll be quiet," he whispered in my ear. The amber and musk scent of him washed over me like honey.

And my body reminded my mind of its desire. And my heart reminded me of the love I had for this beautiful man.

As I rolled over and straddled Jimmy's thigh, I also remembered what I'd been told since I first joined the Party: a revolutionary never knows which day her life might end.

We hadn't celebrated Solstice the night before, but here? Just after dawn? I guessed we could celebrate it now.

As my lips met his again, I moaned a little, deep in my throat. Our sex was quick and quiet. Taking care of one another's needs. No bending the bedroom walls out, this time, or candles tipping over on the floor.

Just two people who needed one another, stealing a moment for some sweetness between battles. I filled up with Jimmy like I was drinking water from a spring.

"Wash me clean," I murmured as he entered me.

"I love you, Jaz," he replied.

And there was light and darkness. Water and stone. And a healing of a place in my heart I didn't even know was hurt.

As I fell back onto his body, breathing hard, resting in the crook where his shoulder sloped into his neck, he let out a long, contented purr.

"That's one thing I love about sharing a bed with a big cat."

"What's that?"

"The way you purr." I smiled.

He purred louder in my ear and I laughed, then kissed him one more time.

"I'll go get us coffee."

I threw a purple and blue dashiki over my head, and made a stop at the bathroom to pee and wash my hands, then braved the kitchen, hoping my father had already left for work.

Not a chance.

My father, William, was settled in the built-in kitchen nook, paper spread out before him, coffee and toast at hand.

"Morning," I said.

"Good morning, Jasmine." He had a strange look on his face. Concern. I hoped it wasn't about Jimmy.

"It's Monday," I said. "Don't you have to work?" He should have been off to the insurance agency by now.

"We have the week off. It's Christmas." He set down the paper. "Besides, with everything that's going on, I wanted to be here for your mother. And for you."

I found two white cups with blue-flowered rims and poured out coffee from the percolator. Coffee in hand, I looked at my father again. He stared at me with serious eyes.

"Let me just take a cup of this to Jimmy. I'll be right back."

As embarrassing as it was to admit verbally that there was a man in my room, I couldn't just leave my father sitting there.

When the solid, non-magical rock of our family was this worried, it meant something was wrong.

Huh, I thought, as I opened my bedroom door. I was going to have to stop thinking of people as non-magical. Doreen, Patrice, and Drake were proving things were otherwise.

"I need to go talk with my father. You okay in here?"

"As long as I have coffee, yes. Can I shower?"

By all the Powers. Of course he needed a shower. Besides, I couldn't just sneak him out my window or the front door. My parents were just going to have to get hip to the fact that I was an adult, and it was 1969. Adults had sex outside of marriage now.

"Yeah. That's cool. There should be towels in the cupboard next to the sink."

My dad stared out the window, newspaper gathered back together, coffee in his hand. I sat across from him and took a sip from my own cup. Dad was never a person you pushed. He came around to talking in his own time.

I just hoped he didn't take too long. The coffee was good, and I loved my father, but I was going to need a shower myself before we left.

"Dad," I finally said. "I want to talk to you, but people are expecting me at a meeting in South Central in under an hour.

When he looked at me, tears shone in his eyes.

"I'm worried about you, Jasmine."

I didn't respond. What was there to say? He was right to be worried. Nothing much to do about it.

"You think I don't feel the things you and your mother do. But I know when there's danger in the air."

He took a swallow of coffee, then cleared his throat.

"I've never said this to anyone but your mother before, but I felt it, two night before Watts burned. I knew something was coming, but I didn't know what. Do you remember that week?"

I cast my mind back to four years before. I remembered the news. The people fighting with police. The smashed windows. The buildings on fire. My parent's hushed, urgent, angry conversations at night.

"I remember you wouldn't let me out of the house, and escorted me back and forth from school. I couldn't even go to the Mansion."

"I kept you and Cecelia home except for work and school for eight days," he mused, staring into his coffee cup. "Myself, too. Until the storm passed."

He looked up at me again. "It started on a Wednesday. What you probably don't recall is that I started keeping you home on Monday, and had laid in extra food, batteries, and the like that Sunday before."

Reaching across the table, I laid my fingers across his big, strong hands. "You knew."

He nodded. "I knew. I've always known. I've always sensed danger coming. Always known just when to prepare."

"But how? And why didn't you learn more about magic?"

He slid his hand out from mine. Waved it in the air, as though waving the very thought away.

"You and your mother and Doreen were sorcerers, girl. My little precognition was nothing compared to that. Besides, I've always hated the politics you all deal with up on that hill. People just need to live. Stop arguing over every little thing."

Well, he wasn't wrong about that. But I still felt stunned, clock ticking, coffee growing cold in my cup.

"So what now?" I asked.

"This thing that's coming? It's the worst I've seen since Watts. And Dr. King getting killed. You're right to try to stop it." He cleared his throat again. "I just hope it doesn't stop you."

I had nothing to say to that, so I just looked out the window, at the sun growing higher in the sky. I really needed to go.

He wasn't done talking. "I've always known your life would be in danger, girl. Knew you had a destiny in you that was bigger than the likes of me could foretell. And I want you to know right now, that whatever you need in the coming days? You ask me for it. And if I've got any way to give it to you? I will."

"Thank you, Daddy," I said. "I will."

I slid off my bench and went around to give him a sideways hug.

"I know my choices this past year or so haven't been easy on you, or Mother, either. But I know in my heart they're right."

He squeezed my waist, then let me go.

"I know they're right, too. Now go on. Your young man's waiting, and I know you have a busy day."

CHAPTER THIRTY
DOREEN

Walking down the sidewalk toward West Oakland, Doreen admired the old houses, the little gardens people struggled to keep up on the weekends or after work, and the Christmas decorations hanging in the windows or on the doors, most of them looking as though they were handmade by kids at school.

Much as she loved Los Angeles and the people there, and much as she worried about Cecelia, Oakland had been Doreen's home for ten years now, and it was clear she wasn't going anywhere.

Doreen wanted nothing more than to take Patrice out for Chinese food and make love to her for days.

But instead, this morning after solstice, she was off to Father Neil's church to meet with Tanya, and then had to get to work at the flower shop. She'd taken too much time off work the past week, and it was a busy season. Doreen had promised to work hard through Christmas Eve.

How she was going to do that and deal with the full moon coming up, and all the magical stuff that needed planning, she didn't know. But she still needed her job, part-time though it was, so that was that.

She rounded the corner and smiled at the paper snowmen someone had strung from a bay tree. Up ahead was the red brick façade of St. Augustine's and the tiny, brick-red painted Victorian house with white trim on the same lot.

Tanya would be working in the kitchen already, getting breakfast ready with Carlos and maybe Leroy. Doreen pulled up the sleeve of her navy coat and checked the time.

The children would arrive in fifteen minutes. She had just enough time to check in with Tanya about what she, Patrice, and Drake had been cooking up.

And then they were going to teach the children magic.

Doreen went around to the metal kitchen door. The scent of oatmeal, cinnamon, and eggs with an undertone of bleach assaulted her, as did the steam in the room. The hood fan over the stove whirred, but couldn't keep up with the amount Tanya and Carlos were cooking up.

"You must miss Jasmine!" Doreen called out by way of greeting. "Need an extra pair of hands?"

Tanya turned and smiled, wiping her forehead with the back of one hand. As usual, a flowered apron covered her taupe business skirt and burgundy-flowered blouse. The steam from the oatmeal curled the fine hairs around her face. Doreen knew the young woman would tsk at that when she used the restroom before heading in to work.

"We're almost done, but you can help us serve if you want."

Pressed hair and pressed clothes, that was the surface Tanya. Underneath her bank teller's exterior was a revolutionary, through and through. Still a little skittish about some of the wilder sorcery and magic zinging around lately, she had finally realized her own two children needed more protection than she could offer on her own.

So she'd come to Doreen and asked for training. There'd barely been time, but from all reports, Tanya had worked hard with Patrice and Drake while Doreen was gone.

So today? Doreen and Tanya were going to test out magic with the littlest kids. While Drake and Patrice had gotten the pre-teens and teens on board, they'd all worked to convince the parents that the small ones needed to be able to hold their own.

Tanya was a big part of that.

Letitia, a young woman Doreen had seen around before, but didn't know well, peeked her head around the swinging door to the community hall.

"Breakfast almost ready? I can hear the kids coming up the street."

"We're on it," Carlos said, ladling oatmeal with raisins into tan melamine bowls. "Tell Terry he can start the reading as soon as they're settled."

Tanya scooped eggs onto paper plates as Doreen hung her coat and bag on a hook and tied on an apron of her own.

"You want to take over the oatmeal, Doreen? I'll start ferrying out the trays."

Ten minutes later, they were all watching the children eat breakfast, smiles on their beautiful faces. Some of the older ones wore white shirts, with little black berets perched on their hair. There were striped sweaters, green sweatshirts, brown corduroy jackets. There were boys and girls, aged six years old through ten.

It didn't matter who they were or where they came from; they all got food to eat. Some of them walked together to Father Neil's. Others had a parent or grandparent who would drop them off, knowing the other children would get their own child safe to school.

This, Doreen thought, was the community every child should have. And the Panthers were building it, brick by brick, and child by child.

"What does Chairman Fred say?" Terry asked.

"All power to *all* the people!" the children answered.

"That's right," Leticia said. "And what do you think that means?"

A hand shot up. The little boy in the striped sweater.

"Tyrone?"

"It means that the people got the power. Not the police. Not the banks…and I think it means all the people got to stick together."

"That's right, Tyrone. That's what it means. We take care of each other and we take care of ourselves," Terry responded. "All the people, black or white, Chinese or Mexican, they all deserve food, education, land, health care, and a right to their own freedom."

Doreen recognized some of the Ten Point Program in that. It wasn't a bad thing to teach children. She just hoped it would build a foundation for the magic she knew they also needed.

"You all done with your breakfast?" Letitia asked.

"Yes!" a chorus replied.

"Then we have something special for you today. Your parents or grandparents all said it was okay," Letitia said. "But I want you to know, like with everything, you never have to participate if you don't want to."

"What is it, Miss Letitia?" asked a little girl, whose hair was in puffy twists held together by elastics with green plastic balls on the ends. It was very pretty.

"Mrs. Doreen?"

Doreen stood up from where she'd been watching, near the kitchen door.

"Tanya and I are going to teach you some magic today. Does that sound interesting?"

The children nodded, though a few seemed uncertain.

"Stand up, please, children," Tanya said.

With a great screeching of chairs and rearranging, they got the children in two rows, facing one another.

Doreen nodded to Tanya to continue.

"Now, clap your hands. As hard as you can!" The adults clapped along, the sound filling the hall.

"Now...stop!" And they did.

"Look at your hands. See how the palms are a little reddish looking? That's the blood beneath your skin, rising to the surface."

"Ewww!"

"Far out!"

Doreen smiled and stepped forward to speak.

"Just like clapping your hands together brings blood closer to the surface, it also brings energy to the surface. Do your hands feel a little tingly?" There were nods. "We're going to call that energy. And energy is the building block of magic."

A little hand raised, just halfway. It was a girl in a yellow dress and a red sweater, white knee socks half falling down her brown legs.

"Yes?" said Doreen.

"But what's magic?"

"That's a good question. Magic is our ability to use our energy to change things."

"That's it?"

"Well, we'll learn more about it over time, but that's enough of a definition for now."

Tanya spoke again. "Are you ready to practice something else?"

"Yes!"

Just as Drake and Patrice had taught the older children to toss balls of energy across the rows to one another, Doreen and Tanya taught these younger children now.

They rubbed their hands together, then imagined balls of energy forming there. Then they tossed the balls at one another, squealing and laughing. Some of the children ducked. Others threw as hard as they could.

These children took to it more quickly than the older ones did. Imagination was the seat of this sort of magic—not the Elemental sorcery some people were born with, and not the Temple magic that took years of study, but the basic magic anyone could do.

Magic for the people.

That's what these children had.

That's what Doreen wanted every child to have. And more.

"Okay!" she said. "Who wants to learn something else?"

Chapter Thirty-One
Jasmine

Since 41st and Central was still a wreck from the shootout, we were meeting in the John Huggins Free Breakfast for Children and Community Information Center.

The community information center was in a red bungalow over on West 55th, not far from headquarters and the small storefront where they were putting in the Bunchy Carter clinic.

John and Bunchy were both dead. Black Panthers killed in some operation that stunk like Federal interference.

I swear, these people were an inspiration. Just a few weeks after a SWAT team busted through their door, shooting up headquarters in a pre-dawn raid, they were still feeding children and setting up a free medical clinic.

But it's what we do. All oppressed people do. Tragedy happens, but things still need doing. Life goes on. The people are nothing if not resilient.

It made me feel proud as we unlatched the curved, wrought iron gate and walked up the driveway set next to a green lawn planted with a few scraggly flowers.

Security recognized us from where they stood on the porch, a rifle-toting man on each side of the door. They raised their fists in greeting.

"All power to the people," the tall, thin man on the left said.

"All power to the people," Jimmy and I replied.

We were nodded in by another man on security just inside the door and walked into what was once a double parlor, but was now set up with a long table in each room, and low shelves and filing cabinets hugging the walls. Stacks of the The Black Panther newspaper were piled on top of the shelves. A dirty chalkboard filled up half the space between the double parlor doors.

Almost every seat at the front parlor table was already filled and cigarette smoke drifted through the air. We were clearly a little late. As I walked around the table to a chair, I took in the rest of the room.

A lot of faces I knew, and some I didn't. No Ericka or Elaine. They must have been on another assignment. That was too bad; I was looking forward to working with more Panther women.

Someone had burned the coffee in the kitchen. I could smell it. Guess that meant I wouldn't get a second cup unless I made it.

And I wasn't about to.

Bright Emory Davis and Tarika Lewis posters were tacked up on the walls, including one of my favorites. It showed a black woman, curly natural rising up from her head, strong lips, and black eyes. Bright fuchsia rays surrounded her. "In solidarity with the oppressed People of the world," the poster said.

I almost gasped, and gripped the curved wood back of the chair I'd been about to pull out from the table. Along with a rifle strapped to her back, in her hands? She carried a spear.

All of a sudden, I could almost feel the wooden shaft in my hands. A gift from the ancestors. I could sense the pounded metal spearhead. A measure of a woman's power.

Gazing at the spear in the poster, I had the sense of it vibrating in my palms as though I held it for real.

And then the image took me someplace else.

My ancestor, a woman with ochre-mud-smeared hair, was walking toward me. This time she held a shell brimming with water. I reached out to take it from her....

"Jasmine!" Rosalia said, snapping me out of the trance.

I jerked, and dragged the chair out, plunking my heavy fringed bag onto the table. I tried to control my shaking, hoping no one noticed. Except Rosalia, who noticed everything.

"Sorry we're late," Jimmy said, scrambling to cover. I'm sure he didn't know what was up, but it was clear something was wrong.

"No problem, man. We just started five minutes ago," said Rafael. He and Gloria from Las Manos had chairs across the table.

Geronimo Pratt spoke. "We need to know what you have planned. I can't run security on some things I cannot see."

"The things you cannot see are up to us," Rosalia countered. "And we are meeting here today to formulate a plan."

"What are we responding to? The attack on HQ? The skirmish in the park? What?" That came from a Party member with an overflowing ashtray at his hands. It looked as if he'd been sitting there, smoking, all day long. A raggedy brother with a high forehead and slightly bucked teeth; I remembered him....

"What's your name again?" I asked.

He took a long drag on the cigarette, its orange tip glowing in the gray haze surrounding his head. "Cotton. And you're Jasmine, right?"

"Yes. My name is Jasmine Jones. And I'm a sorcerer and member of the Oakland branch of the Black Panther Party." Let's get my credentials out of the way.

What the hell was he doing here? Wasn't he one of the men they'd dragged out of Laguna Park?

"I'm surprised to see you here," I said, glancing at him, but turning my gaze onto Geronimo Pratt.

Geronimo returned my gaze. "We think that was a little misunderstanding. But trust me, Cotton here is on probation."

I decided to let it drop for now, even though it didn't sit right with me at all.

"The reason we're here is not because of any one event," I continued. "These events, as you all know, are cumulative. They are an out-and-out war upon our people."

"I think we all dig that, sister," Masai Hewitt said. He was minister of education for the Los Angeles Panthers. I was a little surprised to see him here, at this kind of meeting. But strategy needed his brain, I guessed.

He wore big round glasses, and a neatly trimmed goatee framed his mouth. There was something strong and kind about him. "The thing is, we don't know you well yet, sister. And want to know what you're about. Are you about taking down that motherfucker Nixon? Are you about taking down the LAPD? What are you about?"

"We're about *offense*," I replied. "We're about taking the reins. Not waiting for them to attack us first anymore."

"You remember what happened in Sacramento when we did that?" That was Geronimo speaking.

"I wasn't around for that, brother, but what we wanted to lay out for you today is a way to go on full frontal attack…." I paused, all of a sudden not trusting. Something was wrong.

"When was the last time you swept for bugs?" I asked.

"This morning," one of the men standing security inside the door said.

Dropping into my center, I scanned the room. I trusted that the house had been swept. So what was it?

It was that man. Cotton. I for sure didn't trust him and wondered what in all the Powers made him able to convince a cat like Geronimo to keep him around at all. The man continued smoking, then looked at me and smiled.

Turning in my seat to address Geronimo, I said, "I need him out of here."

"Why is that, sister? You accusing me of something?" Cotton said.

Geronimo was silent, waiting for my answer.

"My sorcery tells me something is wrong in this room, and everything points to him. I don't know how he smoke screened you all into letting him in here after Laguna Park, but Rosalia and I want to lay some heavy shit out on you all, and I'm not going to do it with this man in the room."

The room grew still with tension.

"And the ancestors won't stand for it, either."

Geronimo spoke. "Cotton, would you step outside?"

"I didn't *do* anything, man! I stood with y'all in the shootout, man. You know that! The chick is whack!"

Geronimo stood then, and stared at Cotton until the man shoved his chair back and strode out the front door. Geronimo nodded at the man standing guard at the door. He stepped outside, I assumed to talk to security on the porch.

The tension was not letting up. Geronimo sat back down and spoke again.

"Despite the fact that Cotton was part of the shootout at 41st and Central, and has been known to us longer than you've been a Party member, I am choosing to trust you, Jasmine Jones. For now."

I gave a quick nod. There wasn't much to say. No way I could prove much of anything without lighting up the room. Even that wouldn't prove that Cotton was untrustworthy. It would just show them I had power.

Masai spoke again. "So, you were about to share with us a plan for first strike. How does the room feel to you now?" He arched an eyebrow with the question.

I ignored it, and scanned the room. It felt clean. I looked at Rosalia, Gloria, and Rafael. They also nodded. Good.

"It's fine." I cleared my throat, wishing for some coffee now. And wishing I could ask these people to put out some of the Powers-be-damned cigarettes.

"We found evidence that the FBI is working magic. They infiltrated some of our groups, and attacked us magically as well as with bullets. We've been working on a way to attack on the astral, with magic, but we want to make sure there's backup on the ground in case we need it. Rosalia?" She could take over for awhile.

The hechicera stood in a swirl of skirts and walked to the chalkboard at the back of the room. She began to scratch white lines and curves onto the blackboard with a heavy hand. The sigils. While I'd drawn some of them before, for the cats in Oakland, seeing them visible in front of so many non-sorcerers still made me uncomfortable.

I could see it made some of the people around the table uncomfortable as well.

"These," Rosalia said, slamming the chalk back down. "These are some of the symbols they have used against us. They are also some of the symbols that have built their power, allowing them to attack us, make us weak, keep the people in bondage."

She looked around the table, fixing each person in turn with those citrine eyes, until they all paid full attention.

"We plan to break these symbols," she said.

"And we plan to break the FBI," I added.

A chorus of "What?" and "How?" and "Far out!" raised the decibel level in the room.

I liked a little drama. It made for good propaganda. And we had to sell this shit as if our lives depended on it. And they did.

Then it was my turn to stand. I raised my hands for quiet, and with slight push, shoved some blue ocean fire out from my fingertips. I leaned toward the long table and traced a big blue diamond shape in the air just above the surface, then added the four smaller squares at each point.

"Do you know what that is?" I asked the room.

Silence. I nodded at Jimmy to speak.

"That is Washington DC," he said. "The original pattern the Masons set down, before some of the land was taken back and the pattern was broken."

"What does that mean?" Masai asked me. "What do a bunch of old dead white men have to do with what we're dealing with now?"

"I'll break it down for you. The original people who lived on that land before the white men came—the Piscataway and the Tayac—had their own magic. The white men had to break that magic in order to take over. Take their power. If the magic that founded the city is broken, we have an in. It's harder to build strong, secure magical operations if the original form is weak. This is a weakened form."

I continued. "They've been trying to build a new temple, based on that original form. They keep failing, as far as I can see. And now, they're distracted by us." I smiled at that. "And that's where we take our advantage."

Geronimo was nodding, and so were a few of the others around the room. They understood strategy and how important the power of distraction was in times of war.

I could feel the power building from Rosalia, Gloria, and Rafael. They sent out tendrils, feeding the entity they attempted to call. Quetzalcoatl. We'd discussed this beforehand and I only hoped that it would work.

Rosalia spoke then. "We also have a powerful force they don't know what to do with yet. And we do not wish to give them the opportunity to understand before we strike."

Then Rafael and Gloria stood, and all three sorcerers raised their arms.

And Quetzalcoatl, the Feathered Serpent, flowed into the room.

He waved and rippled in the air behind the table, moving in a circle around the edges of the room. Two of the panther shifters changed then and there, growling and coughing deep in their throats. Some folks ducked their heads. Others smiled in wonder.

"As we were saying, the magics have been gathering. We've already seen what happened with los federales in Laguna Park." Rosalia said.

Quetzalcoatl took that moment to eat the energetic map of DC I'd left floating above the table.

That was that.

"If that's the power you have in your arsenal, I guess we're in," Geronimo said. "When does this all go down?"

"Two days," I replied. "We plan to strike on Christmas Eve."

Geronimo smiled. "Good plan. They won't be expecting that."

"They won't expect an attack at all. But if they were looking for one, they'd expect us to attack tomorrow night, on the full moon." Rosalia smiled back. "So when nothing happens? They'll figure they have time."

"So we have between now and Christmas Eve to organize." Rafael said, exhaling. "That's not too much time."

"It's what we have," I said. "The Powers are moving and things are locking into place. We've got to be ready."

"And tomorrow night? You'll get some help," Rosalia said. "Tomorrow night we gather. We do a blessing for the people."

"Right on," Jimmy said. "Right on."

"All power to the people!"

CHAPTER THIRTY-TWO
JASMINE

Jimmy needed to stay and meet with Geronimo and the rest of security. I kissed him goodbye and headed out the door, nodding my thanks at the two brothers on the front porch, still standing guard.

Cotton was nowhere to be seen. I hoped he'd gone somewhere far away. I also hoped LA leadership was actually going to deal with the man, but I had other problems to deal with.

It was a bright Los Angeles day. The temperature felt like a glorious sixty-eight degrees. Cool, edging toward barely warm.

It made me want to run off to the ocean, to stick my toes in the pale yellow sand and my hands in the briny water.

Instead, I was heading for more meetings at the Mansion. Now that my mother was the newly elected head of the Association, at least I didn't have to deal with Terrance Sterling anymore, though I did wonder where he'd disappeared to.

That didn't set right with me. Made me uneasy. A man like that shouldn't just disappear. And Helen coming back, all disheveled and out of whack, fighting for his honor?

That left a bitter taste in my mouth still.

How could a person go so wrong? Terrance, I kind of understood. The man had always thirsted for more power, and not just the sorcerous kind. But Helen?

I think I'd always hoped her integrity would guide her, and she would do right by us all. Turned out, Ice Queen or no, she was weaker than we thought.

It took courage and a type of inner certainty to break free.

I shook my head. No time for regretting might-have-beens.

Jingling the keys to our borrowed truck in my right hand, I pushed all of those thoughts firmly to the back of mind. If we were going to pull off this operation and get all these people organized, I needed to concentrate.

I rounded the corner onto the acacia-lined street where Jimmy had parked the green El Camino, breathing in the moisture from a sprinkler watering a vegetable bed and patchy lawn in front of a yellow bungalow.

Sending my attention down beneath my solar plexus on a breath, I smelled something beside water, trees, and grass. I broadened my attention, seeking outward from the edges of my aura.

There it was…. I was smelling something underneath the tang of leaded gasoline that always lingered in the air, underneath the acacia trees and damp vegetation.

It was the dried-out, papery scent of snake.

"Damn you," I muttered, dropping the car keys into my big fringed bag.

Did I have…? Yes. There was a crystal in my pocket in case I needed extra oomph. I slipped the long crystal point into my hand, just in case.

A shape detached itself from the shadows of a tree. There he was, bold as brass, walking toward me, dark glasses a permanent fixture above his narrow nose and pale lips. His hair was movie-star perfect, as usual, and his black suit looked freshly pressed.

I hated him with every fiber of my being. There was nothing good about this man. Not his magic. Not his interest in me. Not his fucking job with the FBI.

"What are you doing in this neighborhood, honky?" Not a word I often used, but *by any means necessary,* right? And language was one weapon I had at hand.

"Waiting for you," he replied, unbothered by my taunt.

It took a lot of effort to not rub the spot in the front of my shoulder where he'd planted his barb. The hollow didn't hurt now, but the memory remained.

And the damn Fed and I still had an undeniable connection that I wished would go away. Rosalia wanted me to exploit that, to use it to track him down.

I'd been avoiding it.

He stopped two yards from me. Way too close for comfort. Everything set off warning bells. All the fine baby hairs stood up on my arms and the back of my neck.

I flexed my fingers, hands held loosely at my sides. Ready for action.

But maybe that connection-that-wouldn't-leave would come in handy.

More than once, I'd wished I could look into this man's eyes. I'd cracked his glasses once, and seen one pale blue, frightened eye, blinking in the sudden rush of light. It looked like one of those creepy pale fish that live in underwater caves.

Maybe I didn't want to look into those eyes after all.

"I don't have time for this," I said. "What do you want?"

"To broker an agreement."

I stopped flexing my fingers, and took a breath. Reached for some Ocean, just in case.

"I don't understand."

He offered me a tight little smile. "I'm sure you don't."

"Don't mess with me, man. I'm in no mood for you."

The Fed actually laughed, a crackling, creaking sound. Weird.

"I think we both want the same things," he said.

"How do you figure that?" I wasn't too comfortable standing on this South Central sidewalk, talking with a Fed. But I sure as hell wasn't going anywhere with him. And I didn't want to lead him to the borrowed car.

Not that it mattered. The asshole seemed determined to find me no matter where I was. There wasn't really any personal security when you couldn't hide your location.

I was going to need to work on that.

"Neither of us is too fond of my boss," he said.

Well, well, well. Why in the Powers was this man tipping his hand?

"And who might that be?"

"Jasmine!" It was Jimmy. I heard him and what sounded like two other sets of feet jogging toward me. A rifle ratcheted behind my ear.

Damn. Bad timing.

"I'm just having a little conversation with this Federal agent," I said, without turning my head.

I could smell Jimmy beside me. Amber and musk. And the cigarette stink of the other men. One of them was breathing heavily. Geronimo needed to whip his security forces into better shape.

"What were you about to tell me?" I asked the snake.

"That we're watching you." He tilted his chin up. "All of you are under surveillance. Twenty-four hours a day."

And then he actually had the gumption to turn his back on us and walk away.

"Jaz…" Jimmy said low. "You okay?"

I watched the sun bounce off the man's suit as he walked away. He wanted something. I could feel it. And that something had changed. He no longer wanted to kill me.

What in all the Powers had shifted? I tried to sniff the difference in the air. Tried to taste it on the back of my tongue.

I couldn't place it. But it had something to do with the damn sigils we were getting so close to cracking. I just knew it.

"I'm fine," I said, finally turning to look at my lover's concerned face. "I swear, that man just will not die."

"You've tried to kill him?" one of the Panthers said.

"Done my best. More than once."

He gave me a nod of respect.

I turned to Jimmy again. "You done with your meeting?"

He glanced at one of the other men, who nodded.

"Close enough, I guess. Some neighbor kid came slamming up the walk, said you were in trouble." He smiled at me then. "I shoulda known you were handling things just fine."

"Thanks for coming to my rescue anyway." I rolled my shoulders, releasing the tension I hadn't even noticed was there. "You never know. Panthers all on board?"

"Yeah."

"Okay, then. Let's get back to the Mansion and lock this operation down."

CHAPTER THIRTY-THREE
DOREEN

Doreen wanted to get back to Tanya sooner, but there'd been too much to do all day. Between phone calls, trying rally folks together for the blessing at Lake Merritt the next night, and the flower shop, it was early evening and growing dark by the time she was en route to Father Neil's church for the second time in one day.

She navigated the streets, walking rapidly in her sensible shoes, pocketbook clutched beneath her arm, heading from uptown to West Oakland. It wasn't a long walk, thank the Powers, because she wasn't sure how late Tanya would be working in the kitchen, if at all.

Doreen didn't really have time for this stop, but she needed to check in with Tanya about plans anyway. But mostly? She'd asked to see the younger woman because Doreen really needed to check in about Drake. She had wanted to talk to the younger woman that morning, but there hadn't been a chance before Tanya had to hurry off to work.

Doreen really needed her help. There was no way Doreen wanted to do any of this without Drake. Too much was at stake. People trusted him now, especially the children.

Doreen just needed to figure out how to get him to trust her.

Doreen hoped Tanya was at the church. She most often was, but there were no guarantees. She was there every morning, then it was off to work, then she got the kids from school, dropped them at their grandmother's, and was usually at the kitchen about now, prepping for breakfast the next day.

But sometimes, Doreen knew, Tanya was at headquarters, helping out there. Doreen hoped that wasn't the case. She couldn't have this conversation in a house full of revolutionaries, even though both she and Tanya would likely end up at HQ before the day was done.

Doreen missed Jasmine. She still felt some slight discomfort without her niece acting as a buffer between the respectable middle-aged sorcerer and the younger people.

She gave a snort. She'd never been respectable. Only pretended to be for the years she was stuck in the bog of grief.

And there was the church, red brick and slightly shabby.

Doreen tried the big metal door around back. It opened onto the big, red-tiled kitchen.

"Hey Doreen!" Tanya turned. "What are you doing here?"

It looked like Tanya was alone, and the whole place smelled like biscuits. Doreen's stomach growled.

Tanya smiled, her pressed hair looking almost perfect even after the day Doreen knew she must have had. A streak of flour marred her cheek.

"Want a biscuit? I just took out a tray."

"I would love one. And you have flour on your cheek."

Tanya wiped at her cheek with the back of her hand.

"I'm surprised it's not all over me," she said. "There's butter in the big fridge if you want it."

Doreen got the butter and a knife and sat down on a tall stool near the long metal counter. The biscuit tasted like heaven. It was flaky and perfect.

"Is there anything you don't do, girl?"

Tanya just smiled again and kept working.

Doreen swallowed another bite, squared her shoulders, and spoke.

"Tanya, I'm here because I need help with Drake. I'm afraid I hurt his feelings and I'm not sure what to do."

"What happened?" Tanya asked, plopping more batter onto a waiting stack of metal trays.

"He wanted something…magical. And I was afraid it was going to be too much to saddle a young boy with. Too much responsibility to be tied into."

"Did you explain that to him?"

"I tried. But it only seemed to make things worse. He actually ran from me, Tanya. Down the street."

Tanya pulled the heavy oven door open with a screech. "It's a hard age," she said. "And Drake is particularly sensitive to things like responsibility and honor. He probably thinks you don't trust him."

"But he *knows* I trust him!" Doreen said.

Tanya turned, arms crossed over her chest, one eyebrow raised.

"Doreen." She said. "He's thirteen. His hormones are probably out of control. He's been beaten up by white boys, attacked by the police, figured out he can do *magic*, and already seen and done things that would have sent most kids running away months ago."

"What are you saying?" Doreen set the biscuit down.

"He asked you for something important to him, after going through all that? After giving you what he has? Of course he thinks you don't trust him."

Damn. Doreen never would have thought of that.

"But he's so young…" she repeated.

"Doreen, you know better than that." Tanya's voice was soft, but chiding. "Bobby Hutton was only sixteen when he was killed. Three years older than Drake."

Doreen did know better. She knew what life was like for a black boy in Oakland. A lot of pressure. A lot of fear.

"Do you think Drake's afraid? Of everything we're facing?"

Tanya pulled the next batch of biscuits out of the oven. "I wouldn't be surprised. I'm scared, and so are a lot of other people. We don't know what's coming, Doreen; all we know is that you tell us something is."

Doreen decided she might as well finish the biscuit, since she wouldn't have time for dinner anytime soon. She watched Tanya work for a while.

"Tanya? There was something else I wanted to ask you about."

"Hmmm?"

"Remember those spiders? Have you seen any?"

Tanya slid a spatula under the biscuits, making sure they wouldn't be stuck fast come morning. Then she paused.

"I haven't seen any spiders. But I've *felt* things, you know?"

"Where?"

"Here. In the kitchen. And the dining room sometimes."

"Like what?"

The younger woman's hands started working again, scraping the last of the dough onto a final metal sheet.

"Like something was watching. Listening. But a team sweeps the church every other day. So it can't be that." She looked at Doreen. "Do you think it's one of those spiders?"

"It sounds like it's something. Just keep paying attention. And if you feel something, tell someone else and both of you scan the area."

"And then what?"

"If you can see it, smash it," Doreen replied. It wasn't a good enough answer, but it was the best she could offer right now. "How are your kids doing with the magic practice?"

Tanya actually smiled, full stop. "Jamal loves it! He's getting really good at making those energy balls with his hands. And Kimberlé is getting better, too. She's so serious about the whole thing, and has made the little spell bags Drake taught her for everyone in our family."

Doreen nodded. That was good. Training the children was the best idea they'd ever had. It meant the magic would continue to spread, family to family, child to child.

And maybe that would actually have some effect on this poor world. More than the hidden sorcery the Association and others had been doing all these years.

Magic wanted to be free. And that just might be the revolution the young people talked about.

A true sharing of power.

Doreen took her plate over to the big industrial sink.

"Let me help you clean up," she said. "Then let's get to this meeting where I have to try to explain our plans."

CHAPTER THIRTY-FOUR
CAROL

Ernesto's bed was starting to feel like it was supported by rocks, and the burgundy-bordered comforter wasn't comforting at all.

Carol was so sick of being in this room, lying on this bed, but all the healers told her she had to stay put for a little while longer. At least she got to sleep next to Ernesto every night, even if they couldn't do much more than kiss without risking further injury.

And that was getting frustrating in a different way.

Carol sighed.

At least she was still part of things, which was groovy. Everyone was meeting in Ernesto's sitting room and she was finally able to sit up on her own. The gunshot wounds had mostly healed, but the ache remained. The ache of the wounds…from the gunshots, plus the emotional ache. The sense of betrayal, and the not knowing.

How in all the Powers had something gotten through the wards? How in all the Powers had someone gotten close enough to the window to fire a gun?

And the question she'd been asking over and over, *Why her?*

Was it just chance opportunity? She couldn't tell yet, but a sense of something she didn't know clawed at her.

"You all right, my love?" Ernesto said, his voice quiet.

She figured people knew they were lovers. It was pretty obvious, what with sharing the bed and all. But neither of them were used to it yet. She and Ernesto. Her former teacher. Her friend. Her colleague.

She was glad they'd made love before the shooting happened. She was glad she was able to share his bed that way.

"I'm just thinking," she said. "I'm still wondering, why me. Like, was that actually the plan? Is there some reason someone wanted to take me out?"

She cleared her throat. "We've always assumed everyone wants Jasmine, and I think that's true, but I'm starting to suspect you're right, that they might want me, too."

Rosalia entered the room, with a swirl of green velvet skirts and clashing silver bangles.

"I heard what you said," the hechicera said. "I have been thinking the same. I think they know you are the one. You are the one who is tracking the sigils. I think they know you understand the symbols, and are getting closer to finding out what they mean."

The small sorcerer came closer and sat on the edge of the bed.

"I actually think, maga, that you understand more than you think you do. I want to take you under. See what we can see on the plano astral. Drawing these symbols is fine, but there is some connection we are still not making."

Carol heard a bustling in the outer room, then Jimmy's voice, that deep panther rumble. And then Jasmine's direct tones.

Her best friend.

"Hey, Carol," Jasmine said, entering the bedroom. "You look like you're feeling better."

"Yeah. If I could just get out of this bed, I think everything would be pretty groovy."

"How long do they say?"

"Another day. Two. I don't know. I'm better, but still weak."

Rosalia spoke again. "We need to have her up and about to attend the ceremony. Everyone must be in attendance. Everyone needs the blessing."

Carol was relieved.

"You mean I actually get to get out of this room? No offense." She looked at Ernesto. His brown eyes looked worried behind the eyeglass lenses. She decided to ignore that. "It's a very nice room, but I'm sick of lying here."

She look at her friend. Jasmine looked good, but too thin. She was always slender, but she was so thin now it was almost painful. Her hair was still a perfect oval. Her clothing was radical chic as usual, but Carol could tell something troubled her. Something out of the ordinary.

"Did something just happen?" she said.

Jasmine nodded and pressed her lips together.

"Yeah, that Fed. He ambushed me."

"What?"

"No. Not like that," Jasmine said. "He was waiting for me. After the meeting."

"Did you fight?" Carol asked.

"No. It was the strangest thing," Jasmine said. "I think that snake just wanted to talk to me. I still can't figure it out."

Her words hung in the air like a big balloon of strangeness.

No one spoke for a moment.

Then Carol broke the ice. "You know, I was just talking with Rosario and Ernesto. And I think I was shot on purpose.

"You were targeted?" Jasmine said. "Shit."

Her friend plopped down in the armchair Ernesto had dragged near the bed when Carol first got shot, before he figured she was healed enough for him to sleep on the other side of the big bed.

"I guess that makes sense," Jasmine continued. "Of *course*. Of course it makes sense. How did we not see it?"

"We weren't looking," Carol said. "Everything's been about you. And for good reason. You're the one that Fed's been after. You're the target. You're probably even the one Terrance was working against. At least we think so. Right? Why would anybody look to me?"

Jasmine put her hands up as if to stop the flow of speech.

"Because you're the one with the key," she said. "You have been all along. Those symbols started to come through *you*. All the rest of us have just been chasing after phantoms. Whereas you're the one who's had the magic all along. You have the code, sister."

"Yeah. But I still don't know how to unlock it," Carol complained. "But you were telling us about the Fed. What do you think he wanted?"

"Well, I asked him that," Jasmine said, "and I think he was about to tell me. But then Jimmy and security rolled up with protection. Which I'm grateful for. But I don't know. He said he wanted to let us know we were under surveillance twenty-four hours. Like he was threatening me. But there was something there besides the threat."

She turned to Rosalia then. The old sorcerer looked at her with citrine eyes.

"Rosalia?" Jasmine asked. "When we were up there in that astral temple, fighting... When we were watching the sigils change and seeing the walls crumble, did you ever get the sense that the Fed was *making* it happen? That he didn't really want to succeed? That he didn't one hundred percent *want* to take me out?"

Rosalia looked thoughtful. She tapped her fingers on the big turquoise ring she wore on her right hand.

"I don't know, hechicera. But I think you could be right. I have wondered myself, why, with all the firepower he brought, trained magicians couldn't us take down. Couldn't put up more of a fight. It seemed too easy."

Rosalia came back toward the bed.

"I know we're strong. I know the power of the people is strong. I know the people will prevail. With the help of the Gods. And with their magic. But I also know that sometimes it has felt too easy."

Carol snorted at that. Gesturing to Jasmine's shoulder. Gesturing to her own gunshot wounds.

"You think this has been easy?"

Ernesto spoke then, gently squeezing her hand hand in his.

"She doesn't mean there hasn't been a price, Carol. She just means that usually, when the Man comes up against us, the cost is greater.

There are a lot more people dead. There are a lot more people destroyed. Communities decimated. Lives taken. We're impacted, sure. But look at how many of us are still alive."

"So what do we do?" Carol asked.

"I'm going to take you under," Rosalia said, "if you are ready. We have to find out more. And I want everyone in this room to bear witness. And I want everyone in this room to know. What we do is important. And I want everyone in this room to understand what's at stake. And what we're working for."

"No disrespect, ma'am," Jimmy said. "But I think we all know. Little Bobby Hutton is dead. They tried to assassinate Fred and Deborah. Hell, they tried to assassinate Geronimo Pratt! Lucky for him he slept on the floor the morning of the raid on 41st and Central."

"Wasn't any luck about it," Jasmine said. "He knew they were coming. He just didn't know what day."

Rosalia nodded. "I understand that you know how things work here on earth. And that there is danger. But what I do not think everyone understands yet is how the danger is everywhere now. On every plane. The plano astral. The plane of earth. The plane of magic. The realms of the dead. And the realms of those who are to come. The descendants."

She looked at Jasmine, "*Your* descendants. It's part of what the ancestors have been telling us all along. And we need to prepare."

Rosalia turned on Carol then. "Are you ready?"

Carol nodded. And took in a breath.

"What do I need to do?"

"Just follow my voice." The sorcerer touched the center of her forehead, very lightly. Removing her warm fingers, Rosalia breathed across the spot they had touched.

And Carol was suddenly floating. Floating in clouds. Floating in white and gray. Floating in shades of peach and pearl.

And floating past her, all around her, were black lines. Dark lines. Squiggles. Shapes. Things coming together and breaking apart. Lines and angles. Triangles and squares. Sinuous curves. Arcs. Symbols. Sigils. Keys.

"I see," she breathed out. "Help me see more."

And the sigils shaped themselves around her. Drawing on her memory. Drawing on a past and a future she didn't even know existed.

Except she'd felt them before. She knew them somehow. Deep inside her. Rosalia was right. It was all here. Carol reached out a hand.

And plucked one slowly turning signal from the air. She looked at it in her hand. The lines so dark against her pale skin.

And then she put it in her mouth. And swallowed it whole. And everything turned to light.

And she was gone.

CHAPTER THIRTY-FIVE
CAROL

Carol floated in a sea of billowing colors, barely tethered to the ground. Purple. Cerulean. Marigold. Silver. Rose. Jade. All moving in a mist that filled the air.

She had tried to take herself back to the place Rosalia had led her the day before, to find the place of sigils, but she was lost now, and had no idea where she was.

All she knew was that Earth seemed very, very far away. She could feel small pockets of her Elemental Power deep inside her bones, but couldn't quite reach it.

"Who am I?" she said into the swirling kaleidoscope. Her words barely penetrated the mist.

The question pinged in the part of her brain that still held half-rational thoughts. Curious. Why not *Where am I* or, more importantly, *What am I doing here and why*?

But to the rest of her, to the Carol that floated in the strange, multi-hued space, the question made perfect sense.

So she asked it again. "Who am I?"

A faint whisper slid into her ears, so quick and sudden she couldn't grasp the words before they slipped away again.

One part of her brain wondered if this was what dropping acid felt like. She knew some kinds of magic workers used drugs to assist them, but sorcerers never did. So she didn't know.

If LSD was anything like visiting this pleasant, colored, floating world, she could see why the hippies were so fond of it.

It was pretty cool, even if it was disorienting. Floating was pleasant, but she hoped her Elemental connection would return after a while.

It was part of who she was. And always had been. But...

"Who am I?" she repeated.

And a figure coalesced, emerging from between the swoop and swish of colors, moving rapidly toward her.

It shifted shape. Lion. Eagle. Human. Fish. Amoeba. Star. Finally, it settled on a vaguely human, vaguely male shape in a long blue robe.

Its right hand held a large brass key. Its left was held, palm out, fingers facing upward, in the universal sign that angels used, indicating the words unspoken, "Be not afraid."

At least, she hoped that was what it meant.

Her own feet floated downward, and she found that there was some sort of floor beneath her toes. It felt like marble, cool and smooth.

"You are the Seer of Time and a Sorcerer of Earth," the figure said, still moving toward her, coming much closer now. Almost close enough to touch.

"Seer of Time?" Carol asked.

The figure stopped. Held up the key. The key began to rattle, to shake, to whirl and hum. It morphed into a glowing cube of green.

The figure held out the cube, indicating that she should take it.

Carol held it in her hand. It was the layered, variegated green of malachite. Ernesto's Solstice gift.

"How is this cube a key?" she asked.

"It holds the form within the forms. It shapes the building blocks within your Element. It forms the shapes you have been seeking to destroy."

The sigils? The Temples?

"Not to destroy," she murmured. "To dismantle. Re-form. Change."

"What is the difference?" the figure asked. "Death looks the same no matter how it comes."

She didn't know.

"Who are you?" Carol asked the figure.

"The Archivist," they answered. "The one who stores the things you need to know, the things you fear to see, and the things you hope may come to pass."

A shiver racked her body. She wanted to slide away. Her heart beat faster in her chest. Arrhythmic. Her fingers tapped against her thumbs in fast succession. *1-2-3-4-1-2-3-4.*

Her feet wanted to run.

"Carol!" Ernesto's voice was calling to her, tugging her backwards, yanking her out of the shifting, colored space.

"Nooo!" She reached out to the Archivist, but they were already gone.

Carol slammed into her body on the bed and jerked, wrenching her shoulder and cracking her head on the bedstead.

"Ow!" she cried out. "No!"

Her breath came in rapid pants. She started to panic. There was too much she still needed to know. Why did she have to come back?

"Carol! Are you all right? I left to get you some broth and I came back and you were gone!" Ernesto said.

She could smell the blended chicken and vegetables. Her stomach growled. Her body needed more food than she'd been able to take in.

With the battle on the way, she needed to be strong. She needed to be here.

Her eyelids fluttered. Her eyes rolled upwards in her skull. She was being drawn back again.

She heard the clatter of a cup on the nightstand.

Felt Ernesto grip her left hand.

"Stay," he said. "Carol. Don't go away."

"Not done..." she whispered.

There was rustling in the doorway.

"Maga!" Rosalia. The clattering of bangles on wrists. The soft swish of velvet.

Two hands gripping her ankles then.

Carol inhaled, a deep, shuddering breath, expanding her belly and her chest.

Her spirit sank all the way down into her toes. Her fingertips. The base of her skull.

And she was back. All the way home. She felt the Earth in the wooden bedframe. On the floor. The Earth of the bones in Ernesto's fingers, gripping her hand. The Earth of the Mansion, and the gardens outside.

She began to cry.

"What's wrong, beloved?" Ernesto said.

"I don't know."

She extracted her hand from his and wiped her face. Then looked into his deep brown eyes.

"I love you," she said.

He blinked. Once. Twice. Inhaled.

"I love you, too."

"You went out again without us?" Rosalia shook her head. "We barely got you returned from yesterday's journey, and we still don't know what that sigil was you took in…. You can hurt yourself by doing this alone."

Carol didn't reply; she was too tired to defend herself.

Rosalia exhaled. Carol had never seen her worried like this. "Okay," Rosalia said, as though she'd made an internal decision. "I want to hear what happened on this journey you took without my permission. The others are on their way. We have much to do before tonight."

"Tonight?" Carol asked.

"Tonight is the ritual to feed the people. To bless them. Make them know that they are strong."

Right. Carol had forgotten.

"How?" she asked.

Rosalia waved her arms at that. "Later. When the others are here, we will tell you. I want to know whom you met on the plano astral."

"They called themselves the Archivist."

Ernesto sat down heavily on the chair next to the bed. "That's one of the big guns, Carol. I've only heard *stories* of people meeting them before."

Rosalia clucked her tongue and paced. "This is both good and bad," she finally said. "It is good they showed themselves to you. That means we have extra help. It also means that you should be coming into extra powers soon."

The hechicera came over and peered at Carol's face, then scanned her body again, this time not using her hands, only her Sight.

"Sí. Your aura is changing," she said. "How do you feel?"

"My shoulder is killing me. I have a headache…." Carol closed her eyes and scanned her own body. "But actually? I feel better than I did before. And not just since the shooting. Something feels different, dig? I don't think it's my body, though. And I can't trace it in my aura, either."

"It is your mind, maga. That is where the difference lies. You shall be able to think and see and know things that you could not know before."

"That's kind of what The Archivist said. I think. And he gave me a gift." Carol remembered. "He had this big old key, and it changed into the present you got me, Ernesto!"

Ernesto reached for the malachite cube on the nightstand and held it up. "This?"

"Yes. The key was the cube, or something like that."

"The cube is the key," Rosalia corrected, tapping her ring finger to her lips. "Where are those papers? We have a lot of work to do before tomorrow, and I think I know now just what must be done."

She trained those citrine eyes on Carol. "I know that *you* hold the key inside you now, maga. The Archivist confirmed it. You are the one who will show us the way."

A polite knock sounded on the sitting room door, and Carol heard the door opening and what must have been half a dozen people piling in.

Then Jasmine rushed into the bedroom, black coat thrown over a purple T-shirt and denim bell-bottoms. She wore silver hoops that almost reached her shoulders and her hair was a dark halo around her head.

Her eyebrows drew together, forming creases on her forehead.

"Carol! I felt something weird happening. Are you okay?"

Jasmine smelled like the ocean at summertime today. Something had lit her up inside, despite the concern she radiated into the room.

Something in her friend had changed, too. It wasn't just Carol.

"I'm fine. Just went on an astral walkabout and got some additions to my sorcery, I guess." She really wished she could push herself up in the damn bed more easily, but her shoulder still throbbed from her body jerking like that.

Ernesto moved so Jasmine could get closer to her friend.

They looked then, eyes raking themselves up and down, each scanning the other.

"Something happened to you, too," Carol said.

"The ancestors," Jasmine said. "Actually, *the* Ancestor. Who got to you?"

"Someone called the Archivist."

Jasmine whistled through her teeth and looked at Rosalia, who just nodded.

Jimmy came in then, carrying in a chair.

"Let's start this meeting," he said. "We don't have much more time."

"Stakes just got raised," Jasmine said to him, then turned back to Carol. "I hope we're up to it."

CHAPTER THIRTY-SIX
SNAKES AND SPIDERS

*T*he man stank of weakness. It made Samuels' skin crawl. He expected weakness from civilians. Encountered it all the time. It was how he did his job: exploiting the fears and desires of people who had little power.

But a sorcerer? The powerful head of the Association of Magical Arts and Sorcery?

The man made him want to spit. Samuels swallowed his bile and picked up his glass of sparkling water, where a small circle of lemon floated above the ice. He focused his attention on the slight tartness of the lemon as he throttled down his distaste for the man sitting across the snow-white-linen–covered table.

They sat in an over-padded leather booth in the corner, just the two of them. The man across from him drank scotch and soda. Another mark against him. Any sorcerer worth his salt shouldn't be drinking on the job as it were. Samuels never drank at all.

He'd been surprised at the message left at his hotel. That Terrance Sterling wanted to meet with him. Samuels was suspicious, but needed to know why the head of the Association—some of whose members Samuels was currently engaged in ongoing skirmishes with—wanted a face-to-face.

So there they were, in some tony restaurant designed to impress the middle class, and serve comforting lunches to the wealthy and overpriced dinners to anyone stupid enough to pay the prices marching down the right side of the heavy paper in its leather sleeve.

Samuels didn't give a shit about it all. If Sterling intended to impress him, he should really know better.

"Why am I here?" Samuels finally asked, tired of waiting through the niceties, and the ordering of drinks, waiting for the beverages to come, then another round of discussing the damn menu with the straight-backed waiter in his black vest and white shirt and black tie.

Alter his eyes to see in darkness, throw some shades on him, and the waiter could have been a spook.

Terrance rolled the heavy tumbler in his hands, shifting the ice through the amber liquid.

"I have a proposition for you."

"And why is that?"

A startled flash marred Sterling's middle-aged good looks. Samuels could almost feel the man resisting the urge to smooth back his perfectly coiffed silver hair.

"I want to offer you an alliance," Sterling said.

Samuels barked out a laugh. "Really?"

"Use as few words as possible," Agent Tolson had taught him during the first year of his training. "A weak man babbles. A strong man measures every word. The less you speak, the more they will reveal of their true nature."

The waiter was back, setting down a piece of grilled white fish and plain salad for Samuels, and a steak, au gratin potatoes, and a side of corn nibblets for Sterling.

Once they'd taken their first bites, Sterling spoke again. "I've been meeting with your boss."

"Is that so?" The information startled Samuels, and sent thoughts scurrying about, deep in the recesses of his mind. No need to let Sterling know a damn thing about that.

"But I don't like him much. Too full of himself. I prefer a quiet man, like you. A man who gets things done."

Samuels sliced off a flaky wedge of fish and placed it precisely on his tongue, sparing only a moment to savor the taste of lemon and caper as he chewed. Halibut. Pretty good.

"And what exactly do you think that I get done?" he asked, before cutting off another slice of fish.

Sterling leaned across the table. For a moment, Samuels thought the man was actually reaching to touch his arm. The tapered pale fingers stopped in the middle of the white linen instead, one silver cufflink winking from beneath the deep teal wool suit.

"Things we both need done," the stupid man replied. "I hate Jasmine Jones as much as you do."

Sterling sat back in the booth. "Ah. Finally. I see that surprises you." He took another sip of whiskey. "Your boss told me all about your operation. But he clearly never told you he had me on the inside, working toward similar aims."

Samuels put his knife and fork down on the table. "What exactly do you want?"

"I want you to work for me."

CHAPTER THIRTY-SEVEN
DOREEN

The full moon rose above them all, blessing the city of Oakland. Blessing the sleeping families, the insomniac worriers, the night shift nurses and bus drivers, the drug dealers and prostitutes, the people camping under the freeway overpasses with no place else to go.

The lights ringing Lake Merritt reflected on the black water. The night herons were nowhere about. Doreen had hoped to see some out hunting. She loved the strange birds. They always looked like hunched-over old men to her.

The Canada geese were most certainly asleep for the evening, not crowding the lawns.

Drake stood at her side. He finally spoke. "I'm sorry I ran from you, Mrs. Doreen."

She put a hand on his shoulder, feeling how small he was beneath his corduroy jacket and red sweater. As Doreen looked down at his button nose and big brown eyes, at the planes that already threatened to take over the sweet roundness of his face, she found that she was fighting tears.

"I'm sorry, too, Drake. I didn't mean to hurt you. In fact, I was trying to protect you. And maybe that's not right. You deserve to decide for yourself if you want the responsibility of carrying magic for the rest of your life."

He stared back at her, half expectant, half afraid.

"I want whatever's going to make me strong enough to *do* this, Mrs. Doreen. This thing everyone's asking me to do now."

She nodded. "Tonight. I'll pass the power tonight. It won't be the same as what I did for Patrice. And it won't be formal—it'll be out here in front of all these people."

They looked at the gathering crowd. Toddlers on shoulders. Men and women holding candles cupped in their hands. Teenagers walking solemnly together.

Folks from West Oakland, Chinatown, Uptown, and East Oakland. Panthers. Brown Berets. SDS. Representatives from the Ohlone nation. Hippies. The Yellow Peril, as they called themselves… It looked as though everyone was coming except the rich white people from the hills.

Doreen turned back to Drake. "Is that okay with you?"

"I need this, Mrs. Doreen. Everything tells me I gotta have it." He stared at the dark lake. "However you say it's right to happen is cool."

"Okay, Drake."

Patrice walked up to them then, along with Leroy, Tanya, and some of the other Panthers.

"We almost ready?" Tanya asked. "The kids and teens are getting into place."

Doreen took in a breath of the night air, and felt the Elemental Fire banked deep inside her. They had planned so much these past few days. Things move so fast. Faster than they used to, it seemed. She wasn't sure if it was growing older, or if time really had accelerated lately. Looking at the young people all staring at her, the lamp and candle glow reflecting off their faces and their eyes, she knew that it was time itself.

Too much was happening. And since there was no way to slow it down, they would harness the velocity of it.

And hope it worked.

"Where's Huey?" She suddenly realized the tall man wasn't there. "We need him here for this."

He was the one who had sacrificed for the land and the people. He had to be here for the blessing.

"He's coming," Leroy said. "Do we need to wait on him?"

"We do," Doreen replied.

And then Huey appeared, walking through the candle-bearing crowd. He looked taller. More solid. Almost glowing. Doreen could sense the panther shifting underneath his skin, wanting to break free. She also felt the strength and authority he wielded, which held the big cat in place.

The ritual had worked. Huey P. Newton was a sovereign of the people. A leader for the time to come.

Fred Hampton had received the blessing of the ancestors as well, and had already shed his blood in sacrifice. Doreen knew that if he had been here tonight, he would likely look the same.

Two sovereigns, and more to come. The Black Panther Party wouldn't brook anyone to rule over the people, but they valued leaders who could serve, and serve with all their might.

"I'm sorry I'm late," Huey said, his soft drawl carrying, pitch perfect, above the noises of the still growing crowd. "I was on a call with Fred in Chicago. They're all set to do the blessing there as well. Los Angeles, Philadelphia, Atlanta, and New York are all in, too."

Then he grinned, hugely. "We're even getting word from Brixton, England, and Dar es Salaam in Tanzania."

The group around Doreen sent up a small whoop at that.

Doreen stepped forward and grabbed Huey, and drawing his face down, she kissed his cheeks.

He looked surprised. Then smiled.

"Who's in charge?" he asked.

"Drake?" Doreen asked.

The young man and Patrice both stepped forward, then beckoned to Tanya, who said, "Be right back," and started moving through the crowd, Drake behind her.

"Children! All the children!" Doreen heard Tanya call. "Come forward now!"

"What do they need us to do?" Leroy asked.

"Start getting everyone into concentric circles, with a big space in the center for the kids. That's how we'll begin," Patrice replied.

Fifteen minutes later, with circles seven deep, the children were all gathered in the center, and the teenagers ringed the outside edge, interspersed with Black Panthers and the Brown Berets. Mario Savio had brought some of the other Free Speech radicals from UC Berkeley, too, along with some of the hippies who'd fought for People's Park.

"Do what we taught you," Drake said, raising his voice into the night. "You are one community, linked together."

The children crossed their arms in front of themselves, grasping the hands of each child on their left and right. They formed a chain together.

Doreen knew they'd been practicing this, but seeing it brought tears of pride to her eyes again.

And look at Drake. A leader if she'd ever seen one. Tanya, too. Patrice had moved to the edge, to make sure the teens were in formation.

Doreen and Huey stepped toward the center then. Two of the children dropped hands to let them through.

As she passed Drake, she looked him in the eyes and said, "You're in charge. And be ready…"

"Yes ma'am."

Standing in the middle of the people, looking up at the Oakland sky, Doreen felt a peace descend that she hadn't felt in years.

Touching Momma's moon amulet, she murmured a quick prayer, calling the ancestors closer.

"We are one community!" Drake shouted.

"We are one community!" the children shouted back.

"Black power!"

"Black power!" the children cried.

"Black pride!"

"Black pride!"

"People power!"

"People power!" the entire crowd replied.

"All power! To *all* the people!" Drake's voice was straining a little, Doreen could hear it, but he was still loud as could be.

"All power to all the people!" she shouted along with the crowd.

"Children!" Tanya boosted her voice, to reach through the crowd. That surprised Doreen. The young woman must have been practicing, too. Or the magic was helping her more than Doreen realized. "Find your magic!"

A crackling filled the air, and some of the children squealed and laughed.

"Link your power, now!"

And a force field radiated off the children's hands, pushing its way out through the crowd. It was answered by the power from the teens. The two fields met, shoving each other up and down into a mighty sphere of protection around the whole crowd.

"It worked," Doreen whispered. Without her, or any other sorcerers helping, the people—the *children*—had just set up a field of protection around the community.

They dropped hands.

The sphere remained.

Magic for the people had just become magic *by* the people.

"Revolution..." she murmured to herself again.

Then Drake looked at her, the serious expression of a leader on his face warring with the impulse to grin. So she grinned.

He grinned back, briefly, then nodded her toward the center.

In the middle of the shimmering sphere of pale yellow through which the cool night, and the soft lake sounds, still came through, Doreen took Patrice's hand and stepped into the middle of the circle.

Patrice held a large mirror in her other hand. The kind with a handle, and an oval piece of glass set into wood.

Doreen stared at her own face in the silvered glass. Slowed her breathing down. Felt the Elemental Fire coiling in her belly.

Then she cast her mind toward the Ancestor who walked the ochre plains at the foot of the mountain, near the trees where the tiny, red-winged birds flew.

Doreen asked her for a blessing for these people. For protection, but for something more.

For the ability to believe they were enough. That they had the strength to overthrow the forces of oppression and build a world better suited for their children's children to live, and love, and thrive.

Taking another big breath, she took her eyes from her own reflection and looked at her lover's face. Such love, such strength, such awe was present in Patrice's round red lips and dark eyes.

Doreen couldn't help herself. She did the natural thing, faced with that amount of love, and leaned in to place a soft kiss on Patrice's mouth, tasting the waxy tang of the red lipstick against her own lips.

Then, gentle hands on Patrice's shoulders, she turned her, until the mirror was facing Drake.

Patrice tilted it downward, until Drake caught his own reflection.

Doreen filled her body with her own power, with the power of Fire, and with the power of the ancestors, who buzzed and tingled at the base of her skull.

Holding out her hands, palms floating just above Drake's head, she raised her voice and called out to the night.

"Ancestors! Hear me! Bring down the powers of deep night and bright sun. Bring swiftness and surety. Bring courage and strength. Bring joy and fierce laughter. Bring the ability to love and to be loved. Fill this young warrior, Drake, with a power great enough to wield and serve the people all his days. Increase his magic. Make him a leader among the people, willing to work at their side."

She looked out at the hushed crowd, who stood in circles around them. "Hold out your hands and bless this boy, no longer a boy, becoming a magic worker and a man. Offer him your blessings and protection."

Every hand raised, outstretched toward the center. A low humming sound began to rise.

Doreen settled her hands upon Drake's head and poured power into his body and the energy field surrounding his small frame.

The boy began to shake, and a slight moan escaped his lips. It went on, and on. Building. Increasing until the magic pumping through him grew palpable in the air.

And then he straightened. Took a breath. Opened his eyes.

Doreen lifted her hands from him and knew that the ancestors had truly blessed this one tonight.

CHAPTER THIRTY-EIGHT
JASMINE

The Los Angeles civic center was packed with people, standing in clumps and circles, rows and arcs, covering the grass and the walkways that divided them.

The Federal building loomed across the street, its sidewalks gleaming with floodlights. The full moon was rising, just peeking around the edges of the WPA-style tower.

Compared to it, the park was in darkness, lit up with individual candle flames.

There were police around the edges, dark shapes with their flat hats and guns. I didn't care. Panther security and Brown Berets were on the edges too, making sure the people remained safe.

But really? Despite the risk of gathering at all, tonight nobody cared about the cops. The people were defiant. The mood was high. You could almost taste the excitement. Just like cinnamon. Sugar. Baking bread. Lightning. Love.

Jimmy had his hand in mine, and I could see Rosalia, talking with Teresa and Rafael from Las Manos, just a few yards away. I had never felt better in my life. We'd even gotten Carol out of that damn Mansion. Two Brown Berets had her set up in a chair, covered with blankets, protected from the chill evening air.

She looked different to me. More solid, maybe. Purposeful. But also as if there were secrets inside her that she hadn't had before. Carol said we'd talk after tonight. There was too much to discuss, she said, and no time to do it in.

"Hope those pigs stay away," Jimmy said.

I just nodded. There was nothing much to say about that. The cops would do what the cops would do. I was more worried about the Feds showing up, watching this ceremony, though I wasn't sure that would happen anymore. I didn't smell any snakes. And it seemed like the man in black wasn't all he was cracked up to be.

That still bothered me, too. Itched under my skin. I was thinking maybe, in some strange way, we *were* working on the same side, even though every part of me screamed that couldn't be right.

There was something still off. I shook those thoughts from my head and focused on what was in front of me: a mass of beautiful people holding candles.

Candle light flickered on brown faces, golden faces, pale peach faces, and skin so dark it looked like mahogany. People in suits and coats. People in boots and bell-bottom jeans. Everyone looking defiant. Everyone looking excited. Everyone so brave it made tears come to my eyes. I loved this.

"Power to the people," I whispered.

"Right on," Jimmy replied. Carol smiled up at us.

"They're all here for this, Jaz," Carol said. "They're all here tonight, ready to take a chance."

"Do *you* feel ready?" I asked my friend. A slight breeze caressed my cheeks and ruffled my natural.

Carol looked thoughtful for a moment, and swept a lock of straight blond hair from her own face. Then she nodded.

"I think I do. I think I finally know."

"You keep that sigil safe inside," I said. "We're gonna need it tomorrow."

"Yeah," Carol said. "We're going to need it big time."

Rosalia stepped forward. Today she carried her large staff festooned with feathers and ribbons. The sorcerer looked like an ancient shaman that had come out from a cave. Or no. Maybe some priestess. That was it. A priestess standing on stone stairs at the base of a step pyramid. Ready to call on the Gods. Ready to call down rain and fire and wind. Ready to shake the earth.

I hoped I'd be like that someday. In my own right hand was the spear the ancestors had gifted me. The wood felt smooth and hard against my palm, and the spear tip glowed in the candle light, winking like a lighthouse. A beacon filled with blue fire and the power of the ancestors themselves.

I didn't know what was going to happen. All I knew was that Rosalia needed us here. The old hechicera had said there would be a blessing for the people who were about to go to battle.

"*It was something we had always done. Something that got lost,*" she had said. "*Something that needs to rise again.*"

I knew she was right. We didn't know what we were building yet. This world of magic. This world where magic was free instead of locked behind rich people's doors, or hidden in huts at the edge of the forest. But I knew the world was about to change. I just hoped that change was good.

I heard the rustle and rattling of the Aztec dancers moving toward the center of the park. A conch shell sounded in the night. Once. Twice. Three times it blew, and the air seemed to rumble somehow, as if thunder was coming.

And a shimmering light moved toward the crowd massed on the civic center lawn. It was the Feathered Serpent, Quetzalcoatl. Its massive body rolled out through the air, shimmering purple and red and gold, shimmering the orange and peach and salmon colors of a sunrise. The whole gathering took a deep breath. The air was sweet, fragrant. It smelled like roses and copal. Like the burning of incense on a great sacrificial fire and inside the people's hearts. And every arm raised itself up, and the candles flickered in the wind, but none of them blew out.

And on a palanquin, a large statue of the Virgin Mary came, carried on the shoulders of young women and men, lit with candles, strewn with roses. And the people bowed, and the people prayed. And Tonantzin was there.

A mighty voice spoke into every mind. *"You are my children and I love you. You are my children and you have my power. The power of earth, and the power to renew. The power to build, and the power to cut down. And the power to love each other daily. That is the offering that I ask."*

"We love you!" some voices shouted back.

I stood stunned, spear in my right hand, left hand clutching Jimmy's.

"Was that Tonantzin who spoke?" I asked.

"I couldn't tell you, baby," Jimmy said. "But this is some powerful shit."

I nodded, waiting. Everyone waited. A sense of expectation filled the air.

Rosalia lifted her staff and shook it. Ribbon streamers and feathers shaking everywhere. Bells rattling. The row of bracelets on her arms clattering together.

"La gente!" she called. "Good people! There have been many battles. You have fought bravely and we thank you. But we are still at war!" she said. "And the war is large and long and we do not know when it will end, so tonight, we come together to ask the blessing of the ancient ones. The Gods of wind and mountain, of dawn and day. Hold out your hands!"

People held up their candles and raised the palms of their other hands up high.

"And in your hands and in your hearts you carry the great flame! And your tears and your blood are the water spilled freely for the freedom of the people. And we ask these spirits here tonight for the blessings of fortitude. Longevity. And strength. And we call down a rain of blessings on every person gathered here, and on every friend and loved one that you touch whether they are here or not. And may these blessings roll out and across this city. Into the barrios and ghettos, and our homes. May these blessings roll out and touch Chicago and Oakland. Atlanta. Philadelphia. Houston. Albuquerque. And the people of Detroit and Washington DC."

The air in the park grew thicker with every word the hechicera spoke. I could almost taste the words on my tongue. I felt the gathering of Ocean, pooling around my feet, rising through my sex, and bursting up to bathe my heart.

Rosalia was still speaking. "All those who fight for justice, *true* justice. All those who fight for love. All those who fight for a place for their children and a better life for all people. We ask these blessings from these ancient Powers!"

And the darkness of night, and the bright candles illuminating people's hands and faces, seemed to me that they shifted somehow. As if the whole world had tilted slightly sideways. I could almost see around the edges of the park, the thin bright line of dawn, and I felt in my heart that it was coming. It was coming. These were the longest, darkest nights of winter, but tomorrow? There would come a new day.

"What is my place?" I asked the sky. And I felt the ancestors touch my brow, and the woman with the ochre-smeared hair and the gap-toothed smile whispered in my ear, *"You are enough."*

Tears rolled down my face, and I sobbed.

I could feel Jimmy's arm slide its way around my waist and hold me close, but I could also still feel the Ancestor's breath on my cheek. *"You are a leader of the people who will learn to lead themselves. You are a leader who must know humility along with strength. You are a leader who will break if you forget that you must serve. You are a leader who will liberate this world."*

"No. No. It's too much," I said. "It's too much. Don't give me this burden. It's too much, too much, too much."

I could hear Jimmy: "Shh...baby. Baby what's wrong?"

But I couldn't talk to him. I was still here with the Ancestor, and the woman smiled then and took a step away. A bundle wrapped up in a bright orange cloth appeared in the woman's dark arms. Something inside of the cloth was squirming. The ancestor held out that bundle to me, where even in that in-between place I still clutched my spear.

And the woman with the ochre-smeared hair said, *"Take it. This is also yours."*

I struggled to move the spear to the crook between breast and shoulder, right as I felt the bundle drop into my arms. The spear tip rested against my head, pointing to the sky, and both hands held the swaddled object.

And I looked down at the sweetest, dark brown face. The sweetest flared nose. And the sweetest eyelashes. A baby. It was a baby.

I looked at the Ancestor.

The woman was still smiling, darkness showing through that gap in her teeth. Her eyes were bright.

"You will give birth," the woman said, and vanished.

And once again, I stood, spear in one hand, lover at my side, in a park surrounded by a beautiful sea of people and candles. The Feathered Serpent was gone, and the statue of the Virgin was quiet.

And so was my heart. For the first time in years, I felt at peace.

Turning, I sought out Jimmy's lips. So firm. Our tongues touched. Offering promises, and a burst of water. He was so sweet. Like honey. He was my sweetness.

"You are my sweetness," I whispered then, against his mouth.

"I love you, Jaz," he replied.

CHAPTER THIRTY-NINE
CAROL

Carol, Jasmine, Ernesto and Rosalia were gathered in the library. Gregory Oluo was meeting with Cecelia, but they expected those two, plus Jasmine's father, William, at any time.

Everyone was bustling, making last-minute preparations. Tonight was the night.

A fire spat and crackled in the big whitewashed fireplace and Carol sat, bundled in a red sweater, in one of the green and blue chintz chairs Ernesto had dragged there for her, shoving one of the cream damask sofas away from the fire to make space.

It was still such a relief to be out of that bed. The blessing ritual had done her good, but she still wasn't one hundred percent healed. She just hoped she was well enough to be of use that night.

Luckily, they didn't have to go anywhere. Other than an evil astral temple.

A clipboard with a map of Washington DC on it was propped on her knees. She stared down at the red and green squiggles of highways and roads, at the larger demarcations of county and state lines. The Anacostia and Potomac formed a big blue Y in the midst of it all.

There there was the big diamond shape she'd drawn on top of it all.

"Coe. In. Tell. Pro. Coe. In. Tell. Pro. Coe. In. Tell. Pro."

The syllables were meaningless, or had some deeper meaning they would never know. But, like the Barbarous Words of Power used by witches, they held power for those who had fashioned them, and for those who used them.

Carol just hoped that it, and the sigils she hoped and prayed to the Powers were correct, was going to be enough. Enough to topple whatever sick system of power had gripped the government.

Oh yeah. Jasmine had a talk with her about that, all right. Saying the government had always been gripped by evil, but folks like Carol just never had to notice before.

Carol couldn't say her friend was wrong. There was a lot she'd been unaware of her whole life.

She was tapping the map in front of her.

"Coe." At the north, with the sigil that looked like a column with a spider-legged sun in the middle.

"In." At the east. Its sigil was the crescent-topped pillar, with a disc at its core.

"Tell." In the south, the column with the sideways-canted N inside a circle.

"Pro." In the west, the Broken Tree. And flashing in her mind, she saw a snake slithering up the central column, rising from the roots.

"Pro," she said again.

"You figuring anything out?" Jasmine asked, tapping her long fingers on her green cords. "We need to be as clear as we can, or we might all end up dead, dig?"

Carol blew a blond strand of hair out of her face.

"It's as good as I've got right now. I don't know. The Archivist…" She paused. "The Archivist can't tell me more than they have. There's the 1-2-3-4 pattern that certainly relates to the map. But the Archivist also keeps showing me that 'cube is the key' thing."

"The cube is simply four in three dimensions," Rosalia said.

"Of course!" Carol said. Once the words were spoken, it was obvious. If she was feeling better, Carol would have jumped up.

It was all coming together, the syllables the brown spider had whispered in her ear, the visions, the sigils, the map…but Carol felt like she was still missing a vital component. And no way was she willing to do this working tonight if she couldn't grok it.

"So," she said, tucking a strand of stick-straight blond hair behind her ear, "I'm getting the dimensional stuff you're talking about. The cube. How the square or diamond shape rises on the planes. But I still don't understand how all this is going to work."

"What aren't you understanding?" Ernesto asked, before picking up some shelled walnuts and popping them into his mouth.

"I mean, I get it in theory. I get that Barbarous Words of Power put us in the proper state, connect us to whatever energies we're trying to call. But I'm just so used to knowing what I'm doing. And with these random syllables? I really don't."

Rosalia looked at her. "Did you know what you were doing when you ended up seeing that poor man, Lizard, in the garden surrounded by flames and snakes?"

"Well, no. But I also didn't try. Right? It just happened."

Ernesto sat, one arm thrown across the sofa back. His eyes were thoughtful behind his gold-rimmed glasses.

"That man, Lizard, somehow knew to connect to you," he said. "He knew you were an open channel and that's part of how this works. All the practice that Temple magicians do means that they become open channels to whatever it is they're trying to call. The syllables they repeat over and over again give them mastery of that particular channel."

"So it's not just *any* channel, it's tuning," Jasmine said. "Is that what you mean?"

"Yes, tuning. And that's what witches do. Magicians do. We even do it as sorcerers in our early training, when we focus on our particular element, right? We all had those chants and songs we sang."

"I thought that was just baby stuff," Carol said, "you know, like nursery rhymes. But magic."

"Well, they *were* nursery rhymes," Ernesto said, "but nursery rhymes designed to get you in touch with Earth. And Jasmine in touch with

Water and me in touch with Air. When Fire finally came forward for me, I had to learn the hard way because I wasn't already tuned."

Rosalia sat on the couch opposite Ernesto. She shook her hands with impatience, causing the bangles on her arms to clatter and spark.

"Sometimes you just have to *trust*," Rosalia said. "Sometimes you think too much, and I'm surprised at you. Carol, you should feel this in your body. You should *feel* how the syllables work. You should feel the resonance."

The hechicera looked around the little grouping. "And that is part of what we must do. We are *talking* too much instead of chanting." She smacked her hands together.

"We need to chant together and feel the resonance of each separate syllable in our chest cavities, and deep in our bellies."

"I heard about some Polish theater cat," Jasmine said, "who got his actors to resonate their speech all the way down to their thighs."

"That is right," Rosalia said. "That is good practice and that is something that you sorcerers would do well to take on."

"So. Should we practice?" Carol said.

"Sí," Rosalia replied.

Carol tried to sit up a little straighter in her chair, wincing a bit. Her shoulder still hurt like hell even though you could barely see the bullet scars anymore. She'd always have a mark there, the Earth sorcerers said, but not as badly as if they'd stitched her skin together. She crossed her legs underneath her, and took a breath.

"Okay, this feels weird."

"No weirder than any of the other preparations we have to do," Jasmine said. "I'm just worried we're running out of time to get this operation as correct as we can."

"Time spent tuning is never wasted," Ernesto said. "My first teachers taught me that."

"Okay, then. I've only ever done this in a whacked-out, tranced-out state, so I'll admit I'm a little nervous," Carol said.

"That is fine. Use the energy of your nerves to focus," Rosalia replied. "You should lead us."

"Cooooeee," Carol began, throat and belly tight.

"Stop!" Rosalia snapped. "*Feel* it first. Feel where it is in your body. Then begin the chant and call on the Elements. Call on your Sorcery to help you."

Carol closed her eyes. She listened to the crackling of the fire. She felt the wood heat and burst into flame. She felt the wood that made the structure of the chair, and the wooden floor beneath the chair, and the broad beams overhead. She felt her friends around her. Their flesh and bones.

Slowing her breathing down, she reached further, to the garden outside. The grass that was kept well-watered and trimmed, no matter what time of year it was. The manzanita copse. The birds, the squirrels, the blue jays scolding just outside the window.

And then she found a place down in the soles of her feet. A place of foundation that rose up to her root at the base of her spine. But yes, it began with a sense of the soles of her feet.

She intoned the syllable after taking in a deep breath.

"Cooooeeee. Cooooeeee." And the sound rose up into her belly.

"Innnnnnn." And the sound resonated and expanded, opening her chest. She could feel it resounding between her shoulder blades at her breast bone. She could feel her throat opening. And the sound rose up and filled her head.

"Proooooooooe."

She began the sequence over again—"Cooooooee"—then paused.

"Start with your feet," she said out loud. "Let the sounds resonate up through your body, like I just did."

And all of them joined her. Breathing deeply, she could feel the mix of their Elements in the room, and she could feel the strange, wild sorcery that Rosalia carried. A sorcery less structured, but even more powerful than any Association magic Carol had felt before.

Rosalia, she all of a sudden realized, was not a Quintessence like Terrance Sterling. She was not someone who took all the separate Elements, mastered them, and combined them. No. She started from the opposite end. Rosalia had all the elements *first*.

She was tapped directly to the Source, and the elements flowed out from that.

"Wow," Carol whispered. "Far out."

"Maga, you must lead us. Yes?" Rosalia said.

"Yes, sorry." Carol ran her left hand over her face, then took a grounding breath. "Sorry. So. Yes, start with the soles of your feet. Focus there. Call your Elements and, as I said, we'll let the syllables, these barbarous words, resonate all the way up."

They took a collective breath.

"Coooooeee. Innnn. Tellll. Prooooooe."

As the last O tapered out, Carol could feel it. Something was trying to form itself in the library. Something reached for her.

Slamming up a wall of Earth, she smacked it back.

"That caught something's attention," she said, feeling sweat beading down her back. She unwrapped herself from the blanket.

"It was bound to happen," Rosalia said. "They know we are coming anyway."

"So how do we keep them from attacking when we start to chant for real?" Carol asked.

Rosalia stood. "We build strong wards. We do all the work we know how to do. And we work inside the temple room here."

"Here?" Jasmine said. "Not at your shop? Isn't this place still compromised?

"Your magic is closer to this Temple magic they are using," Rosalia said. She began to pace from the couches to the bookcases, then turned to look out the huge, multipaned windows onto the garden. "I think your structures will be a better match, and we can build more resonance this way. And our theory is that we match the syllables to the squares. The big diamond shape. And that you, Carol, lead us in connecting them to the sigils."

"And when we do that"—the hechicera turned again—"we should be starting a process that they cannot unravel. And they cannot combat. Because it is their own process done by people who should not have an entry point."

"And when we get to the weak point?" Jasmine said.

"Then you know what to do," Rosalia said, holding Jasmine's gaze for three long breaths.

Carol's best friend looked both determined and slightly terrified. She knew Jasmine had the strength. She wasn't sure that Jasmine was one-hundred percent sure yet.

None of them were.

"Do or die," Carol said.

"Do or die," Jasmine replied.

CHAPTER FORTY
SNAKES AND SPIDERS

*T*he warehouse was gloomy, the way Samuels liked it. He actually would have preferred it to be darker. But the dirt-encrusted, multi-paned windows set high up on the grimy walls would have to do.

His operatives, the men he was training, the serpent bearers and snake men, stood around the big warehouse space in a ring. One man for each quarter, and the cross quarters as well.

They had been sparring again, practicing. Getting ready for what was to come. But he needed them to stand guard for this meeting. It was too important to leave to chance. Samuels felt it deep in his winding intestines: to do the magic required for his plan would require a man like this.

The man with the silver hair, and the sharp, expensive, bespoke suit. The suit was silver today, too, with the faint patterning of paler pinstripes. Set off by a royal blue tie with the Tree of Life tie tack.

A blue scarab faience ring gleamed from the man's right hand and sterling silver cufflinks winked from beneath the edges of his suit coat.

"Terrance Sterling," Samuels said. "Welcome to my office."

Sterling stood in a rectangle of light, peering around the space, mouth tight and brow slightly furrowed, before one of Samuel's operatives shut the big metal door behind him.

He adjusted his cuffs and sniffed.

"Please, come sit down," Samuels said, gesturing to the folding card table and the two rickety wooden chairs on either side.

The leather soles of Terrance Sterling's shoes sounded loud on the concrete floor as he walked towards Samuels.

Samuels could tell that his own dark glasses bothered the man. At this point, Samuels didn't care.

Besides, it was another thing he'd been taught by the Master himself, and by the Master's right-hand man and possible lover, Agent Tolson, the man who'd first recruited him to the secret magical group inside the FBI. They both were clear: you keep the upper hand. Throw your opponent off, however you can. Make your enemy into a friend, however you can.

Whatever means of manipulation you have at your disposal, you use them.

Dark glasses and a grimy, gritty warehouse were the tools he had at hand.

Terrance Sterling drew one of the chairs back from the table, unbuttoned his suit jacket, and sat. Only then did Samuels sit with him.

"Have you had time to think about my proposition?" Sterling said.

"Time enough to wonder what you're up to," Samuels replied. "And to decide that I must be what what you're up to."

Sterling frowned. "I don't understand."

"Well. I'm up to gaining power. I'm up to feathering my nest. I'm up to working magic. And I think you were doing that pretty well yourself for years, and what I wonder now is why you shifted course. And why you wanted to meet with me in the first place."

Samuels looked at the man across from him, clearly a man used to power and wealth. A man who had nevertheless allowed himself to become trapped inside the spider's web.

Samuels leaned across the table. "How did Hoover convince you?"

Hoover. The Master. The stinking, crooning, amphetamine-fueled, potato-faced man. The head of the Temple. The head of the secret operation that had been running the FBI for years.

Terrance Sterling grimaced. "It was a decision that seemed worth making," he said. "You know..." Then he smiled, a false, pasted-on, white-gleaming-toothed smile. "Use magic to serve the country. Be a patriot. Isn't that what you do?"

Samuels just shook his head and stared. Terrance Sterling was not going to take over this conversation.

Sterling stared right back. Used to playing the game.

Samuels snuck his right hand beneath the shoddy card table and sent out a little flicker of magic, a small snakelet from his silver ring, held focused on the man before him. The snake of energy slithered up underneath the cuffs of Terrance Sterling's fancy silver-gray trousers.

He watched as Terrance Sterling's eyes widened, and he watched as the man leapt up and started shaking out his left leg and then slapping at it. And then he watched as the man sent a blast of his own fire.

A yellow fire. Only one of the many Elemental powers Samuels knew the man had at his disposal.

Sterling zapped the thing that was crawling up his leg and stood, a crimson flush staining his face, glaring at Samuels who still sat, perfectly relaxed, across the table.

"I think you need to talk to me," Samuels said.

"I think you need to fuck off," Terrence Sterling replied.

"Tsk tsk. I didn't take you for a man who swore that way."

"I didn't take you for a man at all. Are you going to send those things at me again?" Sterling asked, tipping his hand.

"I'm not sure yet. Depends on what sort of answers you give me."

"You are threatening me? You're blackmailing me now? I thought you wanted to be partners."

"That was your idea, and I'm not opposed to it," Samuels replied. "But I also need you to know I'm still the one in charge. There can be only one master, and right now it has to be me." Sterling screwed up his mouth as if he was going to spit. "I thought you had a master. I thought you danced to Hoover's tune. Just like I was doing. What's all this about, anyway?"

Samuels was winning, just as he had planned.

He leaned across the table, staring into Terrance Sterling's eyes. Even though Sterling could not see Samuels' eyes behind the dark glasses, he was sure the man could feel the weight of his gaze.

"I want to take the Temple down. It's gone on long enough, this reign of terror. There needs to be change."

"Ha." *Terrance Sterling barked out a laugh.* "You joining the Black Panthers? Joining the hippies in the street shouting peace and kumbaya? I don't believe that for a minute."

"No," *Samuels said.* "Not peace. Not kumbaya. But real power. The sort of power you haven't even tasted yet. The sort of power the Master cannot know. The sort of power that only my magic and your sorcery combined can bring to the world."

"And what's in it for us? This"—*Sterling's fingers made scare quotes in the air*—"increased power. This partnership. This joining. What's in it for us?"

"What's in it for us is that we change the world to one of our own making. And we use our magic to make ourselves the richest and most powerful men in the world. And we use our magic to run whole countries, not just scraps of them."

Samuels stood then, shoving the wooden chair back so hard it clattered to the concrete floor. He felt his men shift, ready to move at his word.

"Not just petty associations and secret societies and branches of faltering governments who can't get their heads out of their lily-white asses. Or even win the simplest fucking war."

He wiped his face and held out his hands, gesturing as though, instead of in a rundown warehouse, they stood on a promontory looking out over a vast land.

"We're going to be kings," *Samuels said.* "Oligarchs ruling over the masters, ruling over the masses…and they won't even know it. It will be a land of plenty and ease. They will have distractions unthought of before now. And we will provide it all."

"How?" *Sterling asked.*

Samuels just looked at him for a moment, then spoke so quietly Terrance Sterling had to lean in just to hear his voice.

"By making magic whole again. By joining what was sundered out of hubris and shortsightedness. We will build what Solomon himself failed to build."

Samuels snapped his fingers.

"Men," he said. The eight operatives stepped forward.

Samuels snapped his fingers a second time, and serpents shot out from the men's hands, forming a web. A tangle. A mighty weaving of power, of magic. Sigils flared all around them, and a temple was built, appearing from nowhere, shining. Beautiful.

This was not the Temple of the FBI, but a new temple. A temple with shining columns filled with sunlight. A temple with pools of deepest shadow. A temple built on *power,* with *power,* for *power.*

A temple with plenty for all, if they agreed to benevolent rule—and the slight curtailing of their will.

"This is ours," he said to Sterling. "If you add your Elements, it will become complete. And the powerful shall inherit the earth. But not only the earth. The rich shall inherit all the planes of existence and we will rebuild the world in our own image. Light and dark, Terrance Sterling. Light and dark together means power."

"We'll work together?" Sterling asked.

Still standing in the middle of his vision, Samuels gave a sharp nod. If he couldn't convince Jasmine Jones, this man would do. He wasn't as powerful a sorcerer, but perhaps that would be a good thing after all.

Samuels held out his right hand.

"Are you in?"

CHAPTER FORTY-ONE
DOREEN

Doreen, Patrice, and Drake were in charge of focusing the energy of all the other people who would be feeding the operation that night.

It was Christmas Eve. Everyone was bundled up against the dark and cold December air, out at Lake Merritt again. The air smelled of lake water and the hot chocolate some of the families had brought in thermoses they were passing around, along with cardboard cups. Doreen heard her lover, Patrice, laughing at something in the middle of the growing crowd.

It was a serious night, but that didn't mean hot chocolate and laughter weren't also called for. Dark winter nights needed whatever lightness and warmth people could bring.

Looking at the lights that encircled the lake and reflected on the quietly lapping water, Doreen felt a sudden peace sweep through her.

She knew this was the right thing. It didn't matter how it ended up. Whether they were successful or not. Sure, she feared for Jasmine and Cecelia and the others, but even that fear felt okay to her.

This action felt destined. Her soul needed to do this. All of her work, and even the years she spent in avoidance, all led up to this moment. Now.

She looked out at the faces gathered, breath steaming into the night. The Black Panthers. The Brown Berets. A few of the radical Asian folks who called themselves the Yellow Peril. Some members of the American Indian Movement were there. The Free Speech folks had come back, too. And the hippies. The working people of all races…

They'd invited the Chochenyo Ohlone, the first peoples of this land, to come and bless the gathering before they started. About five of them had shown up, rattles and drums in hand.

The original peoples occupied a place of honor. Doreen was glad of that too. It was good to see the way the people accorded the Ohlone proper respect. The first nations didn't often get that, she knew.

Before they started the main working, which Doreen was going to time on her watch as best as she could, trying to synch with the magic in Los Angeles and throughout the country, Drake had asked to do a ceremony for Bobby Hutton as a reminder of what they were fighting for.

Lil' Bobby was the first official member of the Black Panther Party, and its treasurer. He joined at age sixteen, had been part of the infamous event at the state capitol when Panthers entered the state assembly, fully armed, to protest having their guns taken away, saying they needed to be armed against the violence of the police against their communities.

Bobby was seventeen when he was shot dead by Oakland Police.

Huey and the other Panthers agreed immediately to this tribute. Two of them had even built a half-scale casket.

Tanya and the kids had painted it black and then drawn swirling flowers on the lid. People were gathered right now, dripping wax onto the outside edges of the casket lid and ringing it with burning candles.

"Are you ready?" Doreen asked Drake.

His dark eyes shone up at her.

"Yeah," he said, "I'm ready." Then he reached out and squeezed her hand. "Thank you, Mrs. Doreen."

She just nodded. Enough had already been said. She and Drake read each other's hearts now, connected by the initiation, connected by the power that flowed through all things.

"Go on, now," Doreen said.

Drake stepped toward the coffin and looked at the people holding candles nearby. He cleared his throat. Widened his stance. He even took his hands out of the pockets of his corduroy jacket.

"Little Bobby was killed in the line of duty. He was killed by the Oakland Police, trying to protect us. Trying to protect his community, his family. All of us. He tried to protect Oakland."

Drake cleared his throat again. Doreen could feel his nerves and his excitement, and underneath it all, a current of resolve. Tears pricked the back of her eyes. He was so young. So brave.

"There's bad people out there trying to take all of us down," Drake continued. "We know that. We see it every day. But you've been told now that it's even worse than we thought. Because they're using magic against us and who knows what else? And tonight we're going to try to end that. And we don't know if we'll succeed."

His voice caught a bit at that.

"Go on, now!" a man's voice called toward him.

Drake nodded.

"So. I couldn't let us do this without calling on Bobby. Without calling on the spirit of what we're fighting for. So Bobby"—he turned to the casket—"we remember you. At sixteen years old, you knew what was right. You inspired me, brother. You made me want to stand here today and *do* something. I think you've inspired us all. And we send you off, onto the lake. We ask that your spirit guide us tonight if it can. Mrs. Doreen tells us you're one of our ancestors now. And we know the ancestors bless the people. And so if you can hear us, we're going to ask you now: help us. Show us the way."

Four Black Panthers picked up the coffin and hoisted it on their shoulders. They walked the few yards to the lake's edge and then very carefully lowered it down into the water, where it splashed and tipped before righting itself again. The candles flickered, then grew steady again.

The men pushed it out. Every face was turned to watch as it floated toward the center of the lake. A bright outline of light and death. Purpose and sorrow.

"All power to the people," Huey Newton said.

Doreen felt the land itself respond to his voice.

"All power to the people!" the crowd shouted back.

"The revolution has always been in the hands of the young. The young always inherit the revolution," Huey said, then placed a hand on Drake's shoulder. "This young brother is one of the leaders of this revolution, just like Lil' Bobby was. I've said before that Black Power is giving power to people who have not had power to determine their destiny. Well, tonight, all of us—black, brown, Indian, Chinese, Japanese, Mexican, white—we get a chance to determine destiny for our communities. Drake, Doreen, and Patrice are going to show us how."

Doreen stepped forward. "Thank you all for coming. Many of you were here for the blessing last night. Others of you have been training with Drake and Patrice. Well, Drake is right, we are up against something more terrible than I've seen in my life, and that includes my husband being killed by Los Angeles County sheriffs."

People were silent, the candle flames flickering on their faces. An sense of expectancy filled the air, as though there were coiled springs inside every man, woman, and child.

"My colleagues are getting ready right now to do some powerful magic, a sorcery that has a chance to set us free." Doreen looked around at as many faces as she could see.

"There are never any guarantees. But we're going to give it our all." She smiled then. "And enough stalling from me. Take in a deep breath."

Doreen felt the crowd and their staggered inhalations. She needed to get them in synch.

"Now exhale. And when I count to three, I want us all to inhale together, right? 1. 2. 3. Inhale."

There was a collective inhalation. "Now hold that breath, 2, 3, 4. Then exhale 2, 3, 4. Inhale 2, 3, 4."

Some of the people in the crowd struggled with the pattern at first, but there came a moment in that cold December night where a mighty *shift* occurred. A deepening.

The crowd became one being.

"Feel your friends and family and community around you. Feel the cold air, smell the lake water and hear it lapping against the concrete. Feel the warmth inside you and from the candle flames. And feel what brought you here tonight. Keep breathing."

The people were so alive, and it felt beautiful. *This* was what the world could be like, if only they had a chance to continue.

"Imagine you have a center, just beneath your navel. Breathe and drop your attention there. Now imagine a circle of brothers and sisters getting ready to work magic. Hold that circle in your heart and mind. Keep inhaling this good night air, and as you exhale, imagine your breath, and the candles, and the lake, feeding energy toward them for their working."

The energy was so thick it was palpable. Doreen could almost taste it on her tongue.

It tasted of oranges. Fresh mint. And hope.

It was the taste of possibility.

CHAPTER FORTY-TWO
JASMINE

The temple was warded. We were all in place.

My spear was in my hand, and I felt powerful like I hadn't for a long time. As a matter of fact, I didn't know that I'd ever felt this powerful.

It was a new kind of power. More integrated. And yeah, that damn snake was still connected to me, but I didn't care anymore. I was going to use that to my advantage, like Rosalia told me to.

That Fed thought he was going to work with me. Well, he had a lesson coming and so did that bastard Hoover, wherever he was. He was going down. I rotated my head on my neck and rolled my shoulders. Shook out my feet. Took a breath.

Then I smiled at my mother. She looked beautiful in a simple, green, floor-length tunic topped by a large ankh necklace. She smiled back. I could almost feel the squeeze of her hand in mine from where she was working with Ernesto, gathering some supplies across the room. I felt her reassurance, a sense that she believed in me.

That was good. She and I had been at odds the past few days and I didn't like it.

We all wore long robes tonight. Not our usual. But Rosalia had said that anything that would bring us into resonance with the twisted version of Solomonic Temple magic we faced was going to help. So we agreed.

I wore a blue dashiki, the closest I was going to get to a robe. Ernesto was in orange, the blending of Air and Fire. Carol wore a green djellaba and Rosalia had on a deep purple velvet robe that fell down to her brown feet, which were encircled by silver anklets that tinkled with bells that echoed the clattering sound of the silver bangles around her wrists.

Gregory Oluo was in a goldenrod floor-length Egyptian caftan embroidered with gold thread around the throat.

Even my father was here, which still surprised me. But he had insisted on it. *If my family goes to war,* he said, *I intend to be with them.* Rosalia said he would make a good anchor for us. A still place, a solid place if anyone ran into trouble or needed help.

My father was just wrapped in a black bathrobe over his clothes. *That's as good as it gets for me,* he said. He sat in a corner, and the rest of us took up our places near the elements we were going to represent.

We had taped out a big diamond on the hardwood temple floor with the boxes at each corner. Carol had drawn each sigil on a piece of paper. Ernesto was setting them inside the boxes right now, getting ready. They would focus us, making sure we were clear. We needed to hold the same image in our mind before the working.

My mother followed him, setting lighted jar candles at the top edge of each paper. The colors of the candles corresponded to the Elements at each quadrant. Another focus for our magic. We had to see things as closely together as we could for a working of this magnitude.

Clarity was important in Temple magic, I was finding. It was important in sorcery, too, but sorcery was mostly instinct. Solomonic magic was more structured, even the twisted shit these cats were playing with. You had to have a structure in order to pervert it, I guess.

You had to know what you were doing to bend things to your own ends.

Kind of like that dude Picasso. In one of my college classes, I was shocked to see he could do the most lifelike, beautiful drawings in the world. That was what gave him the freedom to draw the truth.

And that's what we were after. We were going to draw the truth.

"Are you ready, hechicera?" Rosalia said.

"I am." I grinned at her, feeling a little wild.

Carol sat in a chair in the north, still too weak to stand for more than a minute or two. My mother kissed my father and walked to the taped pattern to stand in front of her, ready to take up the calling of Earth.

Ernesto was in the south. Gregory Oluo was in the east. I was in the west, next to that Powers-damned broken tree sigil in its small square. This was the place in the pattern where things twisted and bent. The place I was going to have to slide in to and do the work.

And hope the Element held while I did so. The plan was that I would charge up my crystal tip and leave it on the floor once the circle of the Elemental Powers was set. Hopefully it would be enough.

The spear would travel with me.

And Rosalia? She stood everywhere and nowhere.

I was sure I could already feel her rising on the astral planes, walking through the æthers, gathering information. Finding the clearest path between here and the Temple in DC.

"I need to visualize those rivers again," I said to Carol. "Can you describe for us where they are on the map?"

Carol closed her eyes for a moment, then opened them again. Her blue eyes were shining. Despite still being too pale, she looked strong.

"The Potomac flows from the northwest. The western corner is broken off, using the river as a boundary. The Anacostia flows from the northeast. They join in the big Y shape near the low center of the diamond pattern, and flow together down, directly south."

"And the buildings?" I asked.

"The Pentagon is just to the southwest of the joining, in the broken-off section. That's got to be significant somehow. Because of the broken pattern, it's officially in Virginia, not DC."

"And the obelisk?"

"The fulcrum—the Washington Monument—is just above the V where the rivers meet. That great Y. And in a straight line from there is our target. The FBI."

Okay. I could see it all, and more importantly, I felt it the pattern in my bones, and felt those rivers running through my spit and blood.

"It's all our target, isn't it?" Ernesto said. "The whole pattern."

"Yeah," I replied. "We still don't know exactly what's going on, and Terrance Sterling sure as hell had some connection to the Pentagon as well as the FBI. I fried that pentagon-shaped lapel pin when I knocked him down. Besides, they're all in it together, and we know that. Vietnam and the war at home. That's what we're fighting for. For the people everywhere."

I banged the spear on the wooden floor three times. The sound cracked through the temple room space.

"Let's start this."

No time like the present.

Carol started the pattern, rocking forward and back in the wooden chair. "One!" Pause. "Two!" Pause. "Three!" Pause. Four!"

The Element holders at each corner were to match the beat, weaving their strands in on each number, forming a strong rope built layer by layer. That was just the foundation. Making sure we all worked in synchrony.

I hoped Carol didn't hurt herself. The rocking couldn't have been good for her wounds, but sorcery worked through us all in its own way. We couldn't always choose.

My own shoulder, on the opposite side of the body from hers, pinged in sympathy. It was so weird that we both ended up with shoulder injuries, one of us from a snake, the other from two bullets fired through glass.

I took up the beat, smashing the butt of my spear on the hardwood floor.

Carol changed rhythm, moving faster.

"Call your Element," she said.

Every sorcerer in the room had already called their Elements forward. The space was teeming with power. But she wanted us to say their Names out loud.

"Breath of the World!" Mr. Oluo said.

"Flame of the Heart!" Ernesto shouted.

"River of Understanding," I said.

"Power of Earth Made Whole," my mother replied.

"We weave the Powers, round and round. Encircling our bodies, minds, and souls," Rosalia chanted. "We weave the sorcery of righteous death and vital life. We weave the Powers ancient and reborn!"

"Air!"

"Fire!"

"Water!"

"Earth!"

"All!"

The chant went on and on, until my body shook with it. Gripping the spear shaft, I slammed it as hard as I could onto the floor. Every molecule inside me waited for the moment that would come, I knew not when.

But I was ready.

And then, Rosalia gave a mighty yell and flung our spirits toward the sky.

Wrenched out of my body, I clutched the spear for dear life as I flew upward through the veils. The misty, cloudlike æthers. Then a bright violet swirl.

I was descending then, into a place built of shades of amber. A place of structure.

A temple—their Temple. The one I'd seen before, but grander, larger, more substantial then the one I'd encountered down on the misty plane.

It was recognizable, but barely.

Rosalia had brought us here, by sheer force of her will. She was the only one who knew the way. The only one trained enough to see beyond the veils that a sorcerer like me was used to.

Someday, I would ask her to teach me what she knew. If the revolution ever gave me time.

The air was filled with swirls of golden amber, from rich yellow to umber.

The butt of my spear rang every time it struck what looked like a pale, veined marble floor.

"They must have been working on this place for years," I said.

"Decades," Rosalia replied at my side.

"Why is no one here?" I asked.

Besides my mother, Mr. Oluo, Carol, and Ernesto, no one was here. My father must have been anchoring us only from the temple room in the Mansion. That made sense, I guessed. Bringing him onto the astral would have compromised his safety. It was better that he kept watch over our physical bodies down below.

Rosalia smiled at me. The look on her face was a little scary. "They don't know we're coming yet. They would have expected us last night, or on the Solstice. When we didn't strike then, they must have thought we were not coming. Tontos."

I didn't know what tontos meant, but it didn't sound like a compliment.

CHAPTER FORTY-THREE
CAROL

The sorcery moved through Carol in a way she'd never felt. The constraints of her body were an irritation she fought to ignore.

She wanted nothing more than to be powerful now. She was done with all the ways she had been before. Too careful. Too obedient. Too unquestioning.

She was a sorcerer and Seer both now. She would be reckoned with.

Inhaling, she started deep in her belly, and allowed the air to fill her lungs. She held that breath until blood beat in her ears. Then a slow release. An opening.

And she started the pattern all over again, matching the 1, 2, 3, 4 of the Elements, of the pattern the Archivist showed her, of the four rising on the planes, forming a cube.

A cube with a square on each corner. No. Not a square. A smaller cube.

"Eight small cubes form one large cube. One Temple rises on the planes. What are they building there?"

She tried to feel the resonance between the magic they built between them in the Mansion's temple room and the Solomonic Temple she had encountered.

And from there, she tried to sense the pattern over Washington DC. Layer upon layer upon layer, from earth to sky, they built their magic. Layer upon layer. Built from the power of mind, and no small amount of blood, she guessed.

The blood of the villagers and the soldiers in Vietnam. The blood of black boys spilled on the streets of Oakland, Chicago, and LA. The taste of parents' tears.

And the earlier pattern, laid over the original powers of that place. The blood of slaves. The cries of the first peoples. The wives, and mothers, and daughters, all kept in their places. The rapes, the beatings, the deaths.

And a vision of balanced beauty. A structure that would hold an ideal of freedom, built upon it all.

Eyes rolled back inside her head, Carol could See it all so clearly now, the patterns that had formed themselves for years.

But she could not force others to See them. Not yet. Perhaps that would come in time.

The Powers themselves slammed against her consciousness, cracking her open until nothing was left. Nothing but sorcery. Nothing but movement, and the taste of candle wax and mountain earth. Nothing but darkness and light.

With a mighty pull, Carol's astral form shot up through the planes of existence, the mystic realms, the place where all things entered consciousness and were given form.

A temple of amber waited. Setting her soul down lightly on the marble floor, she realized, for the first time in her life, her soul was free.

And this freedom was what she had been born for. The freedom to help others free themselves.

Her mouth struggled to form the proper shape to speak the words she knew were necessary here. Her consciousness was too overloaded with a sense of *everything* to make one word.

She tried again, moving tongue and lips in such a way to make a sound. "Ahh…maaaa."

Primordial sounds. But not the sounds she needed. Where was the focus from the temple she had left below? The taped corners and the sigils.

The sigils, yes. Where were they here? They could help her. Help her remember what she was here to do.

Mighty amber pillars rose from the marble floor toward…what? A murky, shifting, swirling space of shapes forming and un-forming that confused her.

Okay. Carol was coming back to herself. Calling on Earth, she fought to regain stability.

"I need to be here. Help me."

She remembered, then, what Rosalia had said about not thinking. How could she feel this space without a body? Her body felt so far away.

"You're a sorcerer, dammit. Figure it out."

The others had taken up their positions around the temple space. Carol could sense their Air, Fire, and Water.

If she could sense that, she could sense her body, no matter where it was. And if she could sense her body, she could feel this space.

What did it feel like in her body? She breathed on this astral plane, feeling her physical body breathing down below.

"Fortitude," she whispered. "And leadership."

She tasted the sigil inside her.

Dominion, a voice not her own rang out, tolling like the giant astral bell.

Like the Tarot cards from Mrs. Chisolm's class on magical divination. Dominion was the two of wands, staves crossed, fire meeting fire.

Or two temple pillars, crossing, one against the other, as they built and formed the cubes upon each plane.

The particular twisted nature of this Temple. Not Solomon's temple. A temple that aped the structures of magicians long ago.

A temple built upon dominion, in itself a crushing weight upon the world. The four-patterned diamond laid out on native land. Land that had once been sovereign, complete unto itself, now crushed beneath a temple made by men who thought to impose structure. Men who had followed after the slaughterers. The very men and women who had enslaved, and raped, and tortured.

Structures built on the hopeful ideals of some, and the bones and blood of others.

But what she felt now was even worse to her. More than dominion, more than rule, more than hegemony or mastery, this was...

"Pure domination, with none of the trappings of politeness anymore," Carol murmured.

She took in a heaving breath, filling herself with her own power. Maybe it wasn't worse, she realized. Maybe it was more of the same, only now she could See and feel it.

Filled with sudden fury, Carol shouted, voice filling up the Temple space. "Domination!" she shouted. "We challenge you! Be here now!"

Something cracked then, piercing the space with sound, like lightning cracked the sky in the Minnesota summers of her childhood. Carol stumbled and fell, just for an instant.

"They're coming! Soon!" she yelled at her companions. "We have to start!"

She reached for Gregory Oluo, and felt him reach for Ernesto, then Jasmine. The connection from Jasmine back to Cecelia was weak and strange, that twisted feeling Jasmine had described. If Carol had been in a physical body, the vertigo of it might have made her puke.

How Jasmine was going to walk that twisted road, she didn't know. She just hoped her best friend had the fortitude in this place to do it. And the ability to remain herself in the process.

Wasn't that what every one of them faced right now? They could lose themselves in sorcery at any moment.

Just like Terrance Sterling had.

No time for thought. Just action. No time for words. Just deeds.

The power of Earth poured through her, increasing in substance with each round of the mighty circle.

"Square the circle!" Carol cried out, and felt as the sorcerers shifted their usual pattern, keeping the circle shape and adding an inner flow, the flow that traced the edges of this Temple exactly.

And there was another circle there, Carol could taste it now, riding on car exhaust and electricity; in this space it was like a flow of diamonds, ripped out from the belly of the earth.

She could no longer tell what was natural or not. She could no longer sense what was real.

As the energies built around her, she saw the sigils flare upon the Temple pillars. The column in front of her, with the spidery sun. The crescent topped pillar, with the disc at its core. The sideways canted N. The broken tree.

She felt a slight ping in the blue glass bead on the leather thong around her wrist. Her protection.

Then she looked up. Symbols flashed and moved in the murky sky. One thousand iterations of the sigils slammed toward one another and broke apart again.

"What does it take to form the whole?" she asked.

And then she knew.

The Archivist was right.

Everything rising up and down was a possible key.

CHAPTER FORTY-FOUR
JASMINE

With a giant cracking sound, the energies were flying. Sigils flared on the pillars and every hair on my body stood on end.

The Temple had activated itself, or Carol had done it somehow, and I wasn't sure it was happy about it.

Sorcery poured from Gregory Oluo to Ernesto, to me, and on to my mother. Around and around it went, sigils crackling on the pillars with every pass.

Rosalia was moving rapidly toward me, heading from the southern pillar to where I stood in the west.

"You must *See*," the hechicera said, and whacked my forehead with one bony finger.

My astral body shot further upward, floating over the Temple. And I saw it all.

Don't panic.

The Temple. The stream of red and white lights. The great pillars. The mighty Potomac, kissing the slender Anacostia, forming a cradle of power, then flowing together as one.

The Pentagon, which from this place on the æthers looked like a churning, bristling mass of sharp edges, clacking and clashing. The FBI was a cypher. A black hole. No. Not even black. Gray. As if it were nothing. Hard to look at if you weren't training your eyes along that straight edge from the Pentagon, through the obelisk, and on into the FBI, which looked like an upside-down Master lock.

"The cube is the key," I whispered to myself. That was what the Archivist had told Carol.

This whole thing. The temple that had to be working below on the earth plane, this Temple here…formed together, this was the whole that was the key to whatever sick magic the FBI had wrought.

"Okay. Time to get to work, Jasmine Jones," I said. I just hoped this knowledge would actually help me with whatever the heck it was I still needed to do.

Sorcery was thick in the æthers. Rosalia was doing something in the center of the Temple floor. She was braver than I was, heading directly into the eye of the storm like that. But I had no time to think. I had to do.

The power of Water filled me to my edges, then spilled out everywhere. I directed it along the twisting stream of magic in front of me.

My mother's face was a mask of concentration as she caught the braided sorcery, added Earth, and passed it back to Gregory Oluo.

There was actually no differentiating the Elements now. The space almost shook with them, causing the Temple to spark and shake. Carol rocked back and forth, then side to side, still setting the rhythm of it all. Her hands outstretched as though she could feel the sigils on the pillars with her fingertips.

Rosalia whirled in the center of it all, a maelstrom herself, skirts flying, bangles flashing. Her citrine eyes were trained on whatever magic formed itself above.

"Here I go," I said to myself, and took a breath, because even without a physical body, the molecules of my spirit knew what breath meant and responded just the same.

Moving forward, toward my mother in the north, I slid and then flipped. Everything lurched and gave a half turn sideways. Then another. It was like walking on a Möbius strip, or one of those freaky Escher stairways. Up was down and down was up and I couldn't tell when or how it changed.

And coming toward me was that Powers-damned snake of a Fed, fool grin on his face, walking easy, as if there was nothing to it.

I wished I had my crystal, then remembered the Ancestor's spear. It flew into my hand on the thought. I steadied myself with it for a moment, then leveled it at the man.

"Stop right there," I said.

The spear tip glowed blue with oceanic sorcery and the shaft thrummed in my right hand. It felt good. And all of a sudden, I knew some people had my back. Through the power of the spear, I could feel the power of the ancestors. And the power of the people.

"I told you we should work together," he said.

The spear in my hands wanted to strike this man who had injured me. This man who had done untold damage to how many of my comrades and friends. I forced myself to stay. To hold. To not slice his head off.

He just stared at me. For the first time, the black glasses weren't covering his eyes. That cold blue gaze speared me like the metal tip of the weapon I held in my hands.

"Get. Out. Of. My. Way." I said.

He held up his hands. "I'm not here to fight you, Jasmine Jones. I'm still only here to offer you a treaty. I'm here to offer you help."

"You sure are persistent when a woman tells you no. What makes you think I need your help?"

"I know the way in," he said.

Shit. That tasted right. Those words had the ring of truth to them.

Balancing on that slender slice of a Möbius strip, I kept getting the feeling with that "cube is the key" business that we were still missing something. There was still an element we didn't have a hold of. We'd gone into this battle with one hand tied behind our back because we had to. Because that was the way things always were.

The odds were always stacked against us, and here was this man standing in front of me—Samuels, he had told me his name was, fitting name for a snake like him. He was offering to actually help, and for once, I believed him.

"What's the cost?" I asked.

"No cost," he replied. "We both get what we want, and I'll be satisfied."

Well, that I *didn't* believe. A man like him was never satisfied with anything, that was for sure.

"Show me," I said. The only way out was through. That wasn't any Sun Tzu, or Frantz Fanon either, but it was true enough.

The Möbius strip flipped again, causing my stomach to lurch. I clutched tight to the spear, not about to let go. Samuels held out a hand. No way. I wasn't going to take that. I'd hold my own hand. Thank you.

Lurching along this strange ribbon that wove between various planes of existence, I saw images rush by me, too quick to hold on to. Too quick to really see.

But I could feel them. I could taste them. The taste of sunshine. Of cordite. Of Earth. The taste and tang of bloodshed and long-running wars. The scent of napalm. Gasoline. Flowers, spring, and Queen Helene's cocoa butter. The taste of Jimmy's lips.

And then we entered darkness.

Shit. Panic rose inside my belly. I held on to the spear. The steel whispered at me, *Warrior*. Right. A reminder. I was here to do a job. This wasn't about me.

Shapes slowly emerged as my eyes adjusted to the darkness.

"It's another temple," I whispered. I looked up, and there above me was the grid. That map of Washington DC. It was the city itself, but seen from underneath. That flow of red and white lights were the cars driving the beltway. The Temple pillars rose up through the cornerstones set by the Masons two hundred years before. They reached all the way down here, to whatever this dark under-temple was.

Along with the square stones at each corner of the diamond, I sensed more, all along the lines, linking the original Temple magic, stone by stone. There had to be more than thirty—thirty-six?—though some of them felt like ghosts of the original magic. Not quite solid.

Damn. If that boundary of thirty-six was broken, no wonder the magic I was standing in had twisted in upon itself. All it would have taken was the slightest nudge, and the intentions of the pattern would begin to mutate, shifting into whatever sickness I was facing.

I sent my attention upward, all the way up to the astral temple, and could feel my friends still pumping out the Elemental forces. Doing their sorcery, ready for battle.

The battle I now had to fight alone.

A strange crooning filled the space around me. I could feel the hairs on my physical body, way down on the earth plane, stand on end.

My mouth filled with saliva, the animal part of me wanting to panic.

"Warrior," I said, and took a deep breath, both to soothe that animal part down and as a promise to the rest of me that we had this. The Ancestor's spear warmed in my hands.

And then I saw him. A strange, pasty-faced man with a potato nose, sweat streaming down his body, staining his white robes a sickly yellow. A face I'd only seen on Aunt Doreen's black-and-white television screen.

J. Edgar Hoover. The man behind it all.

The man I was now convinced had tried to assassinate my friends, attempting to murder them in their sleep. The man who had bombed the Brown Beret's headquarters, and destroyed 41st and Central, who had shot up Fred and Deborah's apartment, who had aimed for Geronimo Pratt's bed, who had called for raids and beatings, who had put my friends in jail and prison.

I heard a panther roaring, busting itself free, slashing at guards, breaking through the bars.

It's time, I thought. *Almost time,* I amended.

There was still a thread I was missing. Much as I wanted to run into that space and stab that wicked man through his still barely human, beating heart, I made myself stay. Feel the Water. Feel the power of these temples.

Whether I agreed with it or not, these magicians had built something here. This twisted magic, a massive working that almost made me sick. It was not designed for folks like me.

What was I missing? What was it? *Feel, Jasmine Jones.*

Feel. Sense. I took another breath and opened my awareness further, broadening it 360 degrees around me, letting my edges sense what it was I needed to know.

There. All the sickly threads that powered the temples, all the way up and all the way down...

The cube that was the key. The key. This cube that was the key...

Well. The one who held the key had become the key itself. Magic always changed the magician. Sorcery always altered the sorcerer. And that stinking, sweating, white-robed man in front of me, crooning his evil croons that sounded an awful lot like the syllables Carol had brought through the æthers?

He was the bloated white spider, tied into this web so tight, it fed on him as much as he fed on it. He was the one who had infected Terrance Sterling and breached our Association wards.

And then I sensed it. This web, these temples, these threads of twisted sorcery and magic? They were the only things keeping him alive.

A sharp scent hit me. Amphetamines. I'd smelled them often enough from some of the white hippies who should have known better, but didn't. Stealing hoarded pills from their mother's bedside stash. Shaking, and grinding their teeth in the parks.

Hoover was an addict, I realized. Good. That was another weakness in this system.

So what I needed to do was take him down.

The spear leapt in my hands. That was the right answer.

I would take him down.

If I took down the web of magic holding the temples together, I took him down. If I took him down, the temples would fall.

"So what's the proper way?" I whispered.

I realized I didn't see Samuels anymore. He had disappeared. Brought me here and left.

There wasn't time to think about it. I just needed to act.

"Tell me what to do," I asked the spear. Blue fire flared, and suddenly my arm was lifting, my hand reaching back behind my shoulder. The wooden shaft thrummed with power in my palm.

And, staring at that white-robed man, that shaking, stinking magician, I cast.

And he turned, suddenly aware of the sorcery hurtling through the air, hands scrabbling to form sigils, mouth working to speak the words of power.

I had cast true. The spear pierced his chest, just to the left of his breastbone, exiting between his shoulder blades. I felt when it passed through his heart.

The blue of my ocean fire sparked outward. Hoover's eyes were open wide and his white-robed body whipped into the air in a rictus, arching backwards, caught in his own web. A golden-green electricity shot from his hands and feet and spat from the crown of his head.

He was being electrocuted by the temple of his own making. By his own magic. The web couldn't hold anymore. Sparks flew everywhere. A great rumbling started.

Hoover spasmed, body jerking as the magic jolted through him. With a rush, I felt the Temple walls collapse around me. I felt the pillars shaking as they slowly turned to astral dust from the inside out. I heard the cracking of old cornerstones.

A sharp tug, and pain lanced the hollow of my left shoulder. I jerked, and the spear fell from my hands.

Rushing back along the silver cord that tethered my spirit to my body, I heard the ancestors in my head.

It sounded as if they were laughing. It was a joyous sound.

Considering it had been their spear that did the evil bastard in, that laughter made me feel just fine.

CHAPTER FORTY-FIVE
DOREEN

The people felt alive, gathered in concentric circles by the lake, burning candles in their hands.

The whole *park* felt alive. The night herons clustered around them, their hunch-shouldered bodies encircling the human crowd.

Doreen had never seen anything like it. She'd never felt anything like it, either, birds responding in that way.

Patrice, Drake, and Tanya had interspersed themselves in the crowd, standing at the compass points. The children and teens they'd been training stood between them, linking their magic to the rest of the crowd. Doreen stood in the south. Her own hands held no candle; she wanted to be free to shape the energy as it rose.

The crowd was tuned together, breathing as one, eyes open to the candles and the night. Two of the Ohlone had brought drums to the gathering, and kept a steady beat in the center of the circles.

Then the rattles joined in.

There was a collective breath. The mass of people focused on one aim: to send magic to the sorcerers working for the people.

The air was thick with magic and intention. It was better than making love. Almost, Doreen smiled. But it was *like* that. That sense of union. That sense of slow-building power. She could see colors weaving through the crowd from her mind's eye. The little sparks of soul from every person gathered here, rising up, forming a web of connection and community.

It was so beautiful. Doreen felt like she was in love. She took a mighty breath in and began to tone from deep in her belly, letting the sound resonate down and up, filling her body with its power.

The people around her took up the toning. Every lung filled, every voice raised itself, and the power built and rose and fell again, and built and rose and fell again, cresting like mighty waves seeking a shore.

It grew and built, grew and built, pressing against the protective sphere she, Patrice, Drake, and Tanya had set up around the gathering.

The night herons began to circumambulate the crowd, walking stiff-legged around them. She felt Patrice and Drake lift their arms and she lifted hers. And every person lifted their arms, raising their hands to the night sky.

She reached with her awareness and felt the other groups gathered, doing the same working. Los Angeles. Chicago. Atlanta. Philadelphia. New York. Cleveland. New Orleans. Dar es Salaam.

Doreen took hold of those streams of power and added them to the rising magic of the crowd around her. She wove it all into her sorcery, building a cone that would funnel the energies up to Jasmine and the rest.

She wove and shaped the energies, her hands touching the edges of the rising power as they built a mighty cone of sound and light.

The chanting tone grew louder. And the chanting was the power of the grass. And the candles and the lake. And Bobby Hutton's casket, floating behind them. And every ancestor that stood with every person present there. And the opossums scuttling on their way, and the night herons doing their dance. And every animal sleeping in the hollows of the park.

And the power built, and it built, and built... all those rainbow sparks above every head. All that sound, all that...every breath from every lung. Every person present there and far away, all one purpose, all one aim, now one being.

One being. One being.

And the tone grew louder still, and shifted upwards, rising, rising, rising to the sky. And her own power, her sorcery, felt as though it would burst out from the palms of her hands and from her fingertips. Scent of cinnamon rising, she let it flow. Doreen let her fire spark and move, resonating with the magic of the crowd. Amplifying it.

"Magic for the people," she whispered into the toning vortex. "Magic for the people."

Other voices near her picked up the phrase.

"Magic for the people. Magic for the people."

Someone started stomping their feet to the beat of the drums. Soon everyone was stomping, dancing, moving in a great, clockwise circle, arms raised up to the sky.

"Magic for the *peo*-ple! Magic for the *peo*-ple! *Magic! Magic! Magic! Magic!* Life! Life! Life!"

And the words wove and changed, point and counterpoint, and then turned into wordless shouting. The crowd roared to the night.

And then the energy crested and cascaded, raining back down around them like a fountain. The energy they had raised blessed each person as it came down and soaked into the earth.

And the night herons stopped circling. And the people released a collective sigh.

Boom! Crackle, crackle, crackle. Boom!

"Look up!" a voice said.

Doreen raised her head, and there above them, fireworks blossomed in the darkness. A cascade of red. Turquoise. Flaming yellow. Then a great whistling sound and another boom, and a multicolored flower rained down over their heads.

The Temple was crumbling. And in its death, it released this gift of beauty.

Doreen started laughing.

"Merry Christmas!" someone shouted. "Feliz Navidad!"

"Hah!" Doreen laughed. Yes. It must be after midnight now. Perhaps these were Christmas fireworks, though she'd never heard of such a thing before.

"Why not?" She grinned.

Looking around the celebration, Doreen all of a sudden needed Patrice. Immediately.

She made her way through the tight crowd, bumping shoulders, grasping hands. Smiling so wide it almost hurt her face. People were hugging and kissing and dancing, and then there she was, her lover, eyes shining.

The most beautiful thing Doreen had ever seen.

Patrice's beautiful dark brown skin lit up with colored light every time a firework graced the sky.

Doreen walked towards her, thinking it wasn't so long ago they'd had their first kiss in another park like this. Another celebration after another battle. She hoped the war was over, but she knew this was just the beginning of their love.

"I love you, baby," she said to Patrice.

"Merry Christmas," her lover answered. And she grabbed Doreen and drew her towards her into the deepest, wettest, strongest kiss. Doreen could barely breathe.

She didn't need to. Kissing Patrice was breath enough.

It was life.

And for today at least, life had triumphed.

CHAPTER FORTY-SIX
CAROL

It was the day after Christmas.

Carol was still weak, but it felt so good to be out of bed, and outside the Mansion.

As Carol and Ernesto walked, hand in hand, toward the arched windows in the old Hacienda-style building, she could see that the coffeehouse, La Piranya, was packed.

Ernesto pushed open the heavy glass door, and Carol followed just behind him. Young people in their jeans and jackets, sweaters, T-shirts, and frizzy brown or heavy, seal-dark hair.

They were all beautiful. And for the first time, Carol was figuring out that yes, truly every person had their own kind of magic. She could feel it in them now, despite what she'd been taught at the Mansion.

Carol thought about her parents. She wondered now what kind of magic they had. She'd never even considered it before. Not before these last few months when everything had changed.

They found a place to stand near the big glass counter and ordered coffee. Maybe she'd make time for a visit. Go back to Minnesota. Go for walks in the snow. Maybe for the new year.

She smiled at her lover. Maybe someday she'd even bring Ernesto to meet them. Wouldn't that be something? Dark Ernesto among the blond, white members of her family. Speaking Spanish.

Carol took her first sip of the black brew. A little bitter, but she didn't want to move through the crush to get any cream. There was no place to sit, so she leaned against the counter to rest, with an apology to the woman who'd made her coffee.

The woman just shrugged and smiled.

Rosalia was speaking to the people. She was telling them the world was getting better, but they still needed to be brave. Carol didn't feel very brave all the time. But she was starting to learn things about that too. That bravery just meant showing up again and again whether you felt you knew what you were doing or not.

The people staring up at the sorcerer were around Carol's age or younger, with a couple that looked like they were maybe thirteen years old.

Thirteen. The same age Carol had been when she left Minnesota and came to live in LA. To learn how to be a proper sorcerer.

Well, if Jasmine Jones had anything to do with it, and Rosalia too, all of these people would tap into their magic. She wondered if it would change the world the way the hippies wanted to.

It felt like it.

Change had to come somehow, somewhere. She figured they just might as well shape it. And with the Temple in ruins, maybe they had a chance now.

"Mi gente," Rosalia said, "there is still much to be done. And we know that your parents have worked hard all their lives to build a life here and we know that some of you are ready to face the oppression that crushes our people. Ready to face la policía. Ready to face even the federal government, like your brother Rosalio Muñoz, who stood up to the draft in Vietnam."

Carol hadn't even heard about that man. She shook her head slightly, suddenly aware of being the only blond head in the room. She still had so much to learn about life outside the Mansion.

"I'm very pleased you have come here today to speak with us. Gloria of the Brown Berets is here to tell us about what they are doing to help the community, and ways that you might help too."

She turned to one of the square wooden tables and nodded at the woman there.

"Gloria, please."

Gloria handed out pamphlets. She was a small woman with an upright spine, and a strength about her that Carol had come to recognize as a hallmark of the Brown Berets. Long dark hair waved down her back. She wore a dark button-up shirt over her jeans, with a long pointed collar and sleeves belling out above wide cuffs.

"I want you to take these pamphlets to your families," Gloria said. "It is information about the barrio clinic. The clinic for the people. We know that some of your families are afraid to go see a doctor. You have been afraid of La Migra. Of deportation. Or you have been afraid you don't have the money to pay."

There was rustling and shifting in chairs as the stack of papers made its way around the room.

"You don't have to be afraid. None of us here are rich"—she laughed—"but we are rich in community. The Brown Berets have your back. There's a place for you to go if you feel sick, or just need help. And the people's clinic is that place. And if some of you want to volunteer after school or on weekends, the clinic always needs help. Checking people in. Cleaning. Organizing. There are many things you can do to help la gente."

A few pamphlets made their way back to Gloria.

"For those of you who live further out," she continued, "or have friends in South Central, the Black Panthers are also opening the Bunchy Carter Clinic. It should be open next week, so there will be two free clinics for the people in our communities. Make use of those resources. Learn how to help each other."

A hand raised.

It was a young man sitting at one of the round tables with his friends, a plaid shirt buttoned to his throat, but open three buttons down, offering a glimpse of the snow-white T-shirt underneath.

"Besides the clinic, are there other ways we can help? Not all of us are cut out to do that sort of work but we want to be involved."

"The Brown Berets also have community meetings like this one to help organize. We have patrols of our neighborhoods to help keep the people safe. And you are welcome to join. It's work, though. You have to train. If you think you can train and become stronger, the Brown Berets welcome you."

She got out a clipboard and passed a sign-up list. The young man was the first to write down his name.

"So that is what I have for now. We can take questions later. But first I would like to ask Rosalia to come and talk to us more about other ways you can help us organize."

Rosalia stood again in a swirl of skirts and clattering silver bracelets. Her citrine eyes looked at every person there. Even looking at Carol, who paused mid sip before Rosalia's eyes moved on.

"There is magic," Rosalia said. "You have seen it. And felt it. And every one of you carries it. Everyone of you who wears a cross. Or the medal of the Virgin. These symbols carry the magic of their own. And you are linked to that magic. And what I come to tell you today is that you can link to *everybody's* magic and make the people stronger than ever."

She raised both her hands to the air, then dropped them again.

"You have all heard by now that we have been fighting bad magic. The policía. The federales. We have been fighting for our communities. We have been fighting for your lives, and we want to know if you will join us, as we help shape a better world, El Mundo Bueno."

Rosalia looked at Carol again, and nodded for her to speak.

Okay. Carol had not expected to have to say anything today. The one white face among the shades of brown. She took a final sip of bitter coffee, and a breath.

Then she set her cup down.

"My name is Carol. I'm a sorcerer. I was born a sorcerer. I carry magic of the element of Earth."

She paused. Ernesto lightly squeezed her arm. She thought. What did she want to say to these people?

"I was taught that only certain special people had magic. That only those of us who were born to sorcery—or who trained for decades to study Temple magic, sigils and symbols, and who practiced through great physical pain and cost to themselves—could work the ways of the other worlds. But that's rich people talking. That's people who want to keep the power from you talking."

They were all paying attention to her now.

"I've learned better," she said, "and not too long ago. I've learned that every single being on this earth has a magic they can access, and we can show you how to access that."

"If you are willing," Rosalia said, "place your hand over your heart."

Carol did so, and noticed almost everyone in the room did too.

"Breathe deep. The breath of life. Feel that heart beating beneath your hand. I am going to give you a little push now so you can feel not only the beat, but the energy of life itself."

Carol felt her own hand grow warm and start to tingle. It lifted itself two inches from her chest, pushed out by the energy of her own etheric body, activated by Rosalia's command.

There were gasps around the room. And laughter. Carol looked. She even saw some tears.

The energy soothed the place the bullets had entered, bringing extra life force to her healing body. A rush of gratitude filled her.

"That's what we're talking about," Carol said. "You dig? You *have* magic. You *are* magic. And with magic, we have a chance to do almost anything."

"Por la gente," Ernesto said at her side.

"We hope you are with us. And anyone who wants to join, please talk with Rosalia. We have another appointment now, but I hope to see you all again soon."

Rosalia nodded again, giving Carol a smile.

Carol led Ernesto back to the heavy door, waiting for him to push it open for her. She felt better, but was still a little weak.

"We have an appointment?" he asked.

"For this," she replied, and pulled him in for a deep kiss.

CHAPTER FORTY-SEVEN
SNAKES AND SPIDERS

*S*amuels couldn't believe the Master was dead.

Much as he had worked to shift the balance of power, and had determined to steal it away...he hadn't really figured Hoover would die in the process.

Which was a stupid oversight on his part. The Master was too far gone to remain alive when the magic he had built from lies and pain, torture and manipulation, disinformation and assassination imploded around him.

Samuels knew now he simply could not have allowed himself that thought, because a thought like that would never have stayed locked deeply enough to escape the Master's notice.

He had to stop calling him the Master. The man's name was Hoover. And he was dead, killed by Jasmine Jones and his own web of magic. The FBI was scrambling, panicked. The Pentagon, too.

Samuels gave a tight smile, then shook his head ruefully. He sipped the smoky whiskey he'd allowed the silver-haired man sitting in a leather chair across the low coffee table to pour for him. Just this once.

He would return to his discipline tomorrow.

Meanwhile, he would listen to Terrance Sterling talk about how Elemental Sorcery worked.

Braiding their magics together was going to take some time.

But now? Samuels had all the time in the world.

CHAPTER FORTY-EIGHT
JASMINE

Jimmy and I were tucked up in my too-small bed again, lying fully dressed on top of the quilt.

Exhausted, I'd stayed in bed for most of the day after we took the Temple down. Jimmy had brought me things to tempt me. Hot chocolate one hour, and ham and cornbread another.

Since we'd all been busy at Solstice, we had a small celebration Christmas Day. I came out for an hour or two before retreating back to bed. My mother did the same.

I think we were both depleted from our battles. But damn, it felt good all the same. There was still going to be work to do, but I hoped that, for a while at least, the heavy lifting was done.

My father baked pies and sugar cookies, and his famous walnut bread. My room still smelled of that because I'd just toasted two pieces, slathered them with butter, and snuck the plate into my room.

Maybe I'd be able to put back on some of the weight I'd lost these past few months.

"When you want to head back up to Oakland?" Jimmy asked, stealing a piece of the toasted bread from my plate.

"I don't know," I replied. "Soon, though. I need to check in with my mother, see if there's anything I need to do down here. And Fred Hampton wants me to come out to Chicago and start doing trainings there."

"You want to do that?"

I sighed.

"I do. It sounds exciting. At least it would if I wasn't so spent. Right now? I also just want to go *home*."

He adjusted the pillows behind his head.

"You going back to school?"

Wow. School. It felt so far away. So unimportant now.

"I have no idea yet, but I guess I've got to decide soon. It's either Chicago for a while or school. I can't do both at the same time. And if I'm not in school, I'm not sure what I'll do for money. I mean, I guess Doreen will let me stay…"

"You could always stay with me. And the Panthers will take care of you, Jaz. You know that, right?"

Jimmy took the plate from my hands and set it on my bedside table. Then he pulled me toward him until my head rested in the crook of his neck and shoulder. It felt good. Safe. I sighed again.

"What do you think you want?"

I thought about it for a while, listening to the beating of his heart through his purple T-shirt.

"I want this. You. I want the Panthers. I want magic for the people. To build a new world, you know? Like, I feel as if we finally have a chance. Like the boot is off our necks, for now at least. So school?" I shook my head. "I guess not."

Jimmy smoothed my natural against my skull. It was already raggedy from being mashed against the pillows, so I didn't mind. His hand felt good. Soothing. I needed a little bit of soothing.

But not too much. Even though I was tired, the wound in my shoulder was gone. When the Temple fell, it had pulled itself out, I guess.

My strength and swagger were coming back. I could feel it. There was work to be done with the ancestors, I could feel them, too.

And there was a destiny for me that I couldn't see the end of. But I knew it was there. And important somehow.

"Maybe I'll go back to school someday. But right now? I think my life is with the revolution."

I sat up again and stared into my lover's eyes. His dark, gold-rimmed eyes stared back at me. I could feel his panther move beneath his skin. I always responded to that. It made me feel strong, like I had to be to stand at his side. And it turned me on, all the way down to my toes.

"The Ancestor showed me something, you know."

"The one who gave you the spear?" he asked, chin lifting toward the wood and pounded metal resting in the corner of my room, next to my desk. After I'd recovered from snapping back into my body, it had been lying next to me on the temple room floor.

"Yeah. She showed me a baby."

I felt him go still for a moment.

"And what did that baby look like?" he asked.

"That baby looked a lot like me and you."

His hands gripped my neck and our lips met. I dug my fingers into the tight curls just above his neck. We kissed long and slow, before Jimmy pulled away.

"I thought it wasn't possible...that shifter, sorcerer mix."

"That's what I thought, too, but the Ancestor was pretty clear. Maybe something's changed. I don't know."

We lay there, breathing together for another moment, before Jimmy spoke again.

"You think we can have kids and the revolution, too?" he asked.

"You know, a month ago, I would have said no. But now? Now I think we can have whatever we damn well please."

"Well, I want *you*, Jasmine Jones. And I hope you want me, too."

"I feel like I might just want you forever."

We kissed again. I smelled the musk rise on his gorgeous skin. And then we were all in a rush, hurrying to rip off T-shirts and bell-bottom jeans, scrambling to throw back the quilt on that too-narrow bed. In a Powers-blessed hurry to make love.

I wasn't ready for that baby yet. Not that day, at least. But I was thinking I was gonna be.

But first, there were kisses to share, and people to train, and things to learn.

There was my lover, whom I hoped to know even better than I already did. There was shape-shifter magic and the ways it met my sorcery. And there were all the ways it blended into this movement we called the revolution.

The revolution shows up in a lot of ways. In feeding hungry children. In healing sick bodies. In marching through the streets. In battling for what is right. In speaking out for justice. In sorcery and magic.

And through the power of two bodies, coming together in pleasure and in love. Through a panther and a sorcerer, who were going to risk bringing a child into a brave new world, even though shifters and sorcerers weren't supposed to be able to have kids at all.

And even though there were people in the world who, just days before, would have said people like us were only good for prison or death, not families and community.

Well, I would repeat to those people, over and over, that their time was over. It was *our* time now.

The people's time.

Black is beautiful.

All power to all the people.

My name is Jasmine Jones. I'm in love with a cat named Jimmy.

I am a revolutionary.

AUTHOR'S NOTE & BIBLIOGRAPHY

This series came about because for many years I've wondered what racial justice in the United States would look like if Fred Hampton had not been brutally assassinated by the FBI and Chicago PD, and if J. Edgar Hoover's COINTELPRO had not purposefully decimated so many groups and coalitions working toward equity, autonomy, and justice.

With encouragement from others, what started off as a 10,000 word short story turned into a four book series.

Am I the right person to tell this tale of sorcery, shape-shifters, and the Black Panther Party? There are likely far better candidates for the task, but the story pushed its way through me nonetheless, for better or worse.

There's a lot of history in this alt-history fantasy. 1968–69 was a time in which so much happened, it is almost impossible to keep track of events. The infiltration, assassinations, psychological warfare, disruption, and attacks on anti-war and civil rights groups by the FBI was far worse and more comprehensive than I could even being to include in these novels. Many of these tactics continue into contemporary times.

I chose only a few key events to highlight in the story, and concentrated on Oakland and Los Angeles, though events were going down in cities across the U.S.

When possible, I used the words of Panther organizers like Fred Hampton and Huey Newton. I also tried to remain respectful of the

Panthers still living and doing good work in the world. That is why so many key historical players are barely mentioned, or appear as very minor characters. I didn't want to put words in their mouths. That is not my place. Many of them have told their stories, and you can find a few in the books below. There is a wealth of information not included here.

If you are interested in more actual history, here is a resource list to get you started:

Film

- *Black Power Mix Tape*
- *1971*
- *The Black Panthers: Vanguard of the Revolution* (this film is controversial among some of the remaining Panthers)

Books

- *The Fire Next Time*, James Baldwin (not about the Panthers in particular, but a great background that frankly, everyone should read)
- *To Live and Die for the People*, Huey P. Newton
- *Revolutionary Suicide*, Huey P. Newton
- *The Nine Lives of a Black Panther*, Wayne Pharr
- *A Taste of Power*, Elaine Brown
- *Seize the Time*, Bobby Seale
- *The Ten Point Program of the Black Panther Party*, https://web.stanford.edu/group/blackpanthers/history.shtml
- *Assata: An Autobiography*, Assata Shakur (Panther history after the time period of this series)
- *J. Edgar Hoover: A Graphic Biography*, Rick Geary
- *Chicano Movement for Beginners*, Maceo Montoya
- *Youth, Identity, Power: The Chicano Movement*, Carlos Muñoz, Jr.

And of course, the repercussions from this time roll forward.

Some Additional Key Resources

- *The New Jim Crow*, Michelle Alexander
- *The 13th Movie*, Ava DuVernay
- *From #BlackLivesMatter to Black Liberation*, Keeanga-Yamahtta Taylor

Many of the Black Panther Party continue to do public work in the world.

- Fred Hampton and Deborah Johnson/Akua Njeri's son founded the Prisoners of Conscience Committee: http://chairmanfredjr. blogspot.com/
- Elaine Brown is an activist and author. http://www.elainebrown.org/
- Ericka Huggins is an activist, speaker, and spiritual teacher. http://www.erickahuggins.com/Home.html
- Bobby Seale is an educator, author, and activist. http://www.bobbyseale.com/
- Angela Davis is a professor, author, and active in the prison abolitionist movement: http://www.speakoutnow.org/speaker/davis-angela

    Tarika Lewis is a violinist, artist, activist, and art teacher: https://en.wikipedia.org/wiki/Joan_Tarika_Lewis

ACKNOWLEGEMENTS

Every published book requires both an author working alone, and a host of friends and community.

Thank you and love to Robert and Jonathan, for helping me build a home all these years.

Thanks to first readers Leslie Claire Walker, Thealandrah Davis, and Luna Pantera. Thanks also to Al Osorio for the occasional series consultation and Mushtaq Ali Al Ansari for spear logistics. These would be lesser books without all of you.

Profound gratitude to The Sorcery Collective for your continued hard work on spreading the word about this series. Much of its success is directly because of your efforts.

Thank you to Dayle Dermatis, editor extraordinaire.

Thank you to Carl of Extended Imagery for the gorgeous covers.

Thanks to my first and third Saturday writing cohort. It's great working with you.

Thanks to Kris Rusch, who told me this wasn't just a short story, but a novel series.

Most of all: thanks to all of the activists and justice organizations who do the work day in and day out. May your lives and work be blessed.

ABOUT THE AUTHOR

T. Thorn Coyle writes books, drinks tea, and agitates for justice.

She is the author of the Panther Chronicles series, the novel *Like Water*, two story collections, and multiple spirituality books including *Sigil Magic for Writers, Artists & Other Creatives* and *Evolutionary Witchcraft*. Thorn's work also appears in many anthologies, magazines, and collections. She has taught people all over the world.

An interloper to the Pacific Northwest, Thorn joyfully stalks city streets, writes in cafes, and talks to crows, squirrels, and trees. Sometimes she gets arrested.

Want to learn more?

Follow Thorn on Twitter and Facebook
Sign up for her monthly newsletter at ThornCoyle.com
Read advance copies of essays and stories via Patreon

24831376R00150

Made in the USA
Columbia, SC
28 August 2018